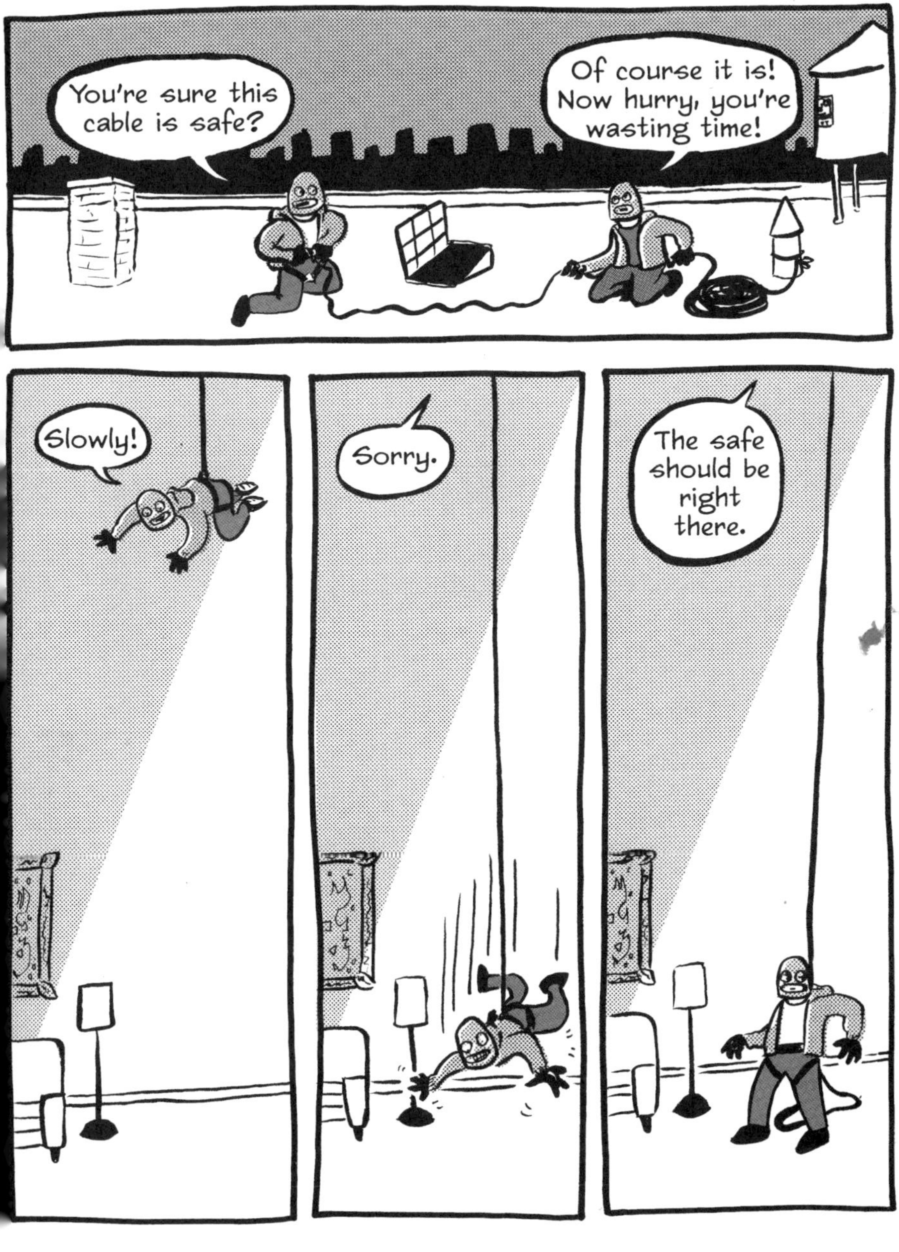

You're sure this cable is safe?
Of course it is! Now hurry, you're wasting time!
Slowly!
Sorry.
The safe should be right there.

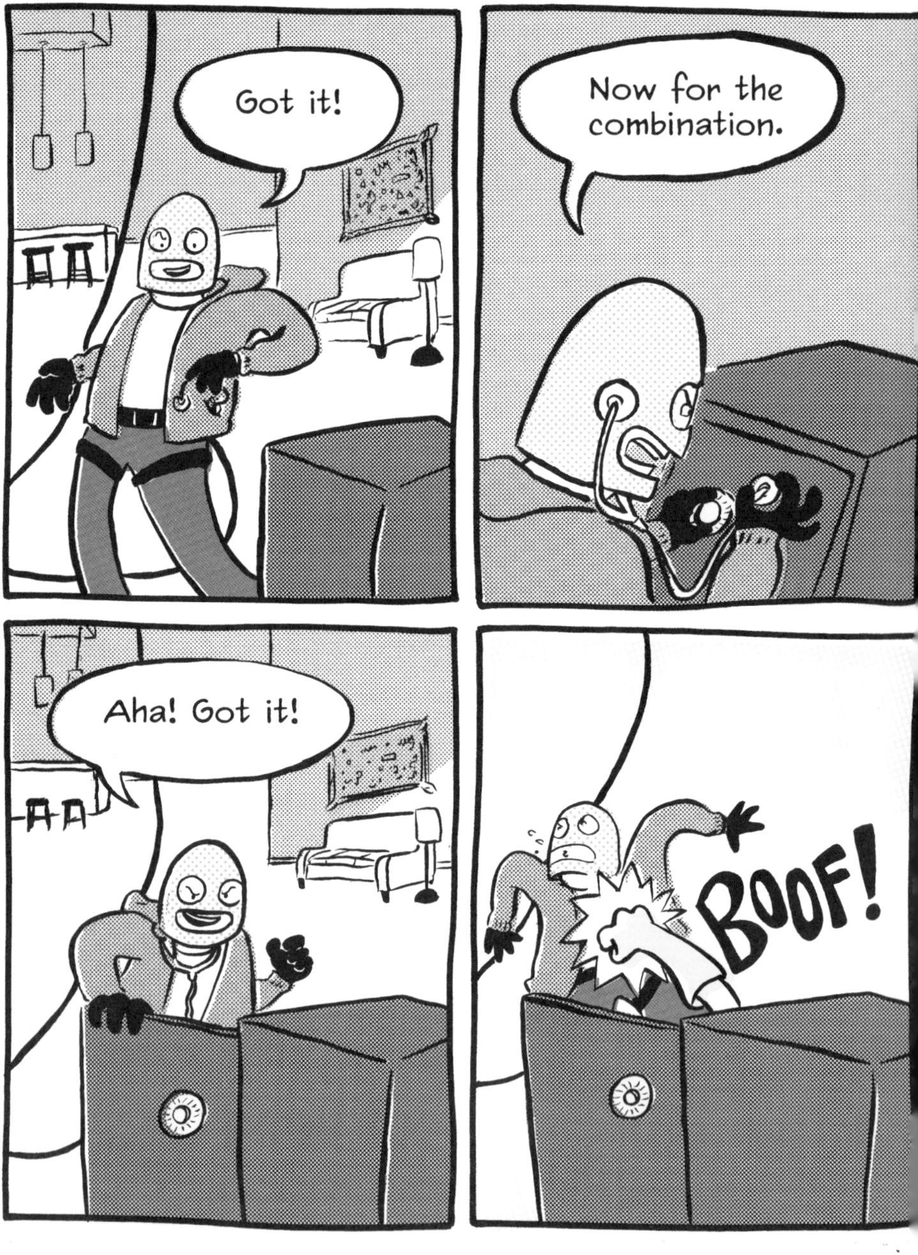
Got it!
Now for the combination.
Aha! Got it!
BOOF!

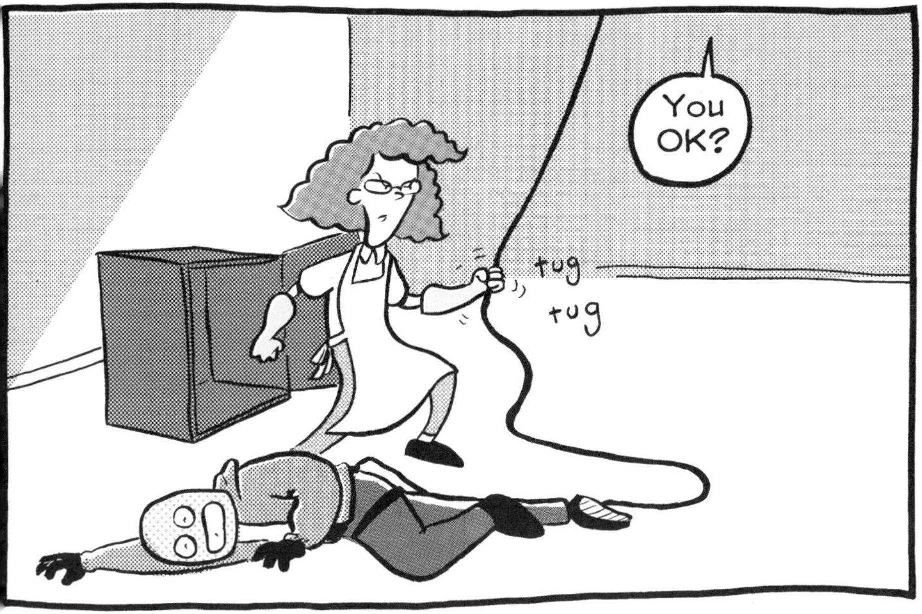
You OK?
tug
tug
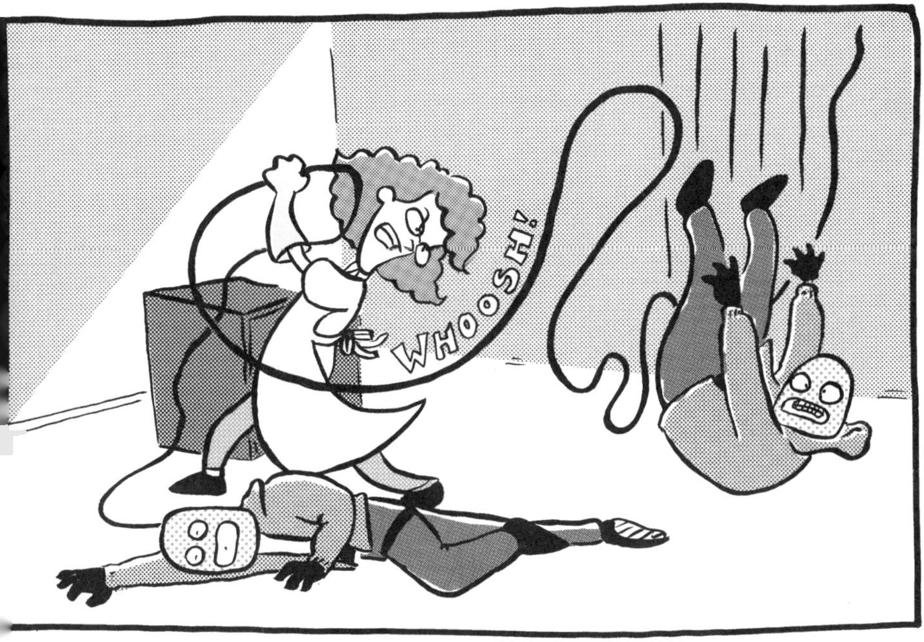
WHOOSH!

LUNCH

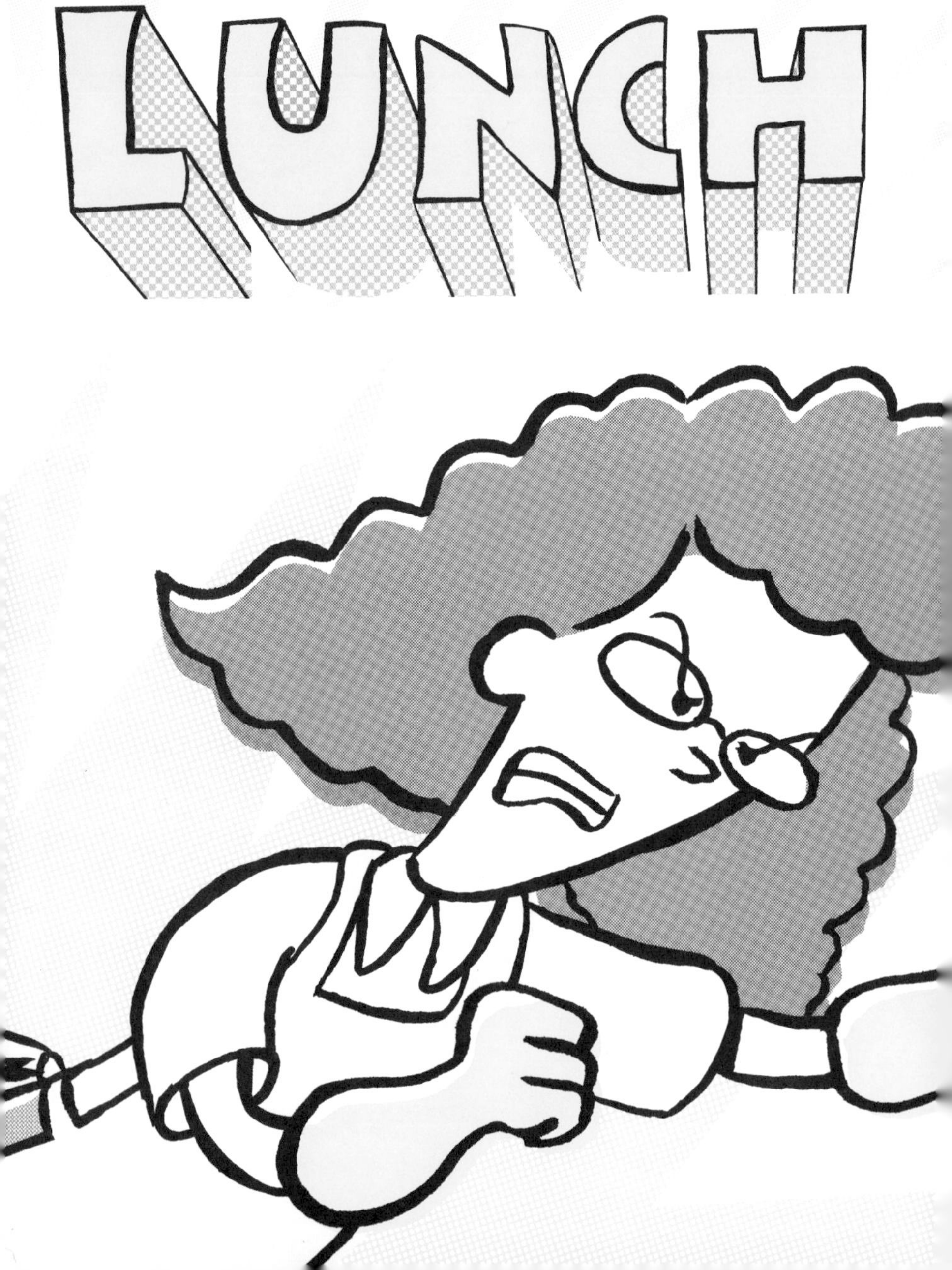

LADY

and the
Bake Sale Bandit

Jarrett J.
Krosoczka

Alfred A. Knopf 🐎 New York

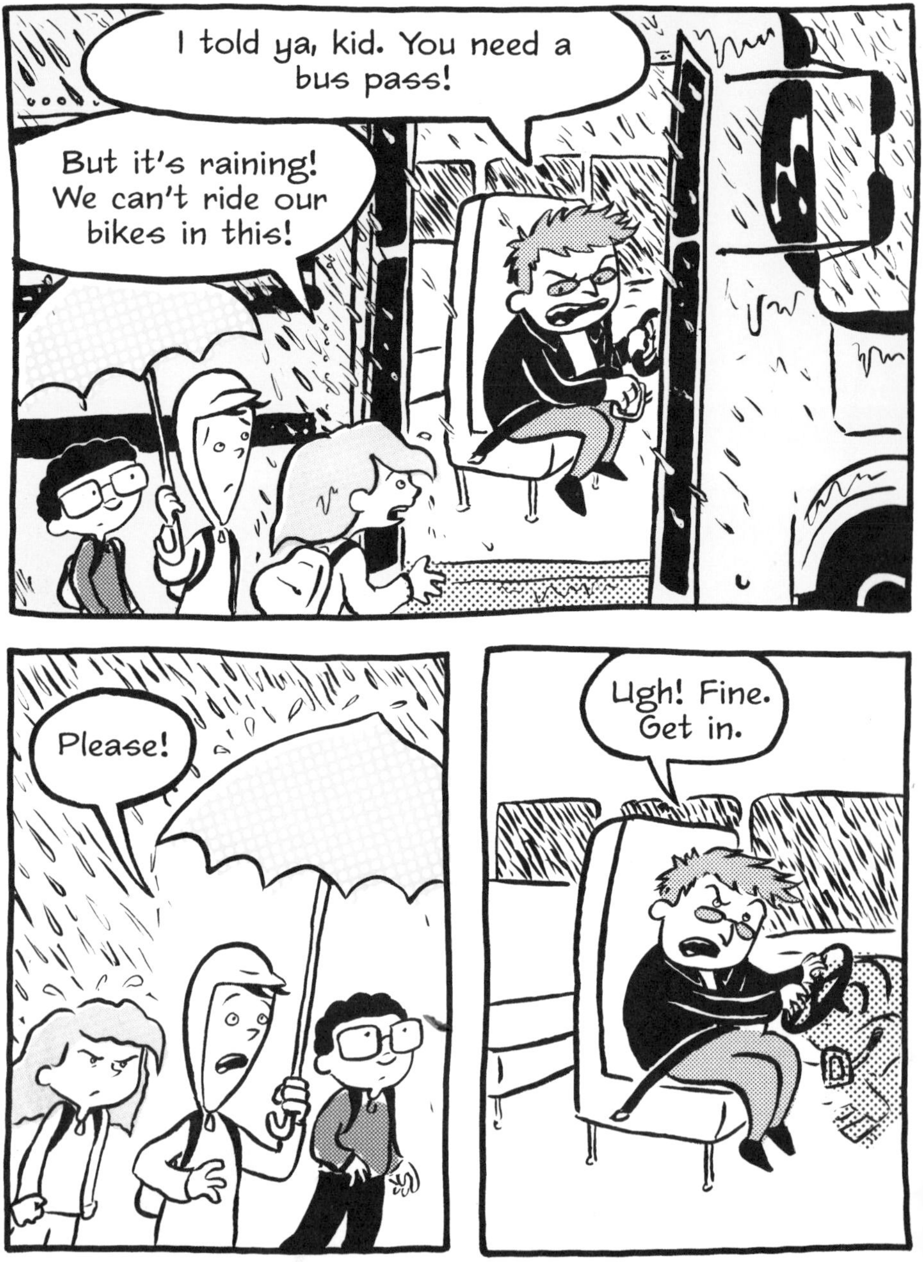
I told ya, kid. You need a bus pass!
But it's raining! We can't ride our bikes in this!
Please!
Ugh! Fine. Get in.

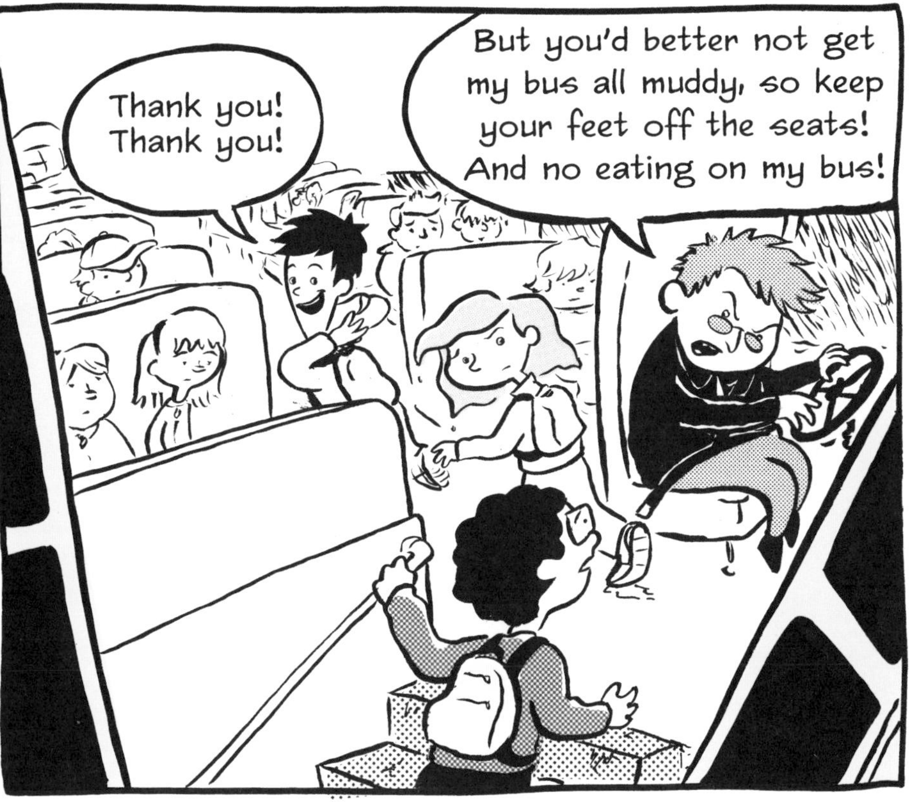
Thank you! Thank you!
But you'd better not get my bus all muddy, so keep your feet off the seats! And no eating on my bus!
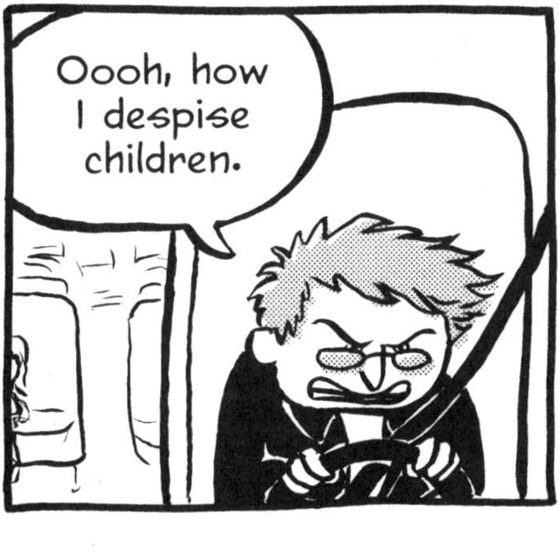
Oooh, how I despise children.
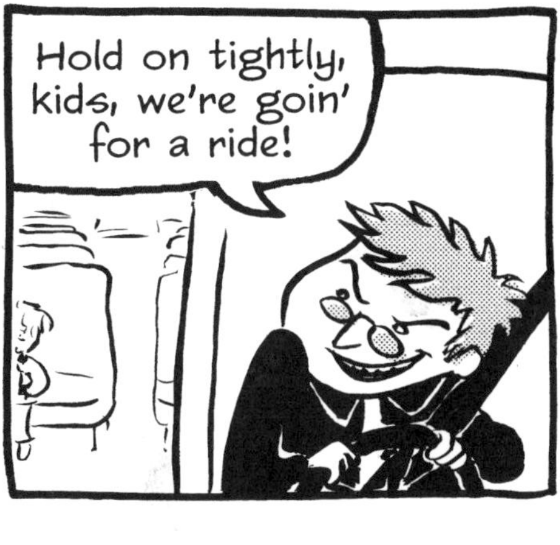
Hold on tightly, kids, we're goin' for a ride!

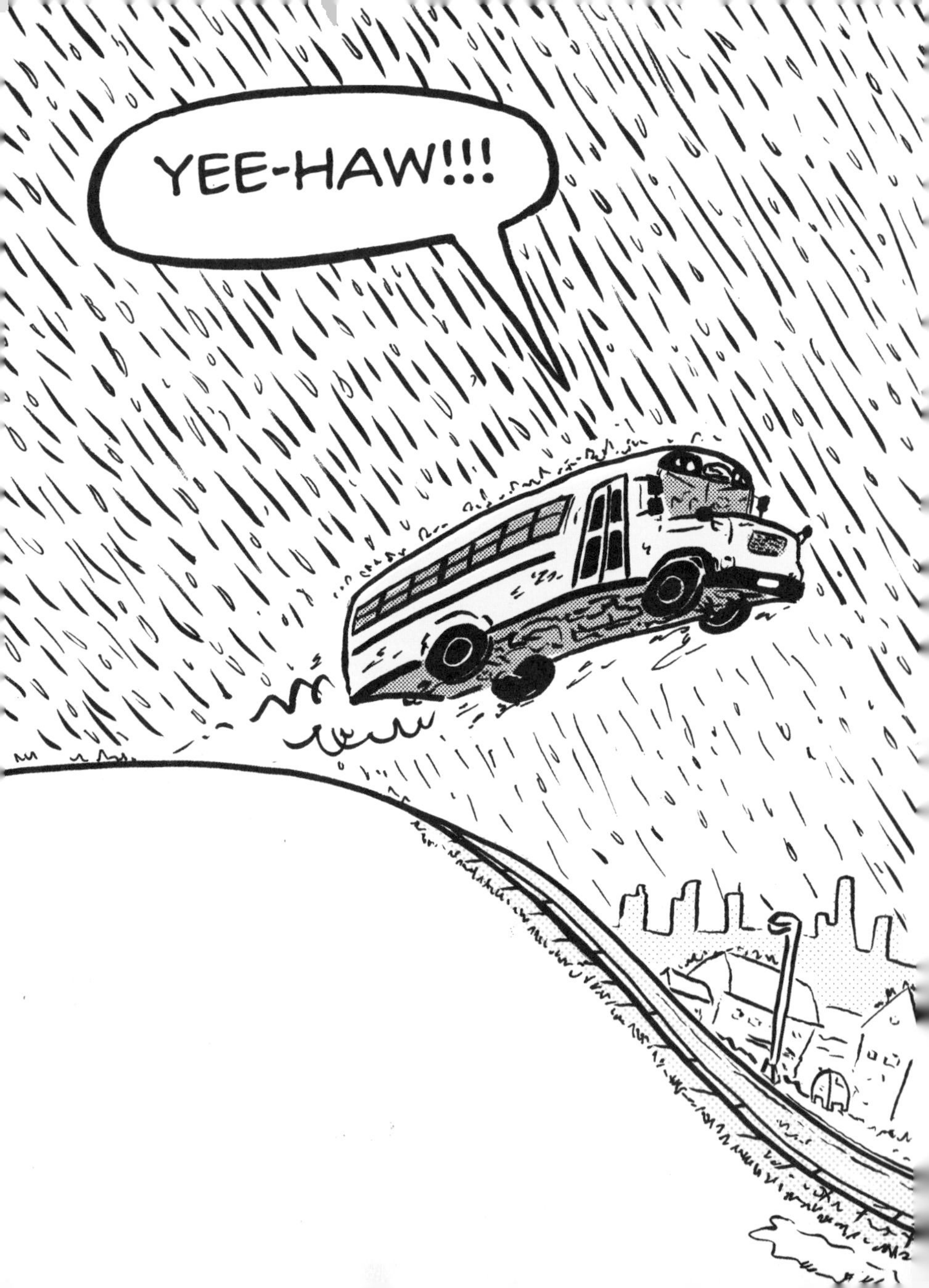
YEE-HAW!!!

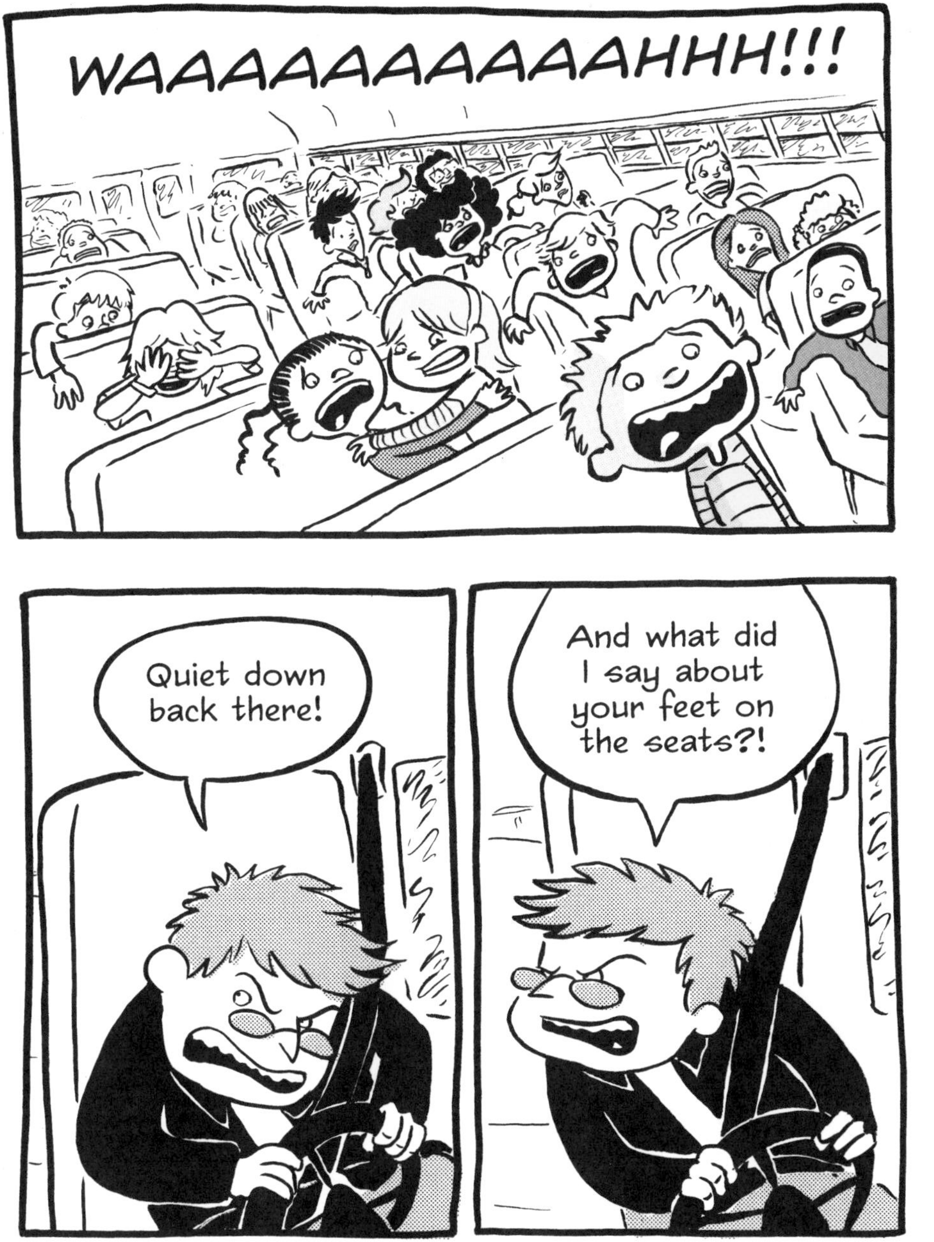
WAAAAAAAAAAAHHH!!!
Quiet down back there!
And what did I say about your feet on the seats?!

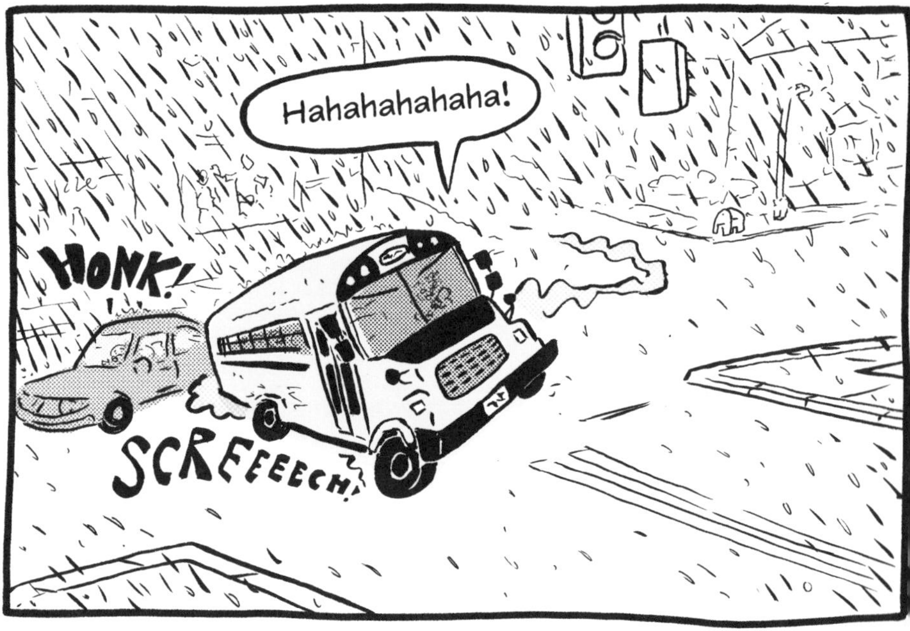
Hahahahahaha!
HONK!
SCREEEEECH!

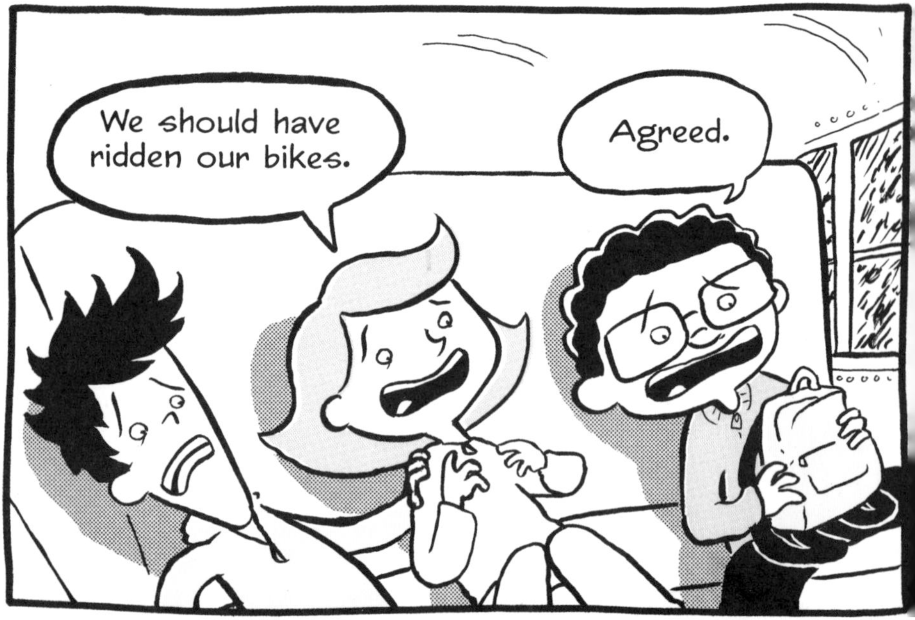
We should have ridden our bikes.
Agreed.

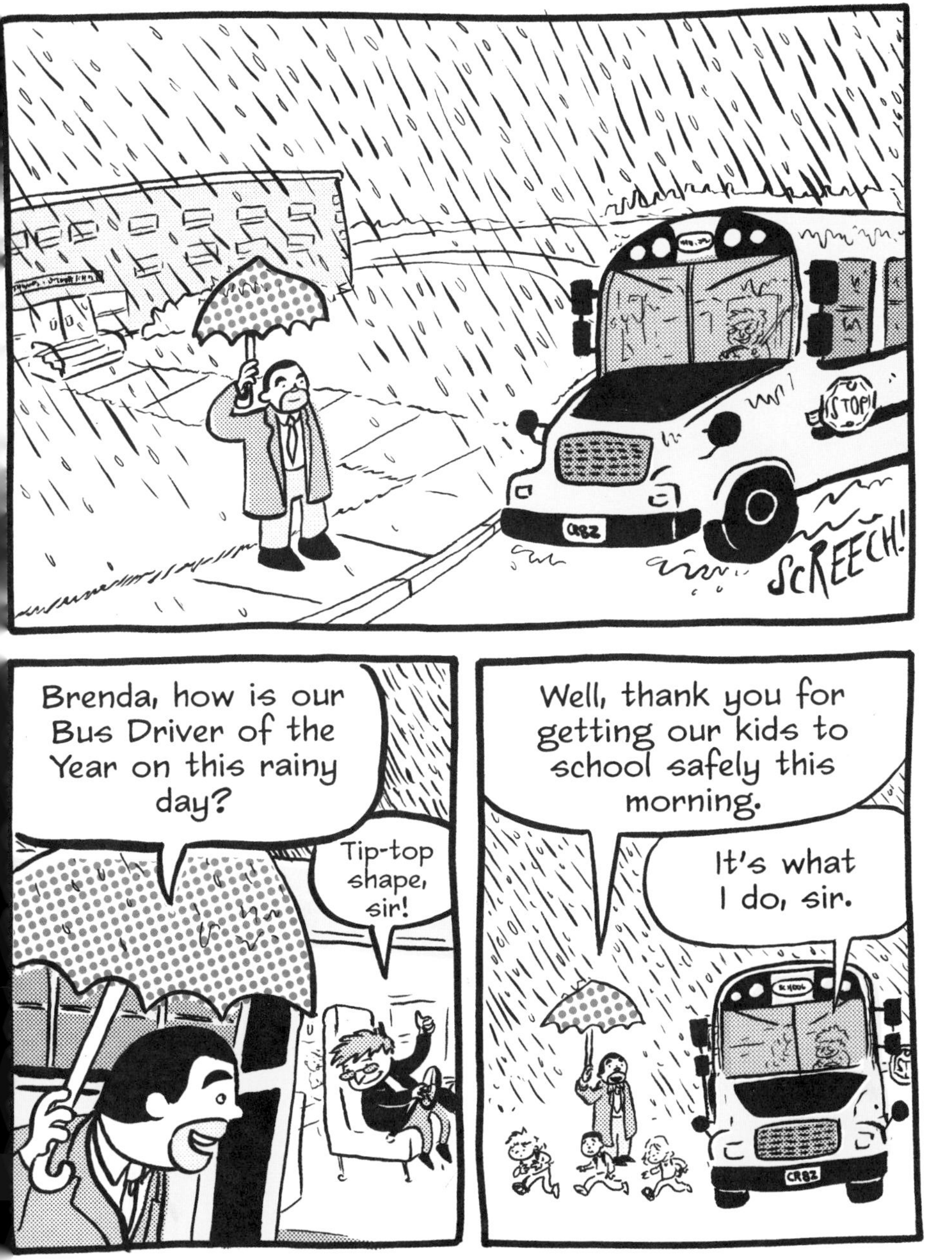
STOP!
CR8Z
SCREECH!
Brenda, how is our Bus Driver of the Year on this rainy day?
Tip-top shape, sir!
Well, thank you for getting our kids to school safely this morning.
It's what I do, sir.
CR8Z

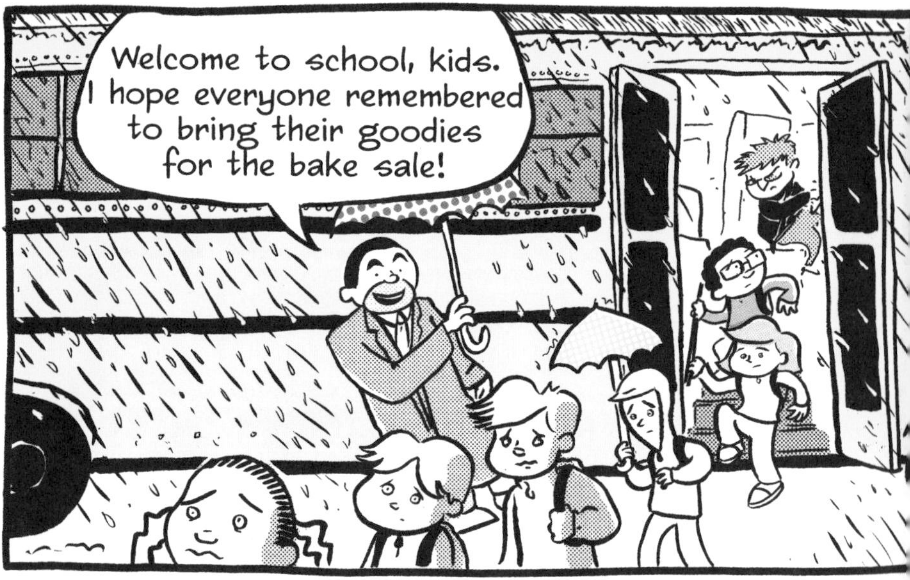
Welcome to school, kids. I hope everyone remembered to bring their goodies for the bake sale!

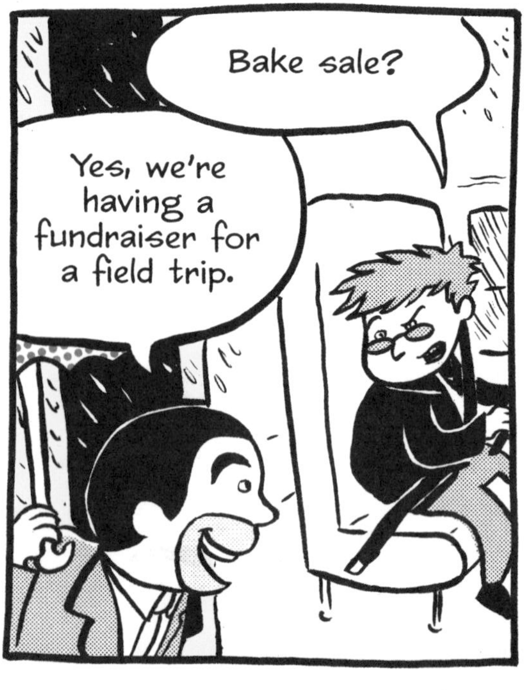
Bake sale?
Yes, we're having a fundraiser for a field trip.

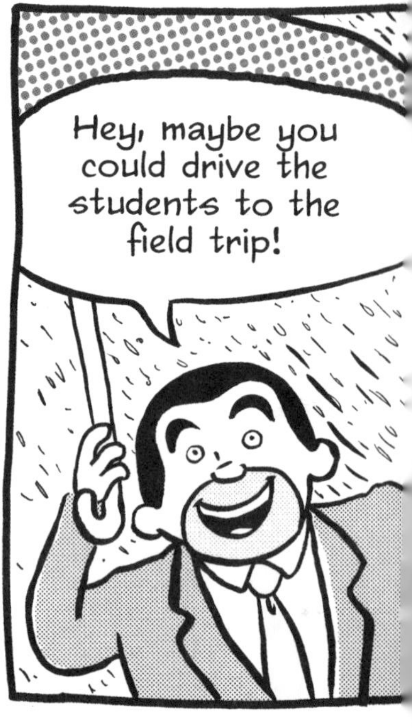
Hey, maybe you could drive the students to the field trip!

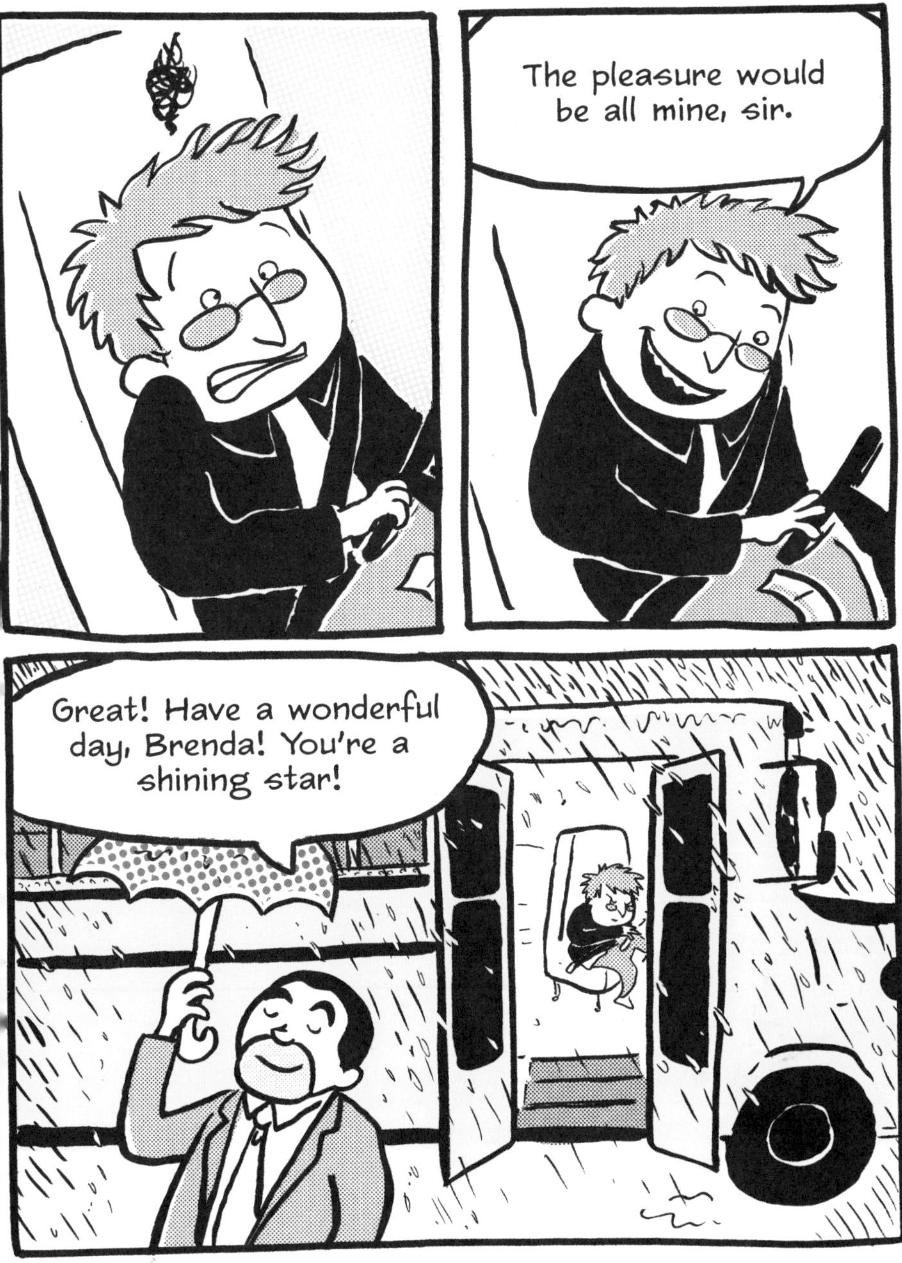
The pleasure would be all mine, sir.
Great! Have a wonderful day, Brenda! You're a shining star!

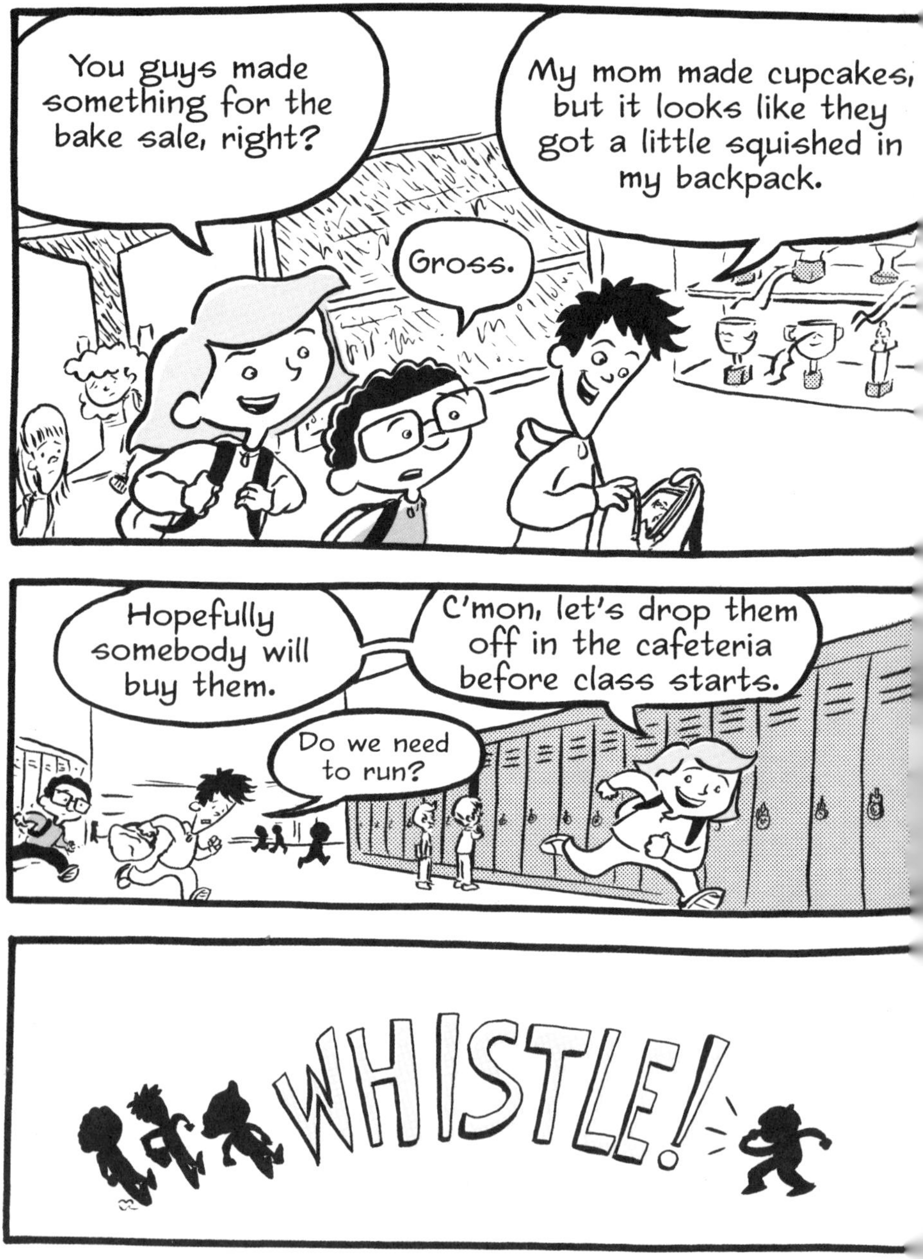
You guys made something for the bake sale, right?
My mom made cupcakes, but it looks like they got a little squished in my backpack.
Gross.
Hopefully somebody will buy them.
C'mon, let's drop them off in the cafeteria before class starts.
Do we need to run?
WHISTLE!

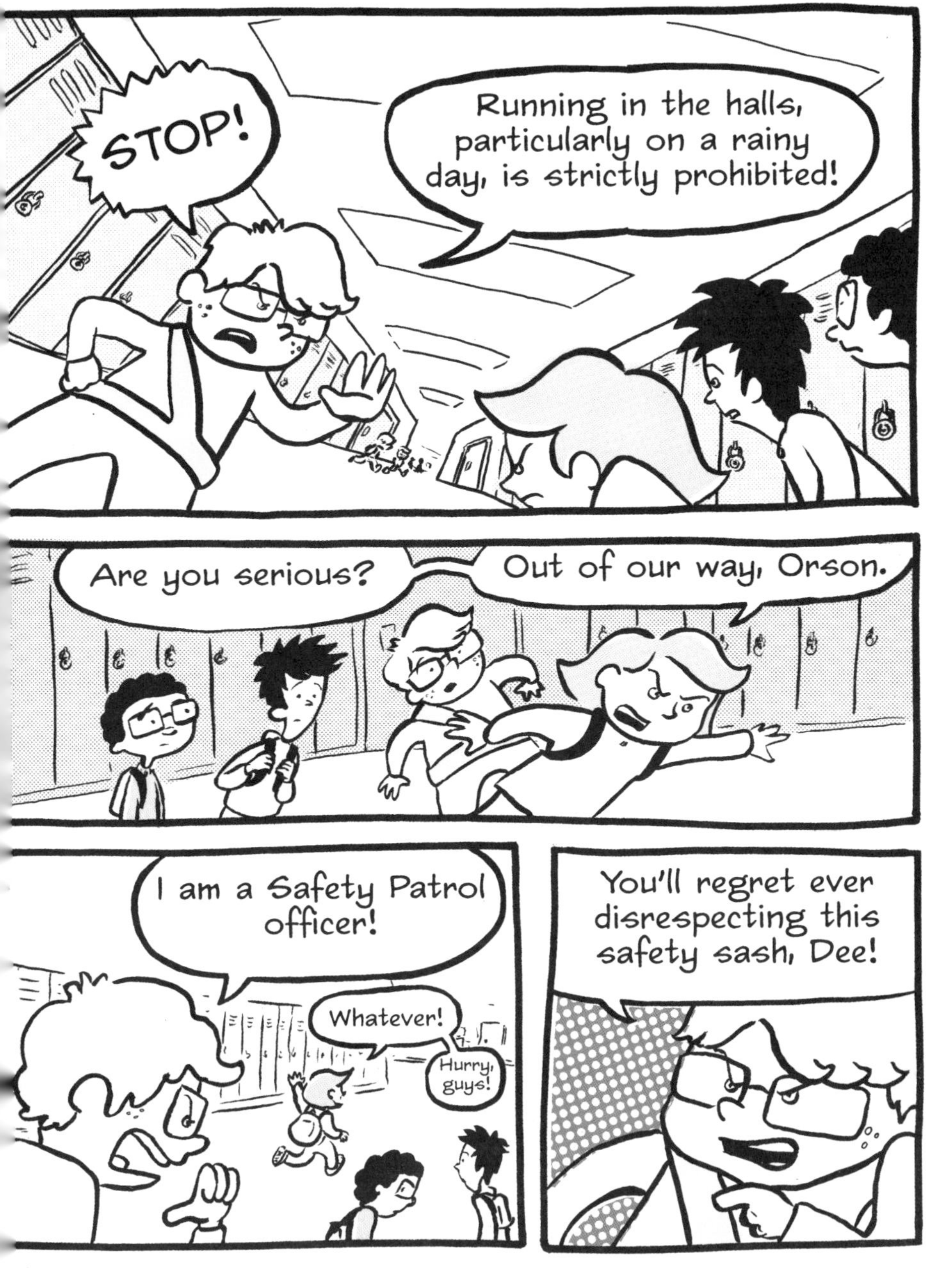
STOP!
Running in the halls, particularly on a rainy day, is strictly prohibited!
Are you serious?
Out of our way, Orson.
I am a Safety Patrol officer!
Whatever!
Hurry, guys!
You'll regret ever disrespecting this safety sash, Dee!

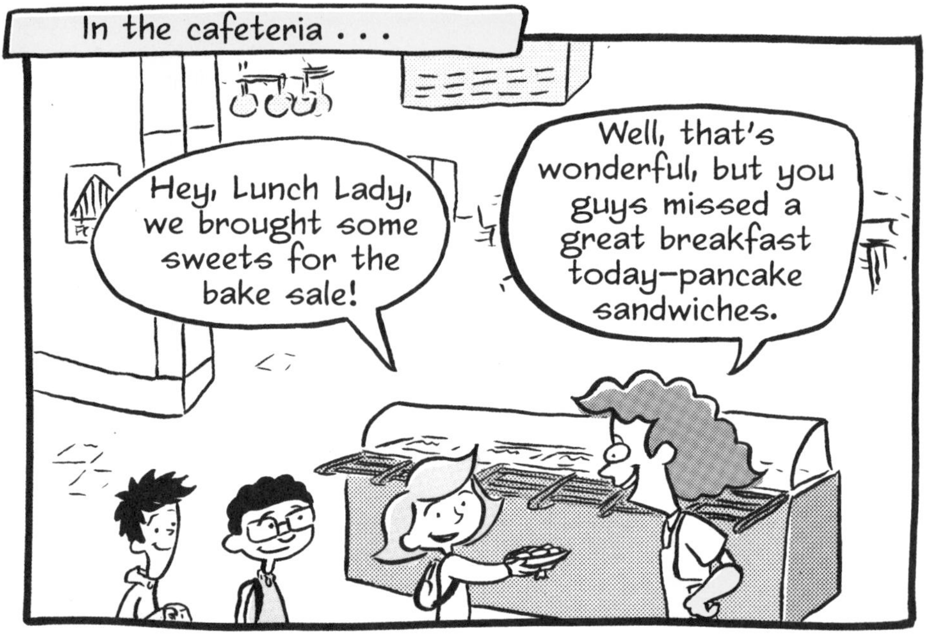
In the cafeteria . . .
Hey, Lunch Lady, we brought some sweets for the bake sale!
Well, that's wonderful, but you guys missed a great breakfast today—pancake sandwiches.

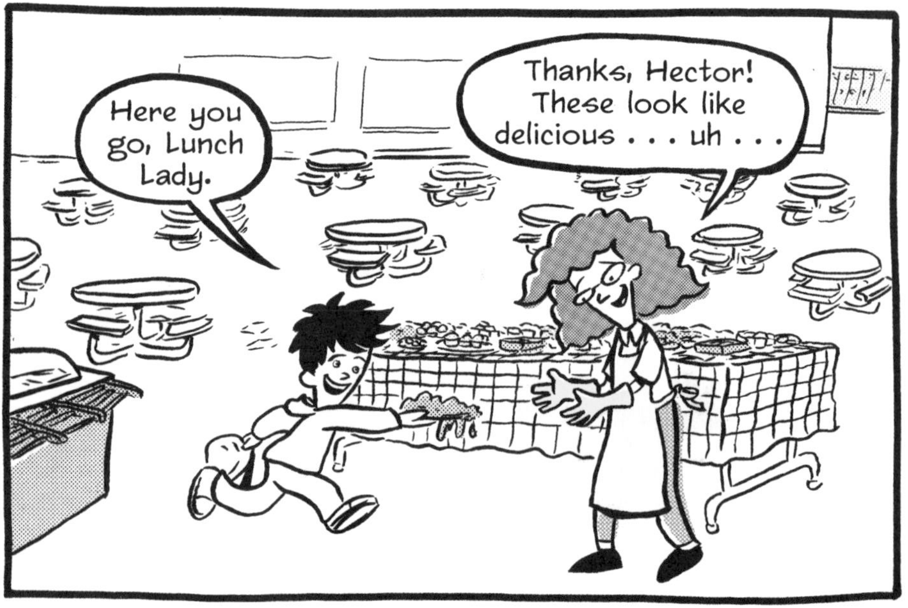
Here you go, Lunch Lady.
Thanks, Hector! These look like delicious . . . uh . . .

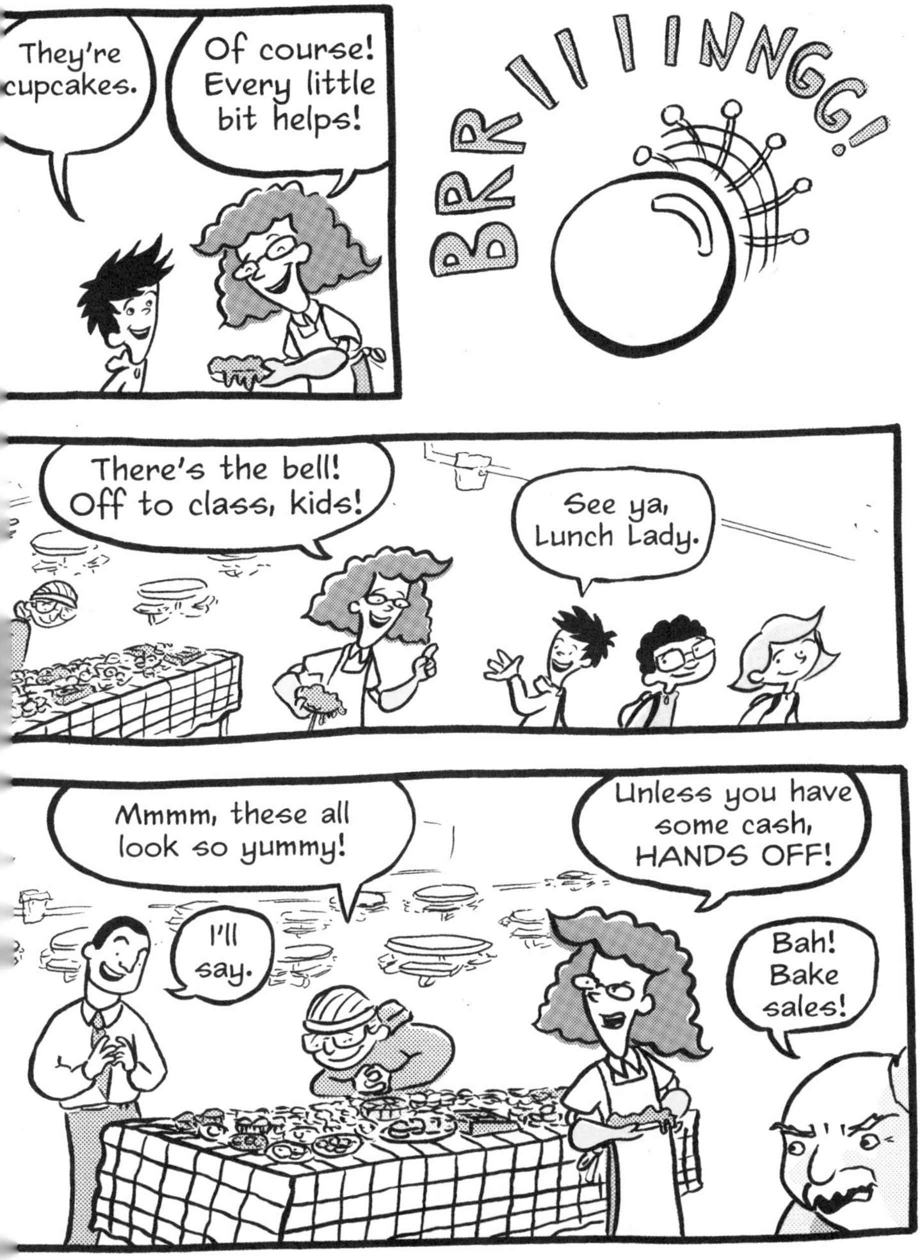
They're cupcakes.
Of course! Every little bit helps!
BRIIIIINNGG!
There's the bell! Off to class, kids!
See ya, Lunch Lady.
Mmmm, these all look so yummy!
I'll say.
Unless you have some cash, HANDS OFF!
Bah! Bake sales!

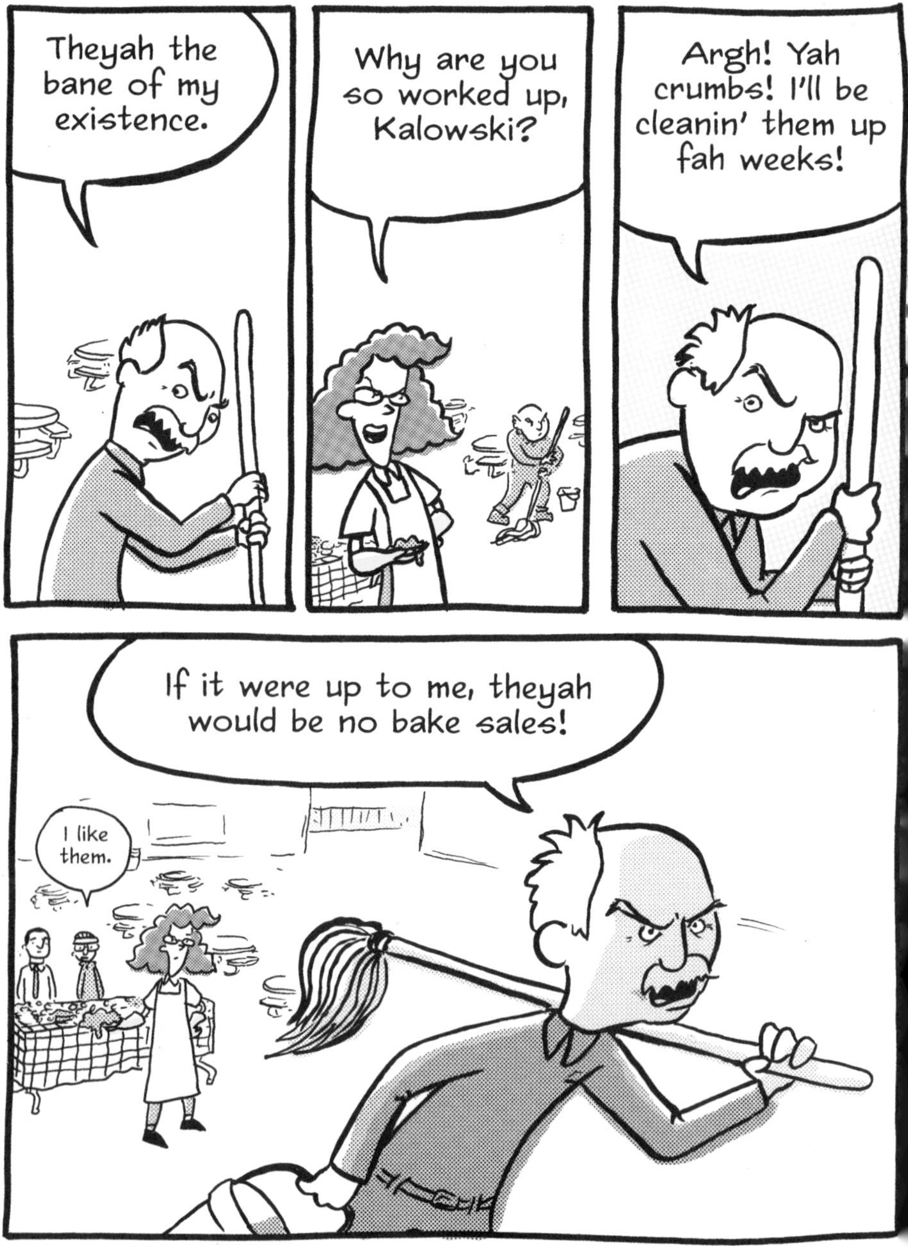
Theyah the bane of my existence.
Why are you so worked up, Kalowski?
Argh! Yah crumbs! I'll be cleanin' them up fah weeks!
If it were up to me, theyah would be no bake sales!
I like them.

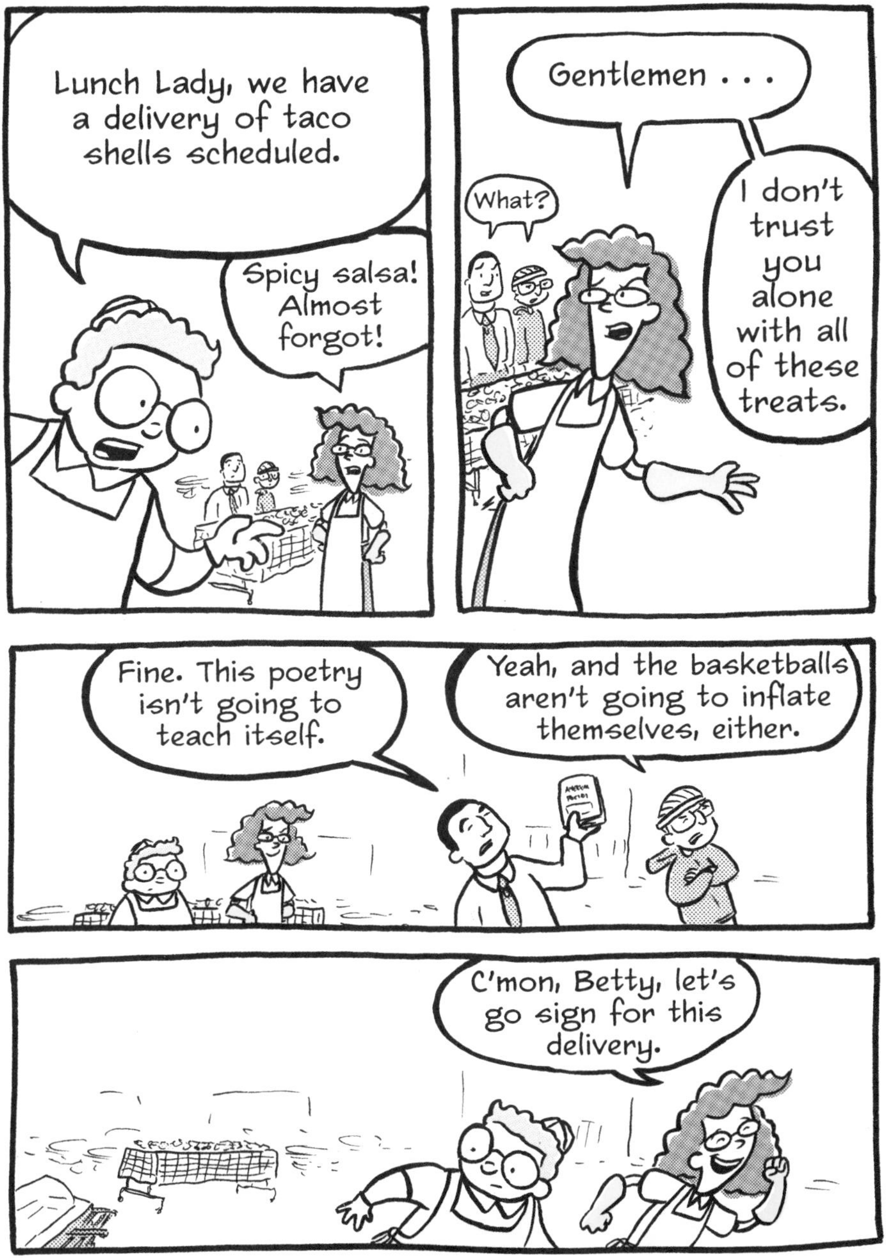
Lunch Lady, we have a delivery of taco shells scheduled.
Spicy salsa! Almost forgot!
Gentlemen . . .
What?
I don't trust you alone with all of these treats.
Fine. This poetry isn't going to teach itself.
Yeah, and the basketballs aren't going to inflate themselves, either.
C'mon, Betty, let's go sign for this delivery.

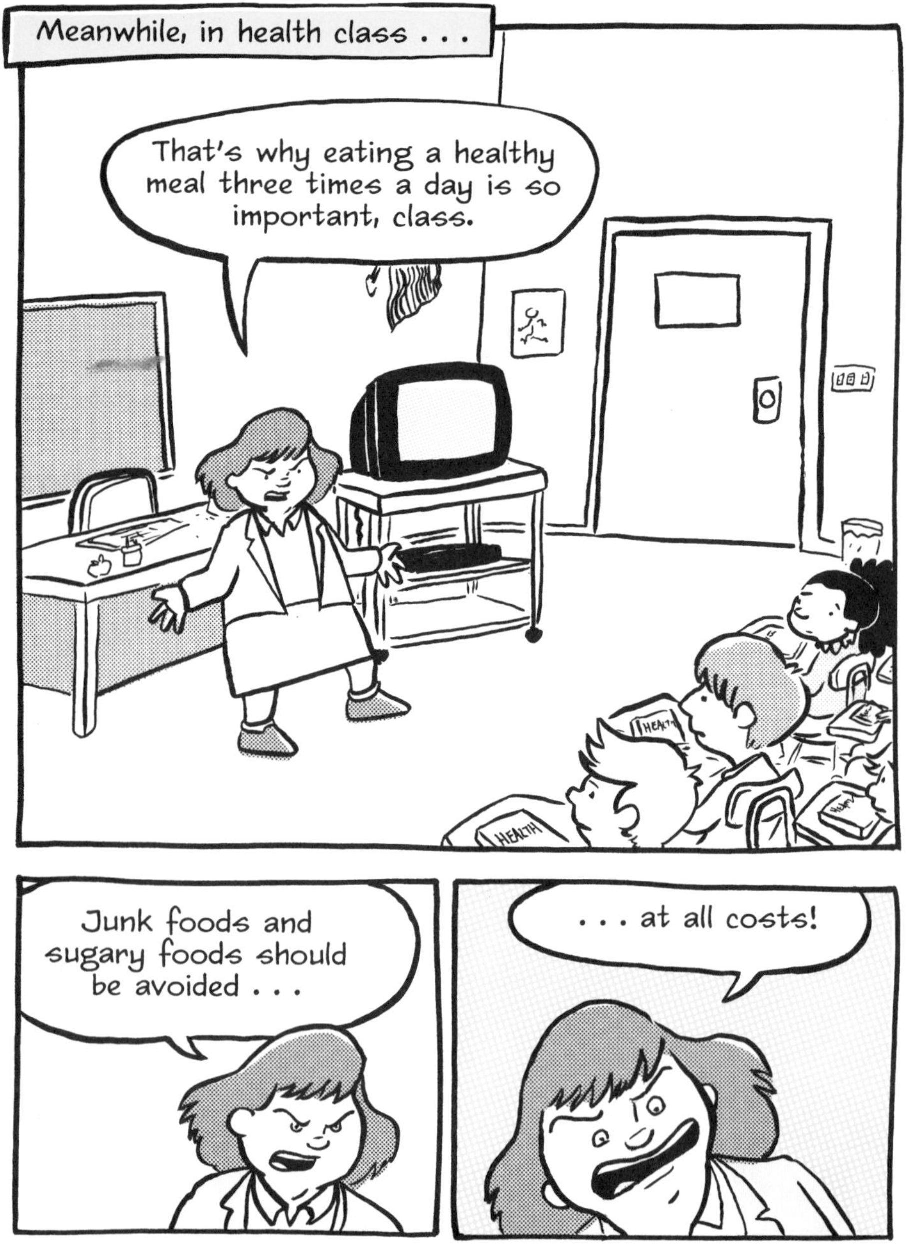
Meanwhile, in health class . . .
That's why eating a healthy meal three times a day is so important, class.
HEALTH
Junk foods and sugary foods should be avoided . . .
. . . at all costs!

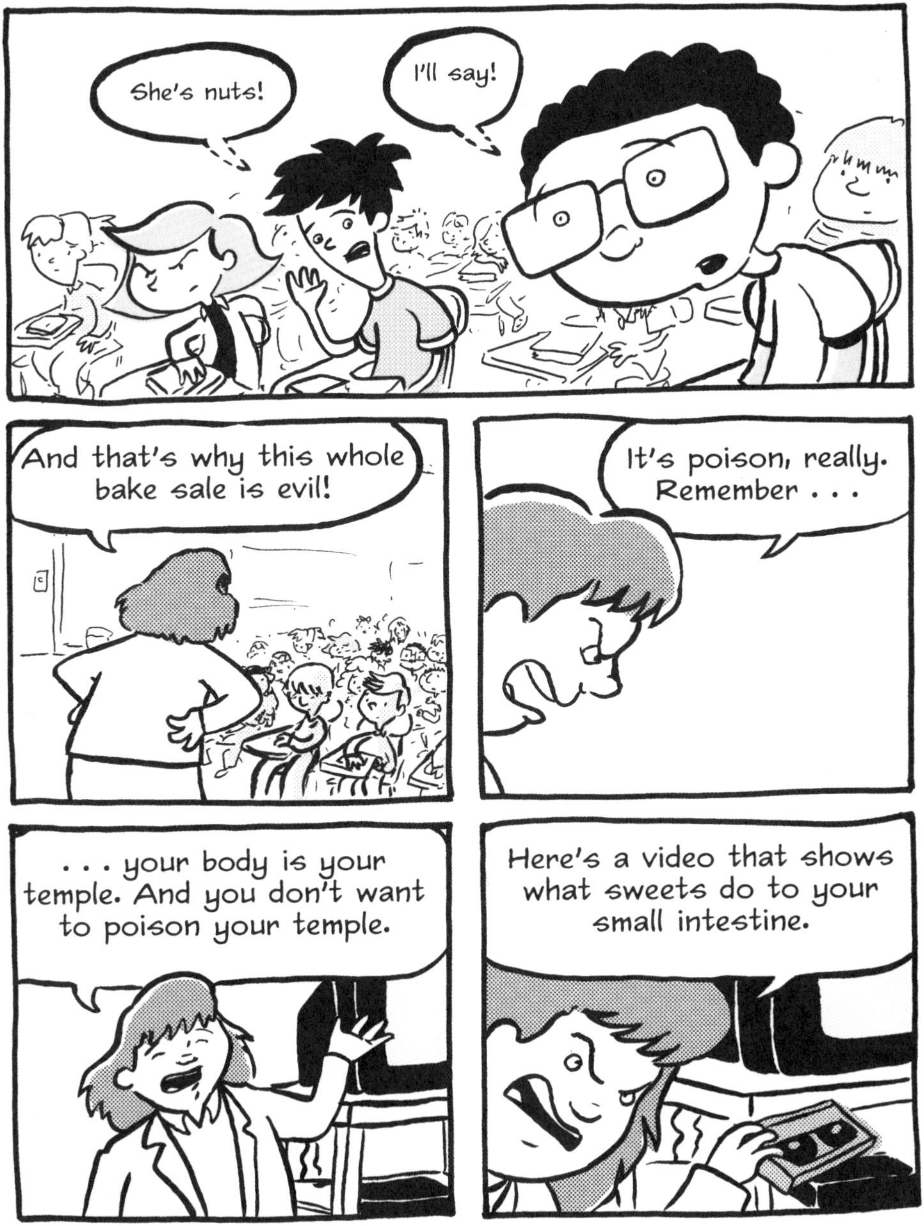
She's nuts!
I'll say!
And that's why this whole bake sale is evil!
It's poison, really. Remember . . .
. . . your body is your temple. And you don't want to poison your temple.
Here's a video that shows what sweets do to your small intestine.

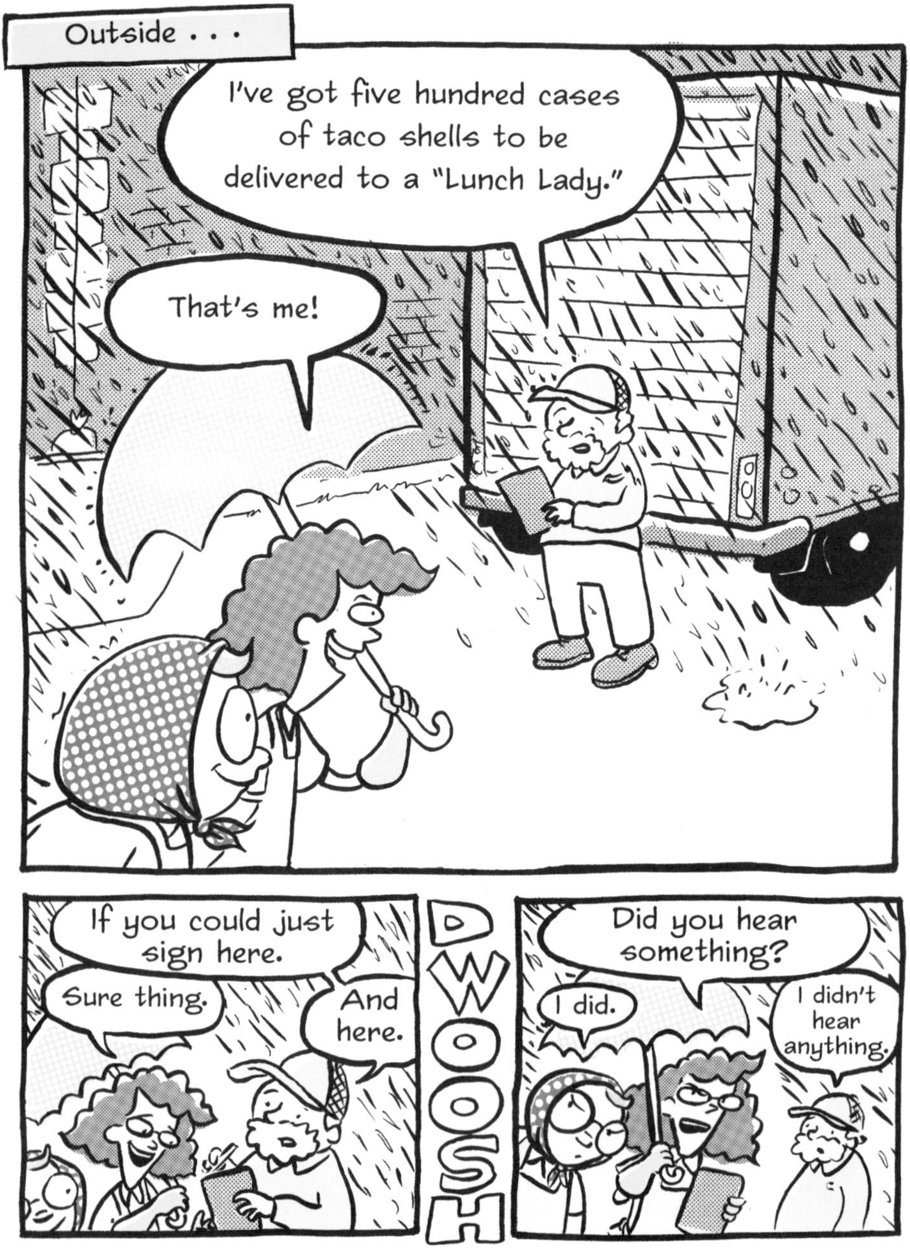
Outside . . .
I've got five hundred cases of taco shells to be delivered to a "Lunch Lady."
That's me!
If you could just sign here.
Sure thing.
And here.
DWOOSH
Did you hear something?
I did.
I didn't hear anything.

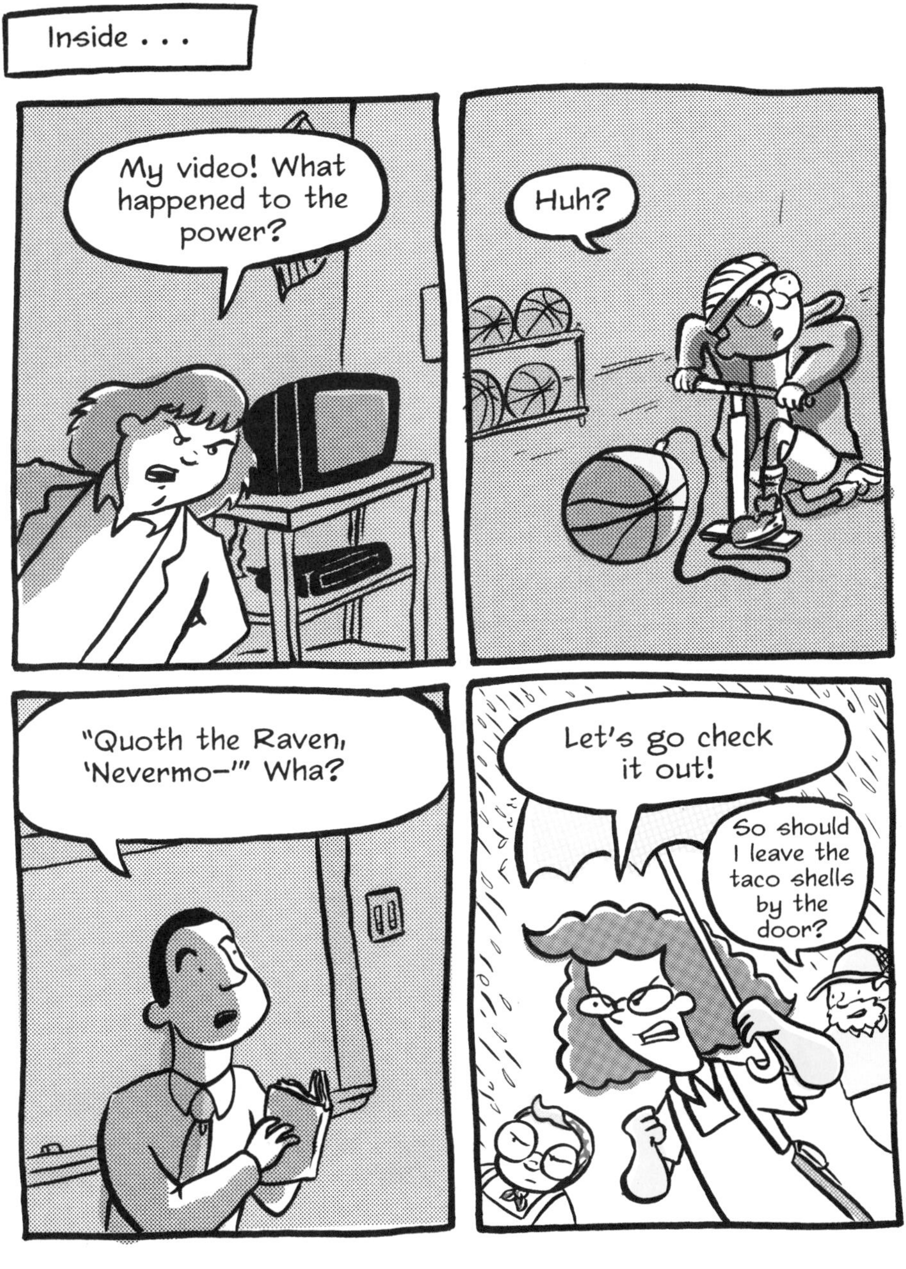
Inside . . .
My video! What happened to the power?
Huh?
"Quoth the Raven, 'Nevermo–'" Wha?
Let's go check it out!
So should I leave the taco shells by the door?

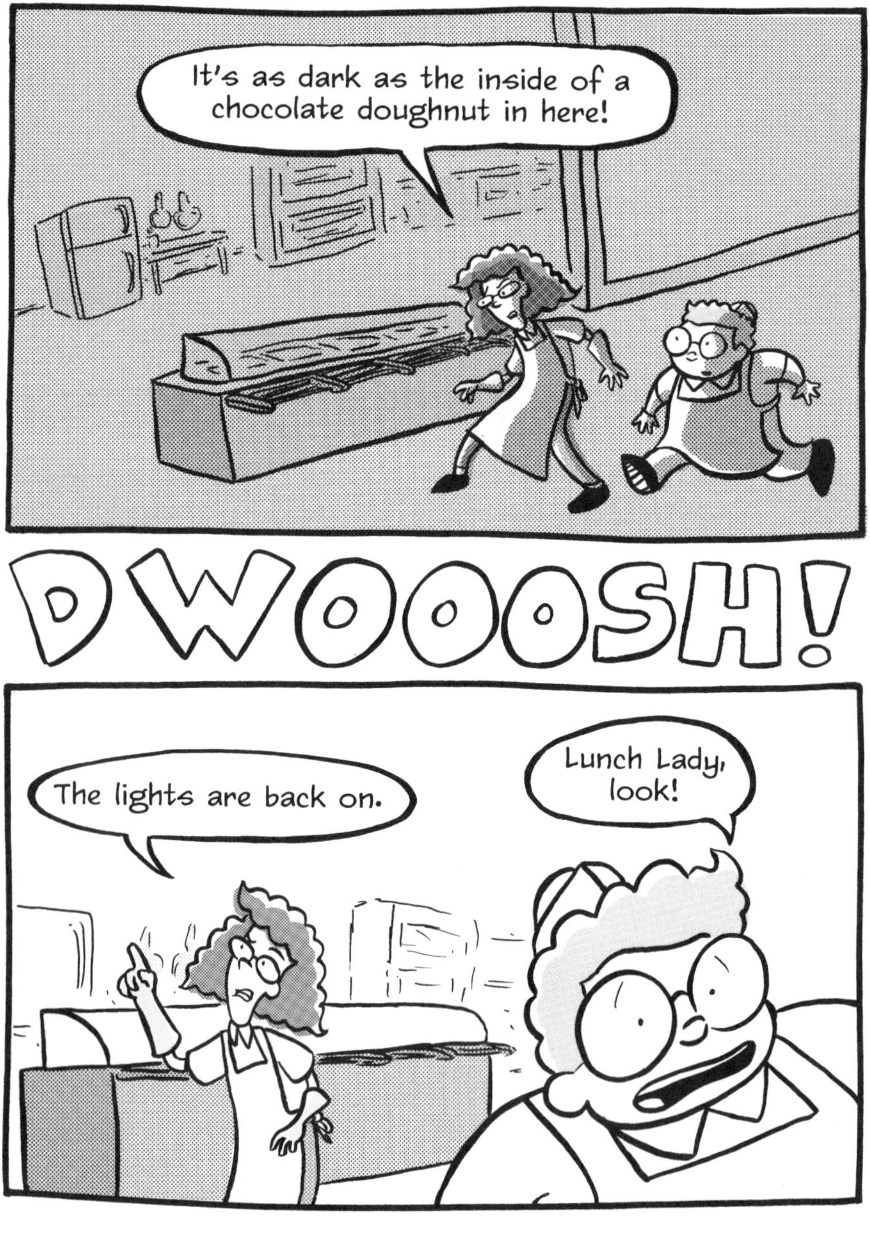
It's as dark as the inside of a chocolate doughnut in here!
DWOOOSH!
The lights are back on.
Lunch Lady, look!

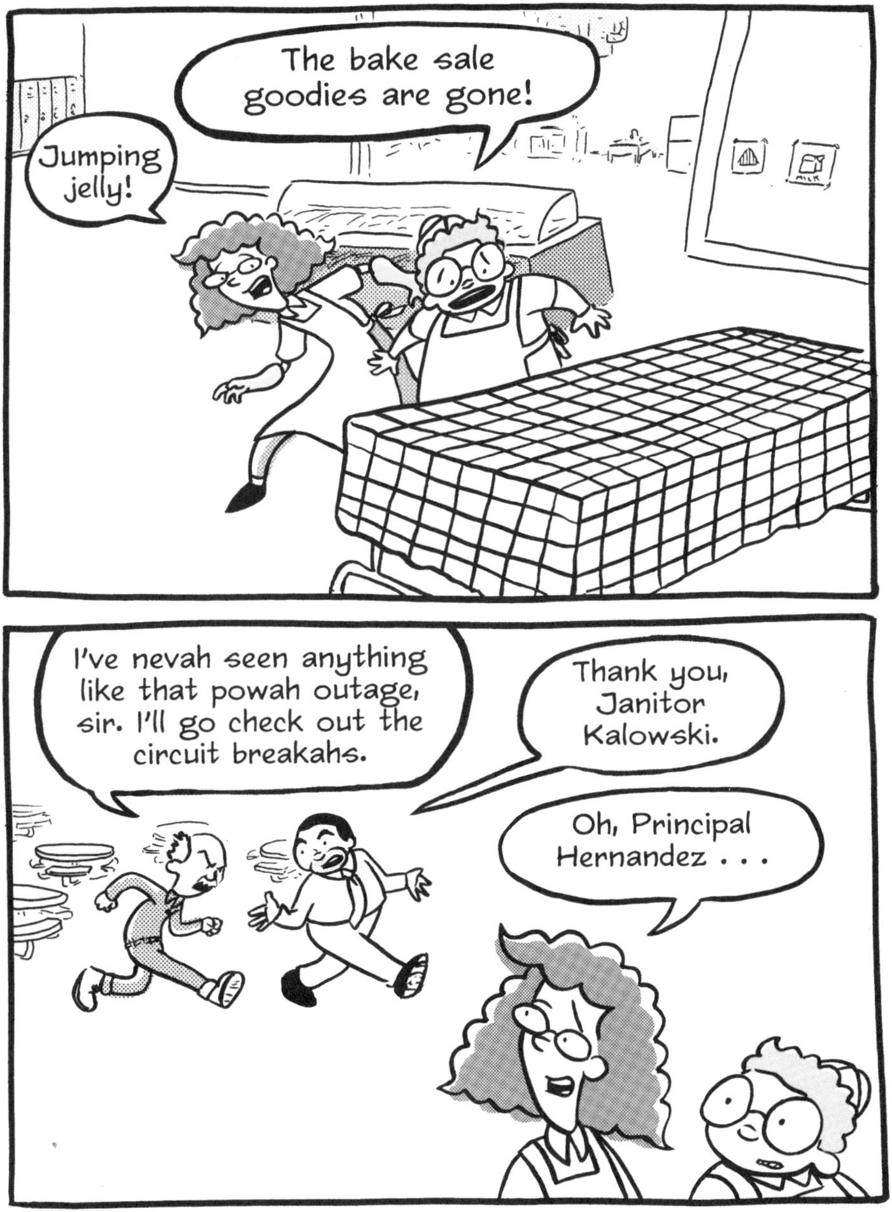

The bake sale goodies are gone!
Jumping jelly!
I've nevah seen anything like that powah outage, sir. I'll go check out the circuit breakahs.
Thank you, Janitor Kalowski.
Oh, Principal Hernandez . . .

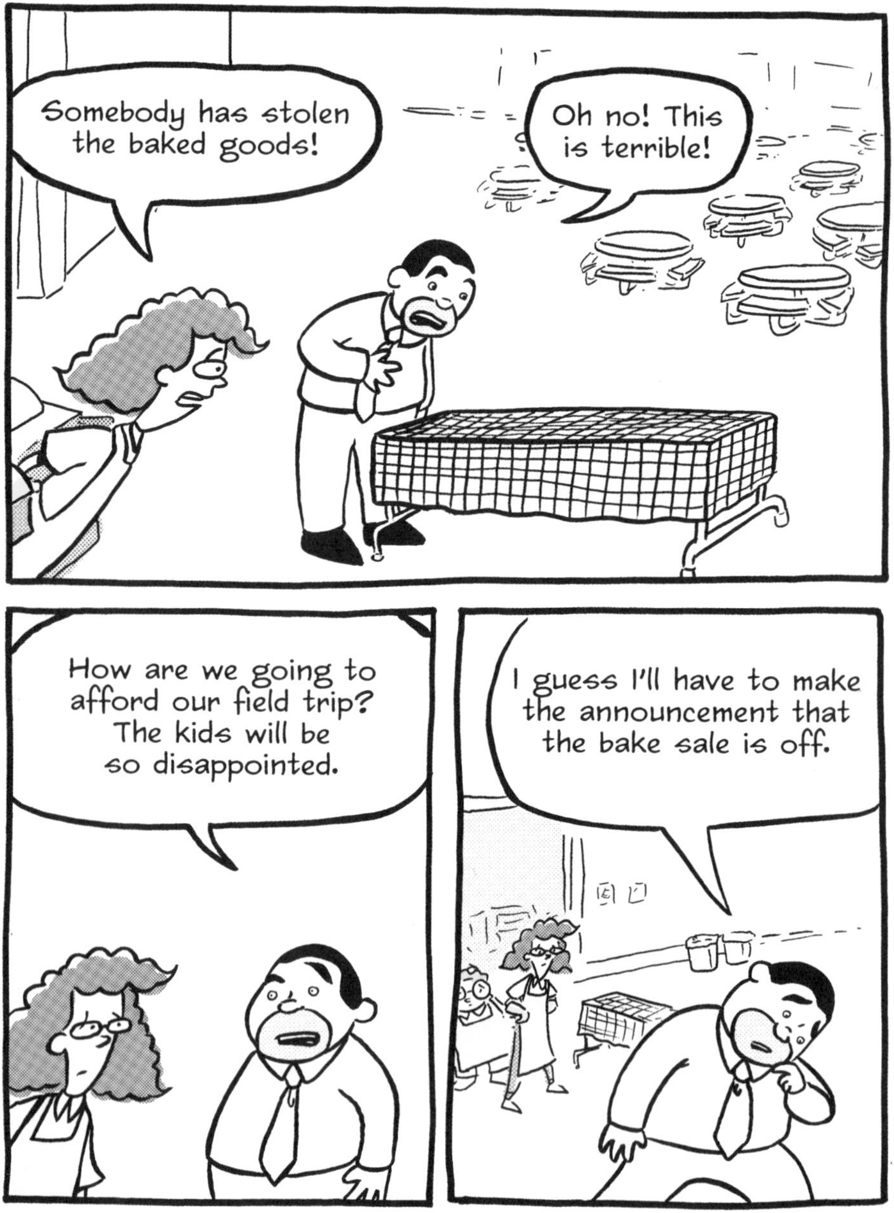
Somebody has stolen the baked goods!
Oh no! This is terrible!
How are we going to afford our field trip? The kids will be so disappointed.
I guess I'll have to make the announcement that the bake sale is off.

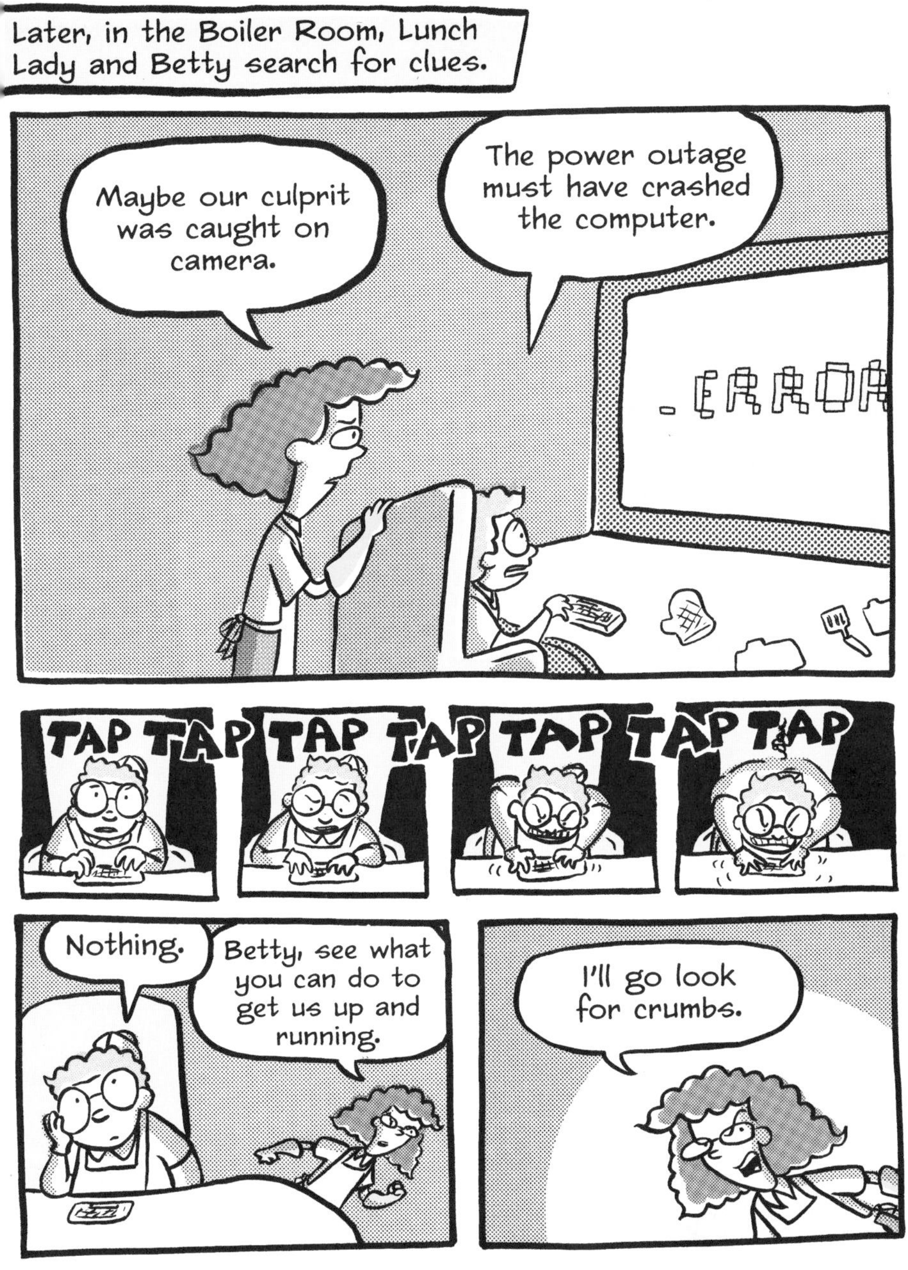

Later, in the Boiler Room, Lunch Lady and Betty search for clues.
Maybe our culprit was caught on camera.
The power outage must have crashed the computer.
ERROR
TAP TAP TAP TAP TAP TAP TAP TAP
Nothing.
Betty, see what you can do to get us up and running.
I'll go look for crumbs.

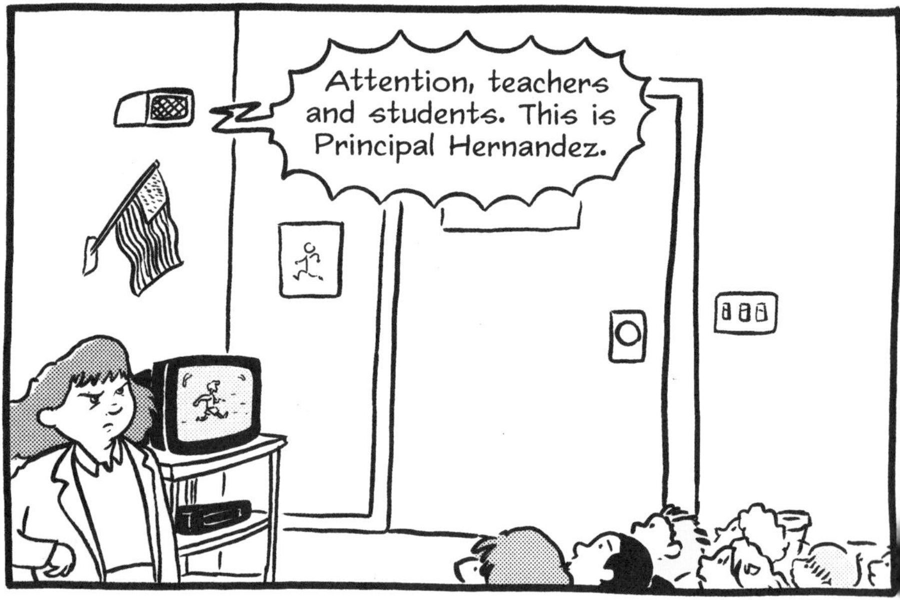
Attention, teachers and students. This is Principal Hernandez.

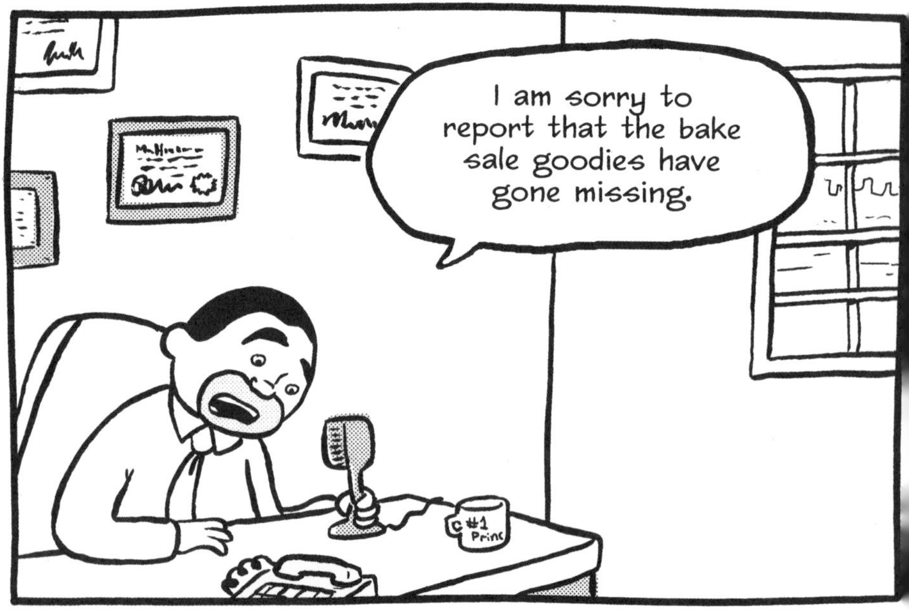
I am sorry to report that the bake sale goodies have gone missing.
#1 Princ

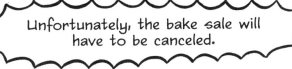

Unfortunately, the bake sale will have to be canceled.

No bake sale means no field trip.

And no cookies.

As Safety Patrol officer, I will solve this mystery!

BRRRIIIIOIIINNGG!

Sit down, Orson.

C'mon, guys . . .

. . . we'll be the ones to get to the bottom of this!

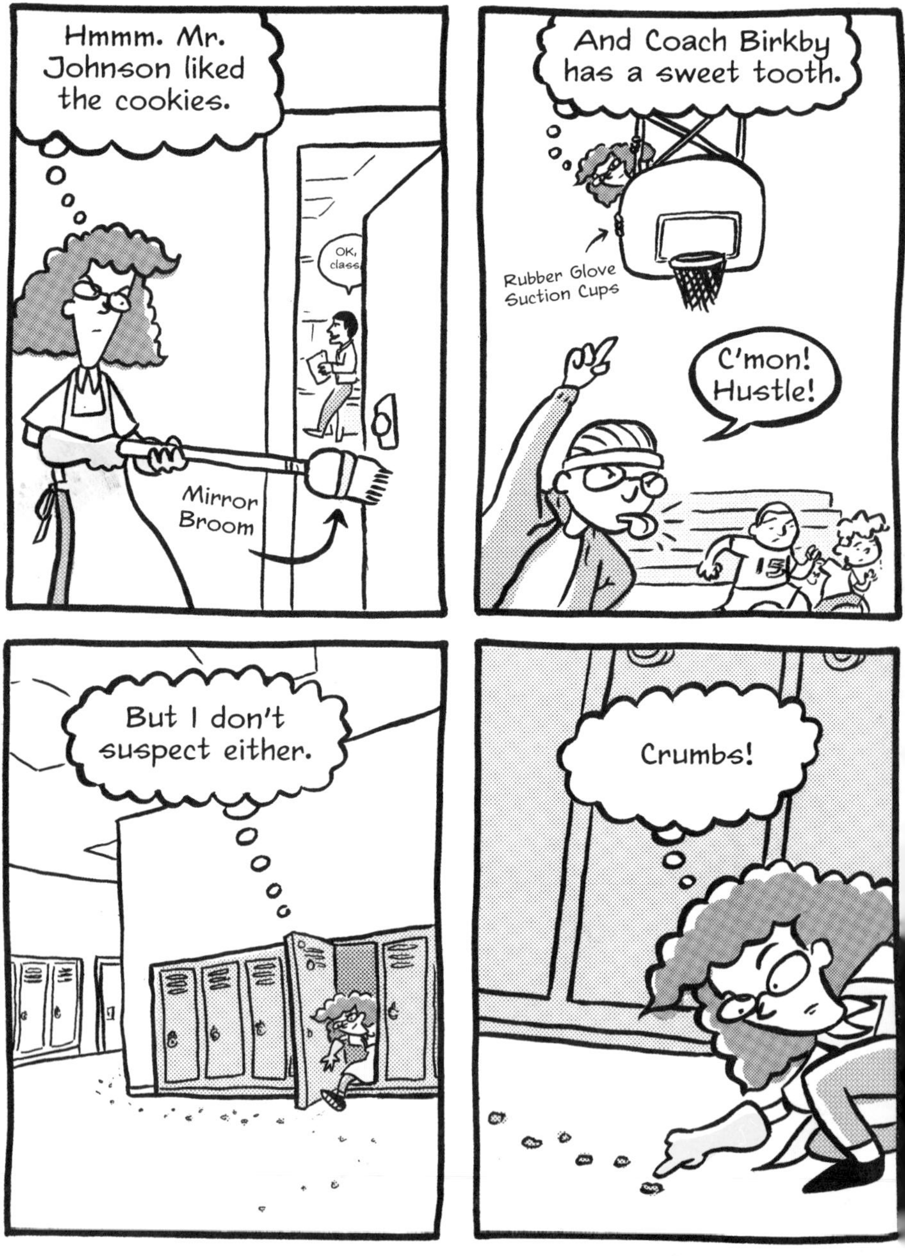

Hmmm. Mr. Johnson liked the cookies.
OK, class
Mirror Broom
And Coach Birkby has a sweet tooth.
Rubber Glove Suction Cups
C'mon! Hustle!
But I don't suspect either.
Crumbs!

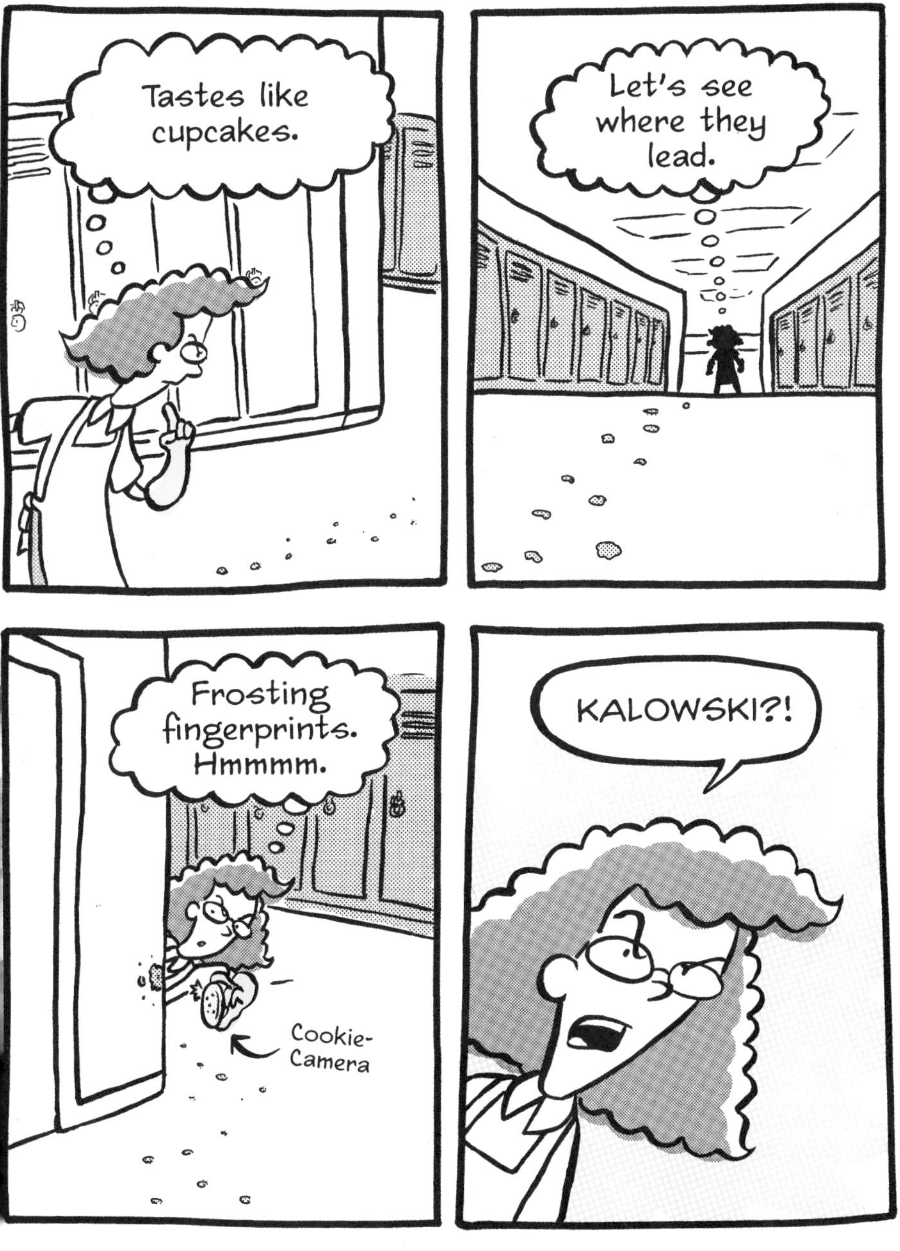
Tastes like cupcakes.
Let's see where they lead.
Frosting fingerprints. Hmmmm.
Cookie-Camera
KALOWSKI?!

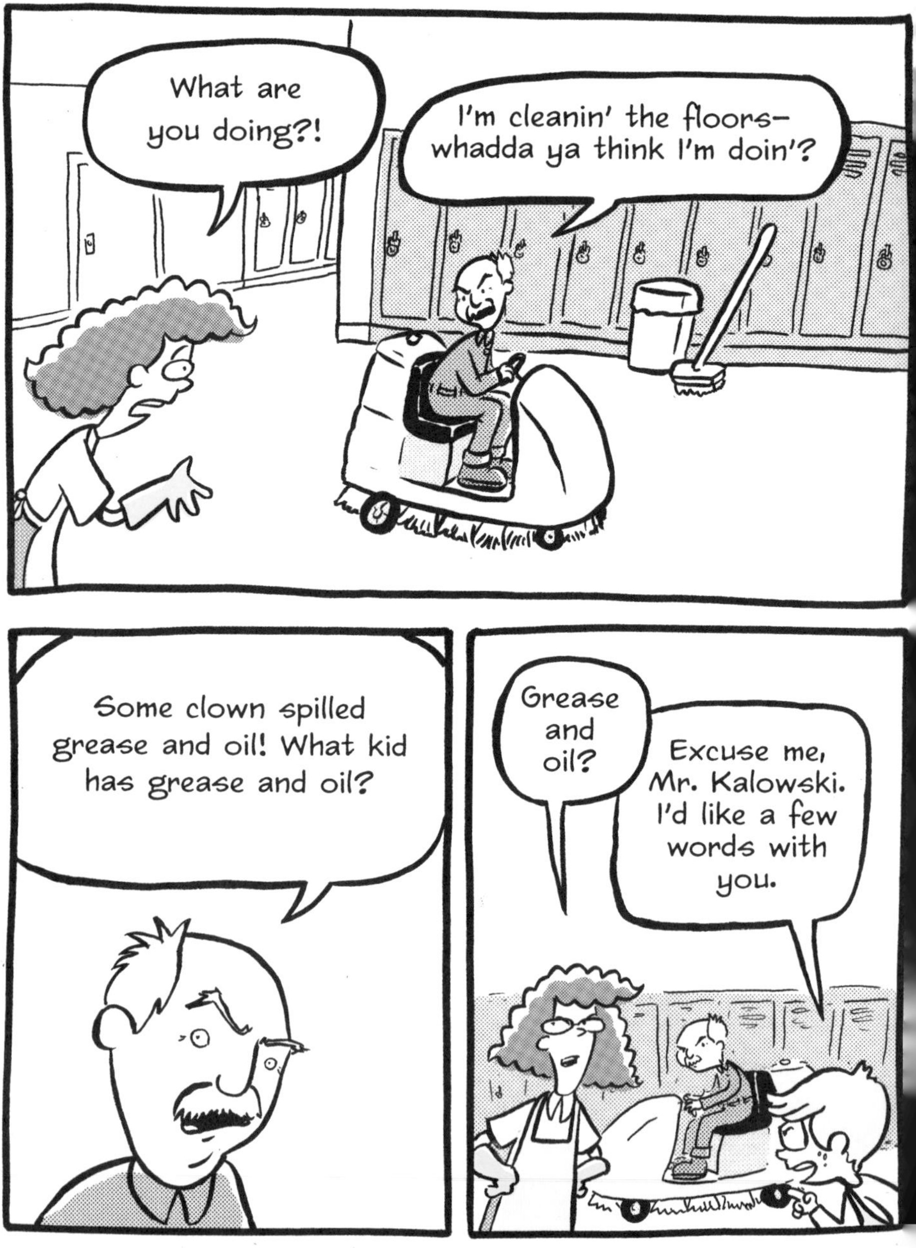
What are you doing?!
I'm cleanin' the floors–whadda ya think I'm doin'?
Some clown spilled grease and oil! What kid has grease and oil?
Grease and oil?
Excuse me, Mr. Kalowski. I'd like a few words with you.

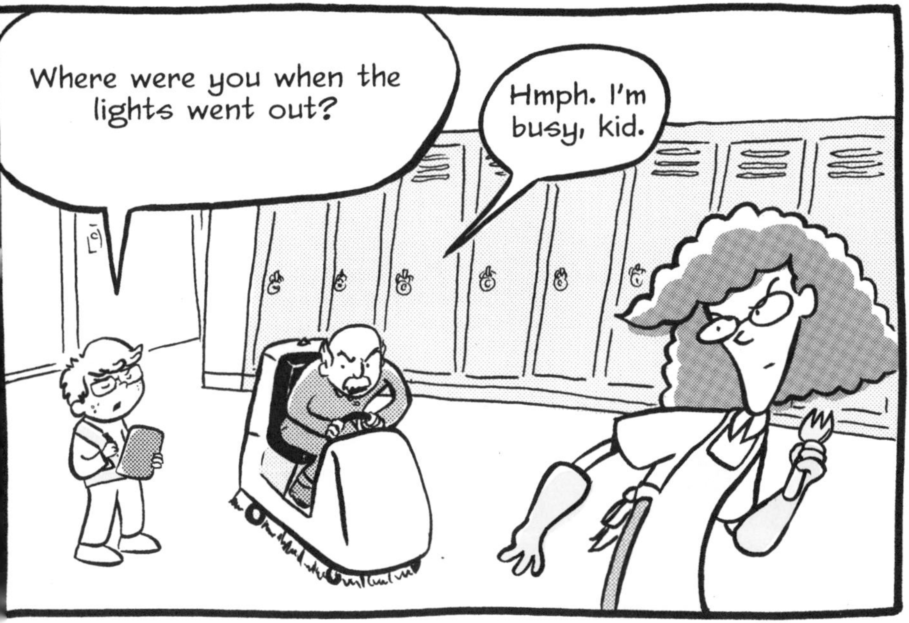
Where were you when the lights went out?
Hmph. I'm busy, kid.

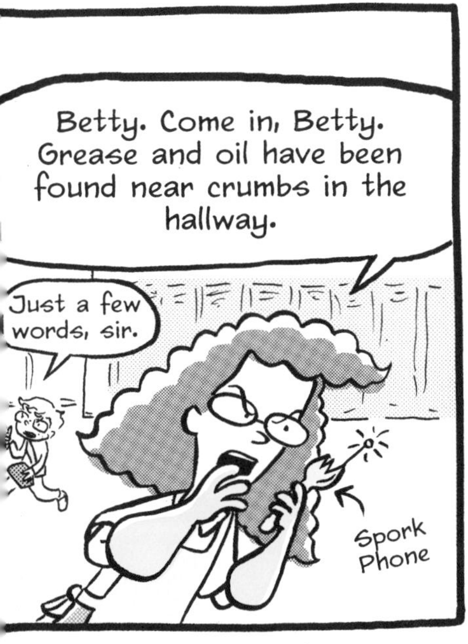
Betty. Come in, Betty. Grease and oil have been found near crumbs in the hallway.
Just a few words, sir.
Spork Phone

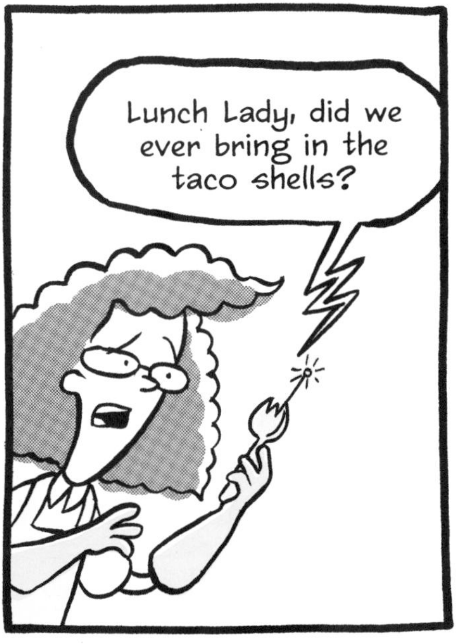
Lunch Lady, did we ever bring in the taco shells?

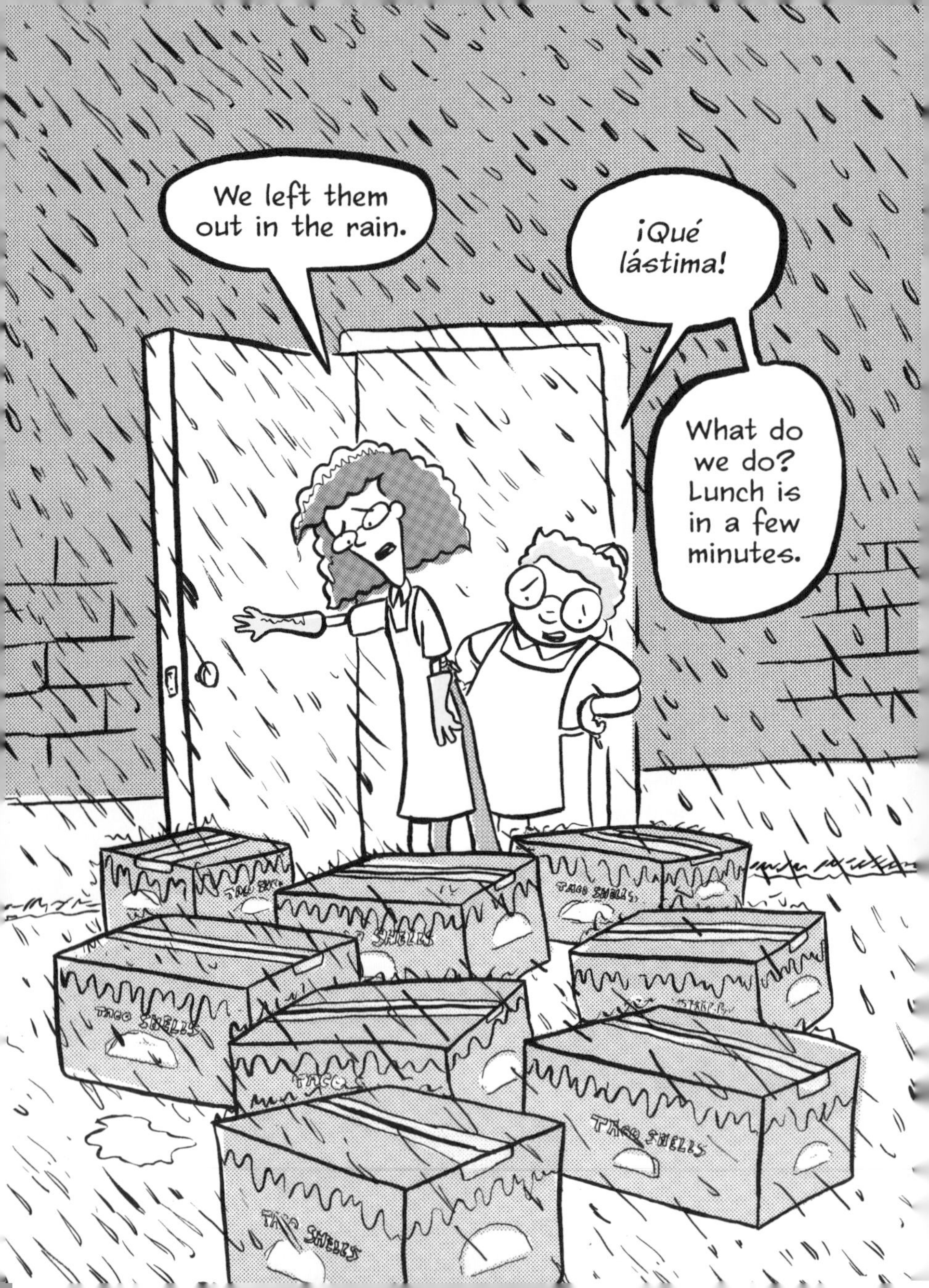
We left them out in the rain.
¡Qué lástima!
What do we do? Lunch is in a few minutes.
TACO SHELLS
TACO SHELLS
TACO SHELLS

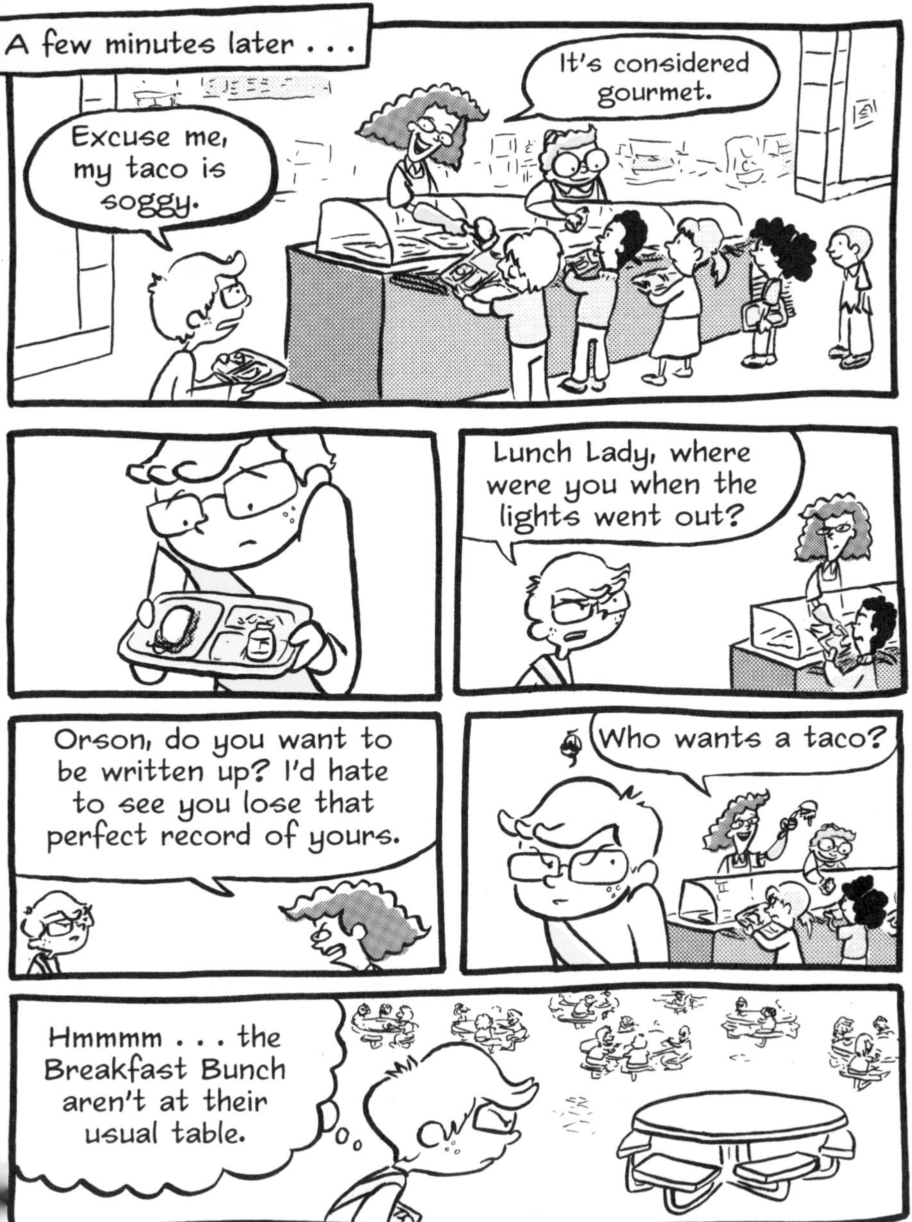
A few minutes later . . .
Excuse me, my taco is soggy.
It's considered gourmet.
Lunch Lady, where were you when the lights went out?
Orson, do you want to be written up? I'd hate to see you lose that perfect record of yours.
Who wants a taco?
Hmmmm . . . the Breakfast Bunch aren't at their usual table.

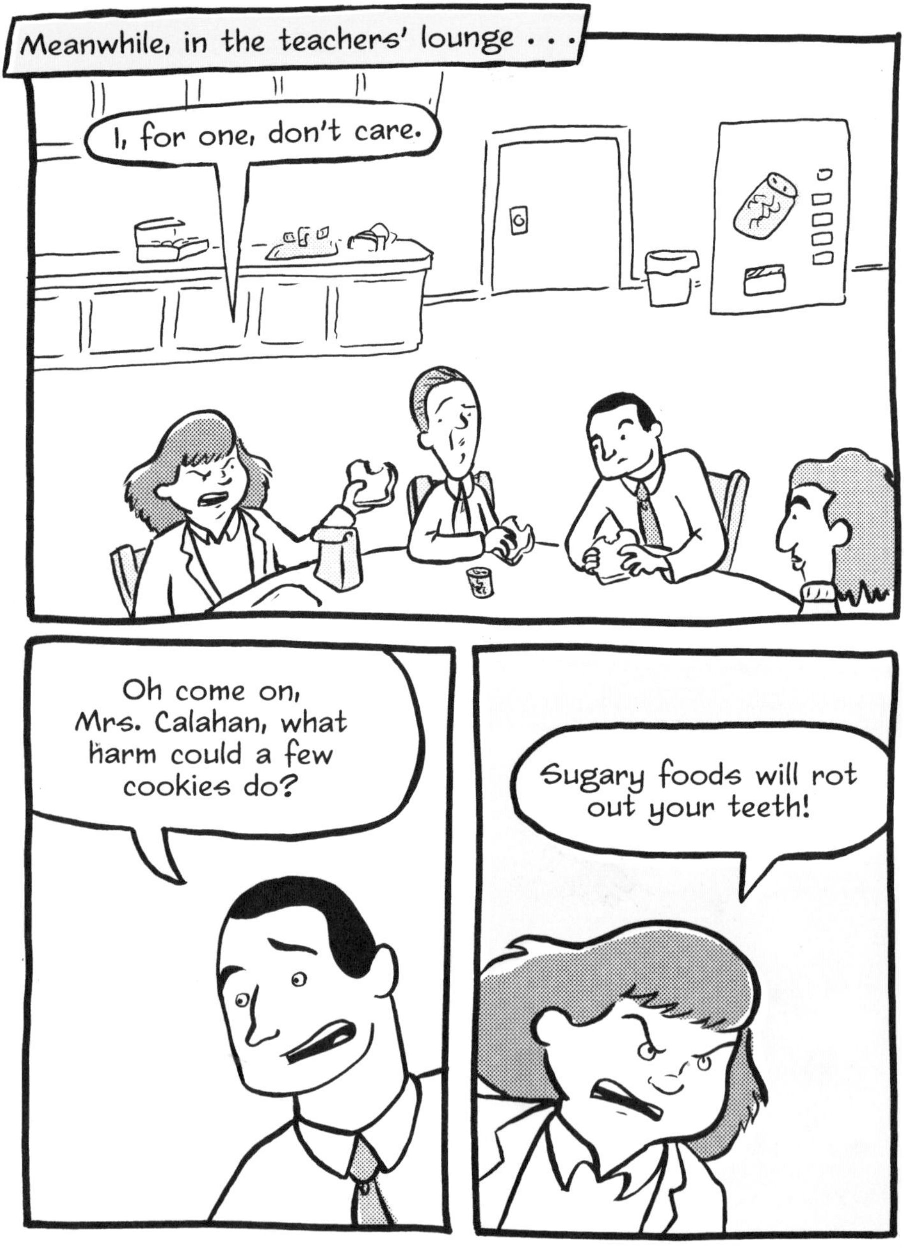
Meanwhile, in the teachers' lounge . . .
I, for one, don't care.
Oh come on, Mrs. Calahan, what harm could a few cookies do?
Sugary foods will rot out your teeth!

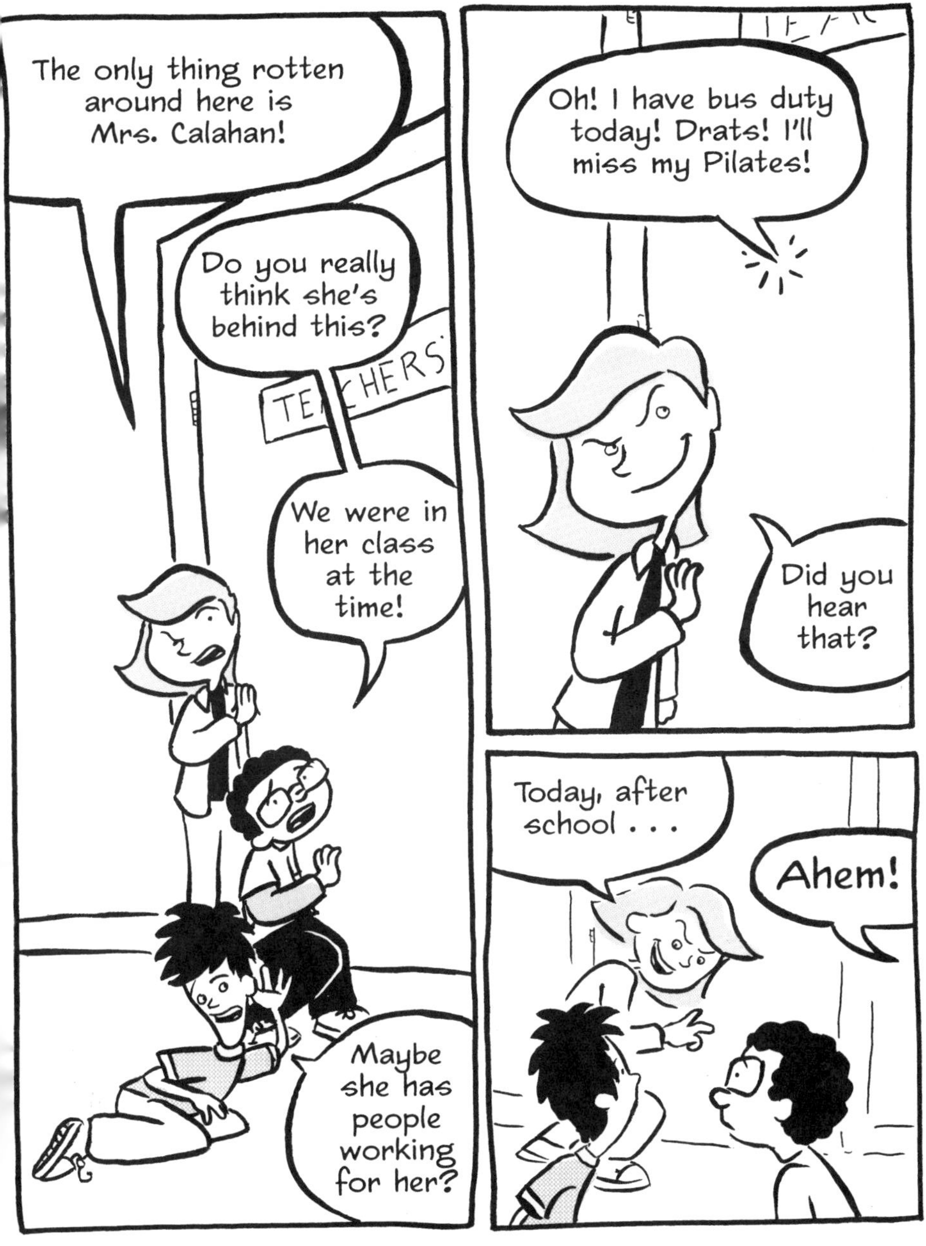
The only thing rotten around here is Mrs. Calahan!
Do you really think she's behind this?
TEACHERS'
We were in her class at the time!
Maybe she has people working for her?
Oh! I have bus duty today! Drats! I'll miss my Pilates!
Did you hear that?
Today, after school . . .
Ahem!

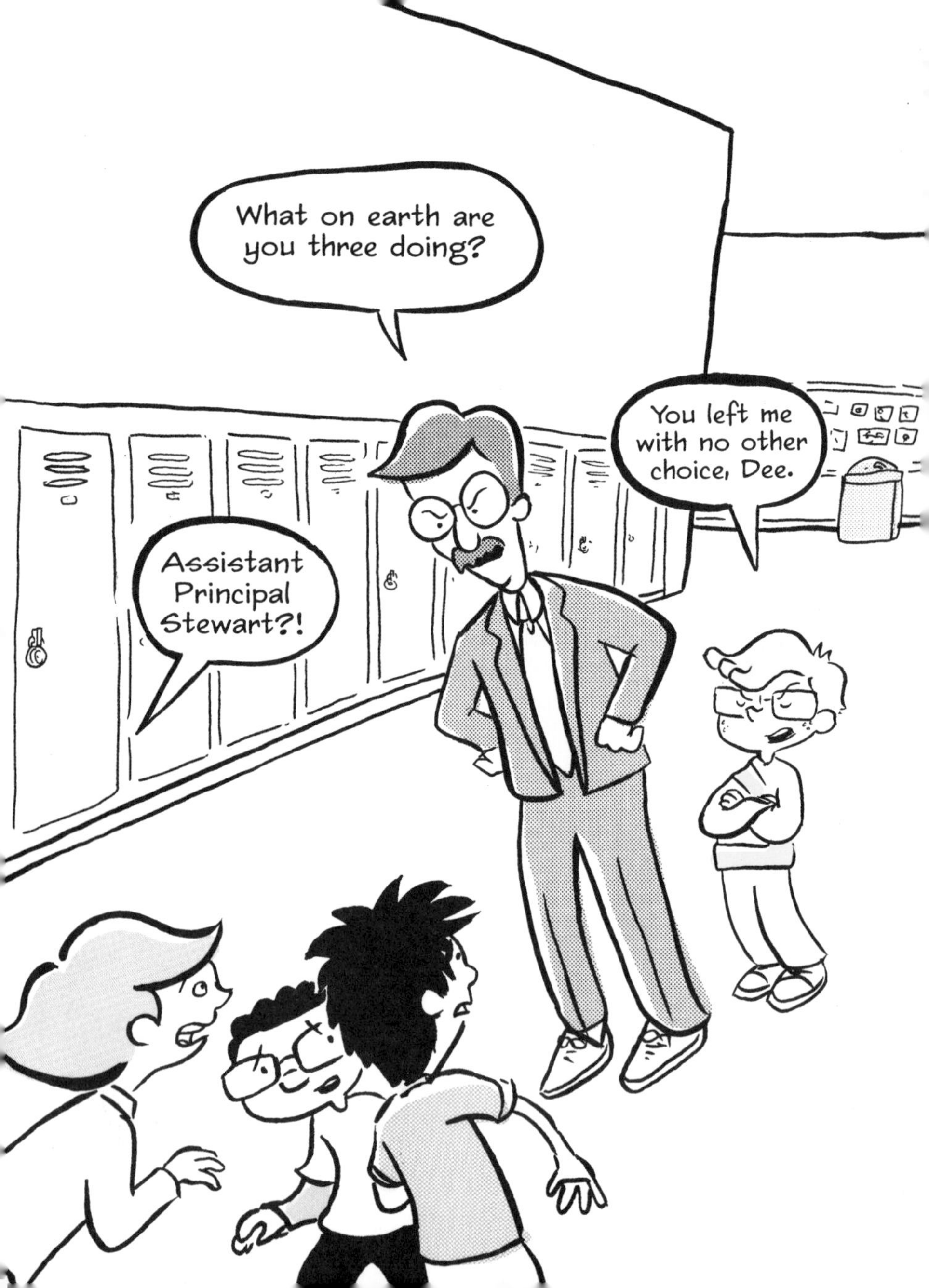
What on earth are you three doing?
Assistant Principal Stewart?!
You left me with no other choice, Dee.

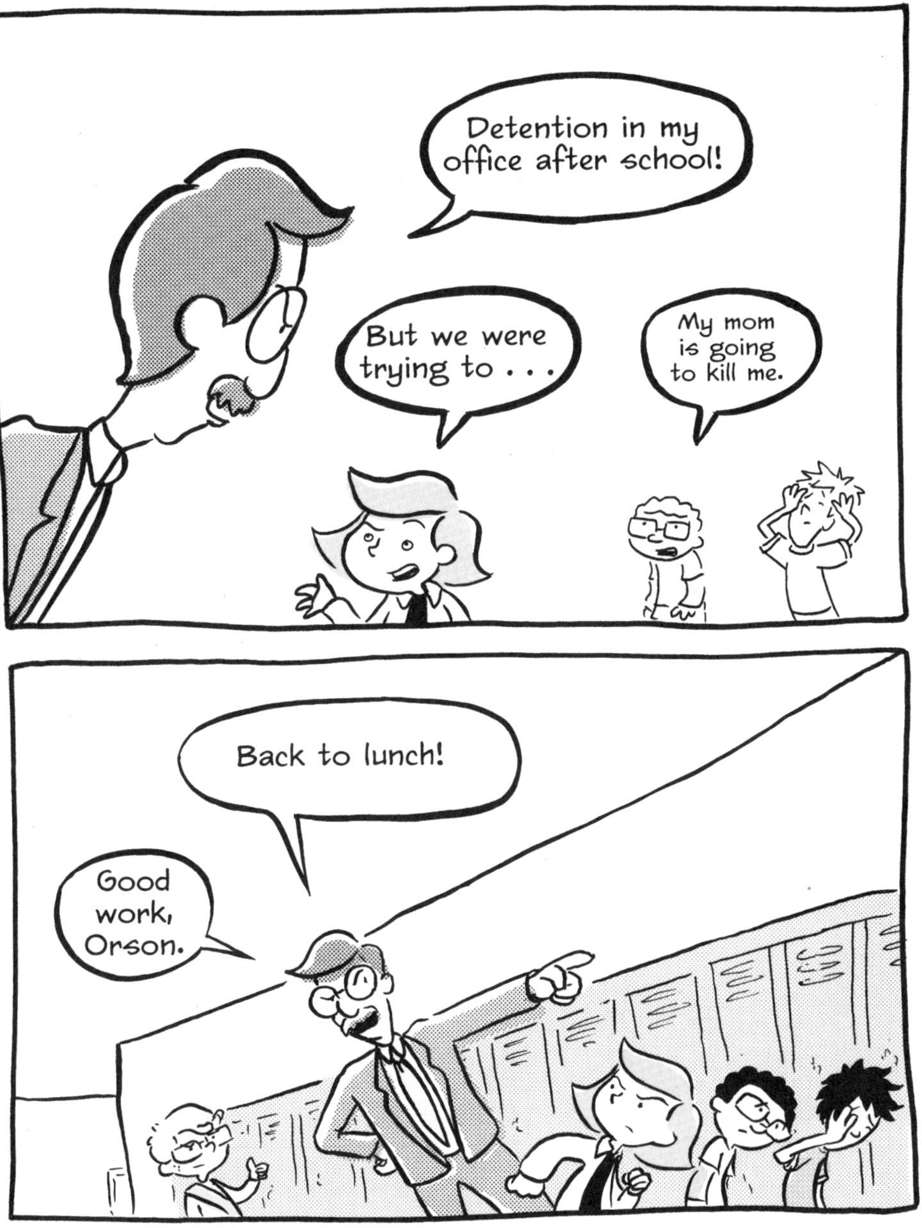
Detention in my office after school!
But we were trying to . . .
My mom is going to kill me.
Back to lunch!
Good work, Orson.

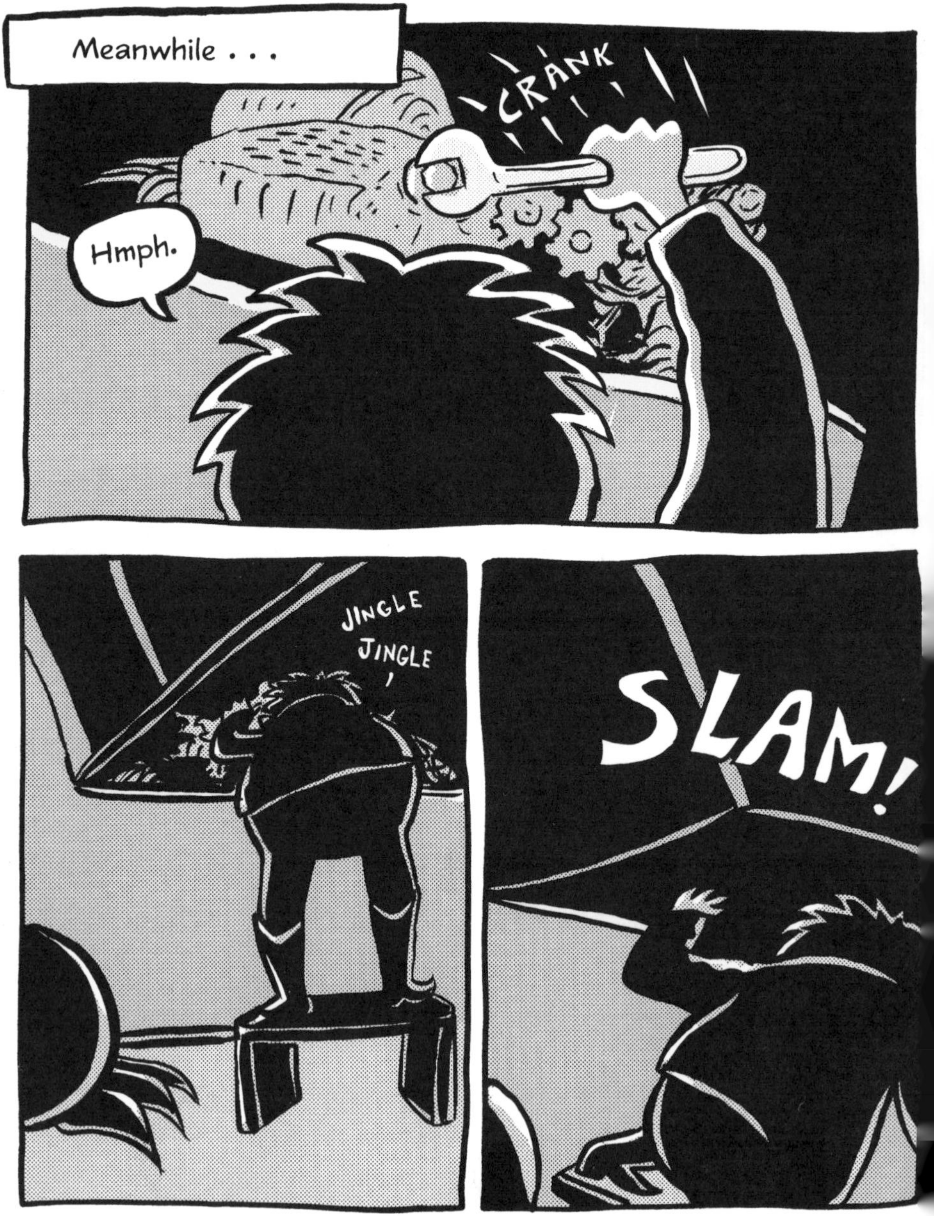
Meanwhile . . .
CRANK
Hmph.
JINGLE JINGLE
SLAM!

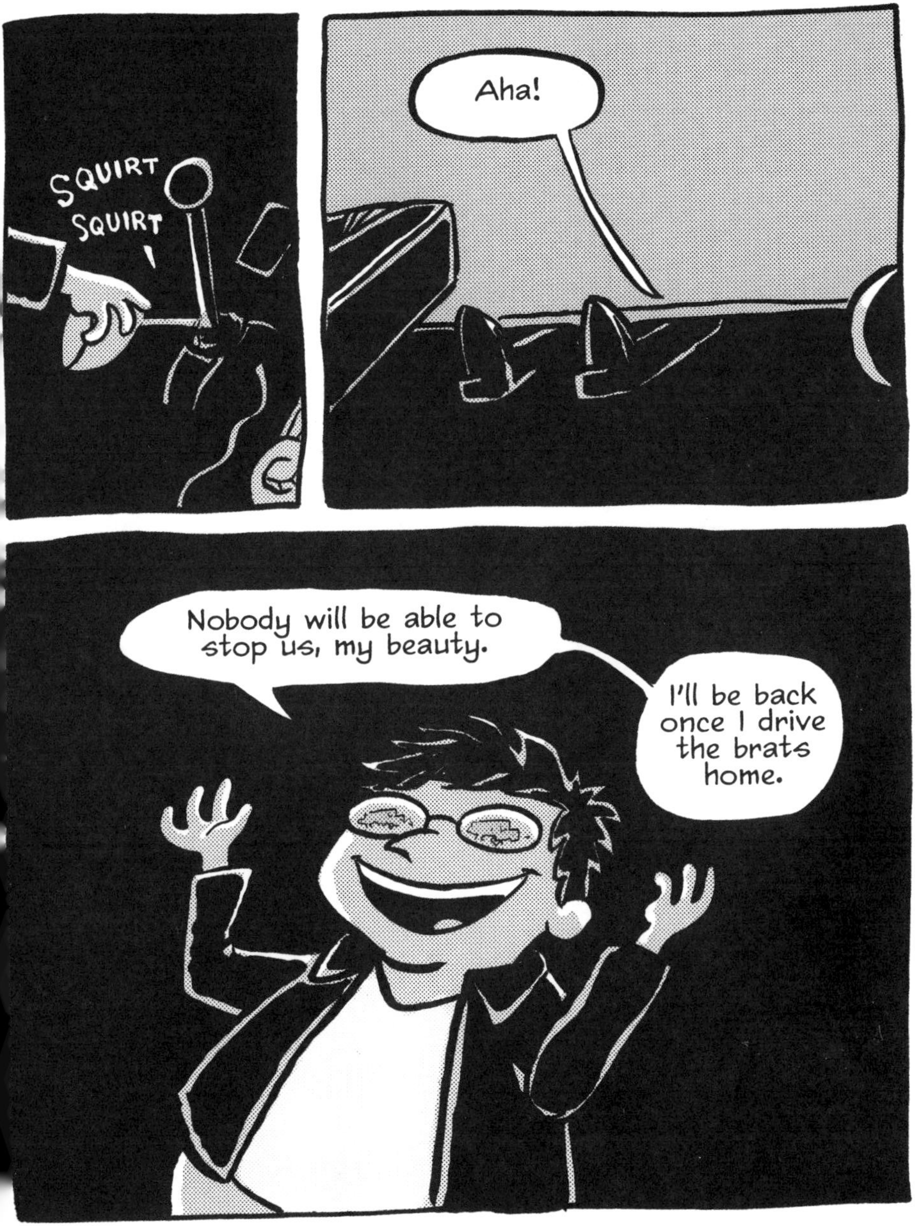
SQUIRT
SQUIRT
Aha!
Nobody will be able to stop us, my beauty.
I'll be back once I drive the brats home.

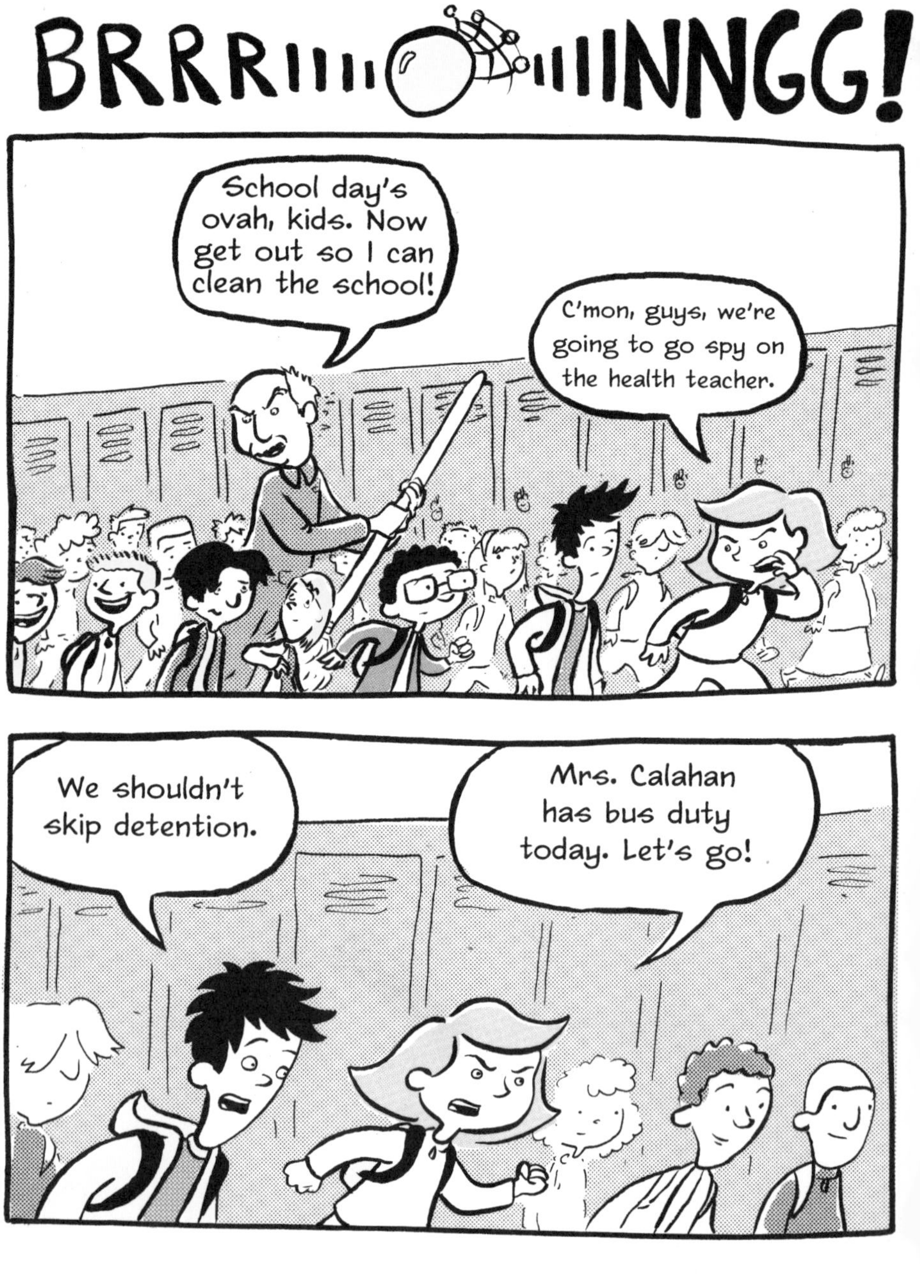
BRRRIIIIII•IIIIIINNGG!
School day's ovah, kids. Now get out so I can clean the school!
C'mon, guys, we're going to go spy on the health teacher.
We shouldn't skip detention.
Mrs. Calahan has bus duty today. Let's go!

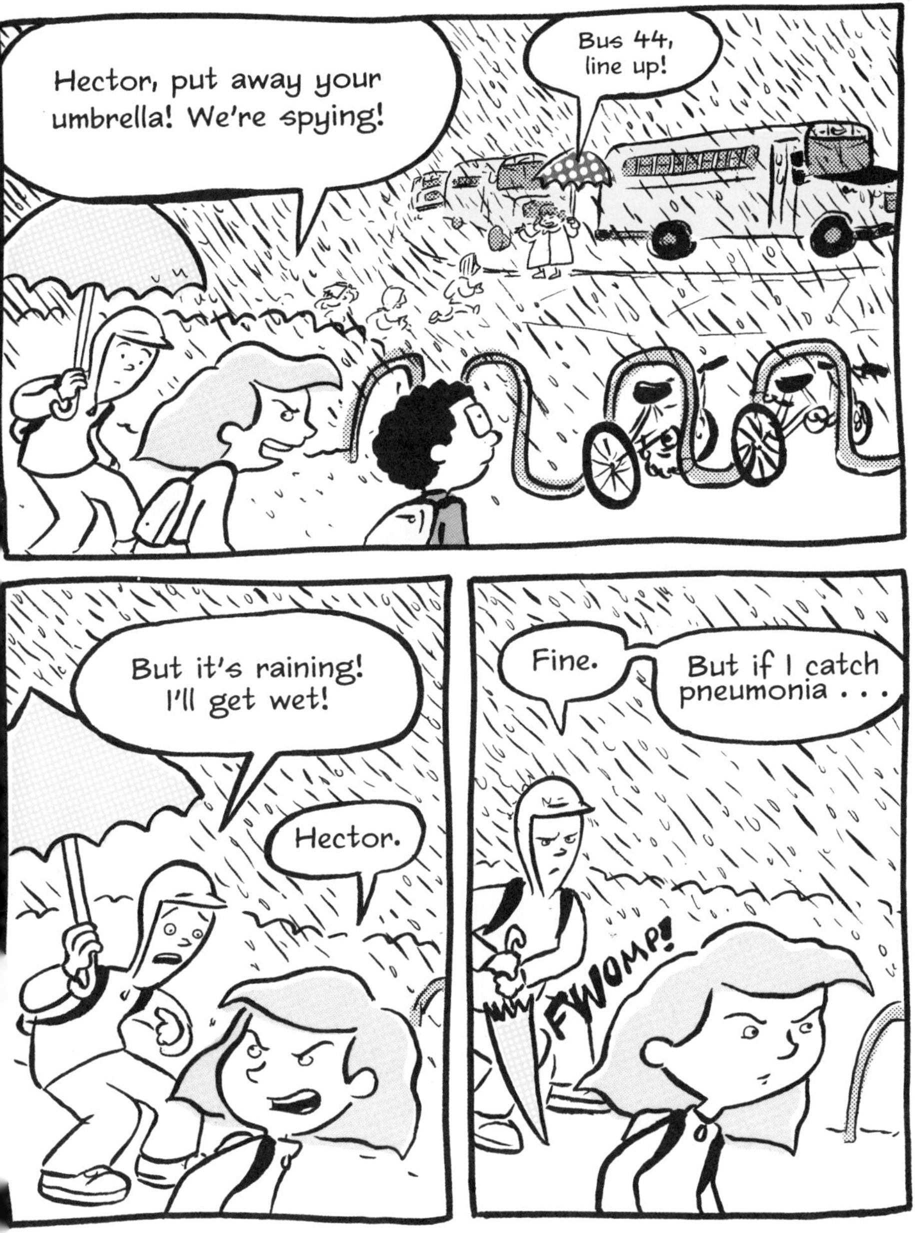
Hector, put away your umbrella! We're spying!
Bus 44, line up!
But it's raining! I'll get wet!
Hector.
Fine.
But if I catch pneumonia . . .
FWOMP!

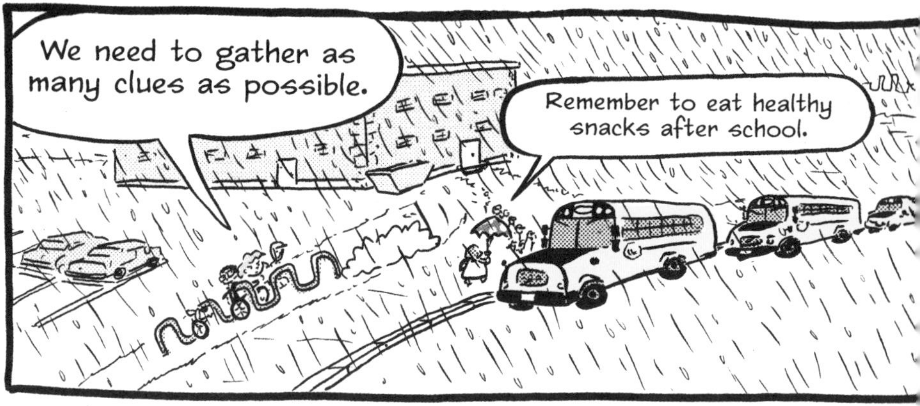
We need to gather as many clues as possible.
Remember to eat healthy snacks after school.

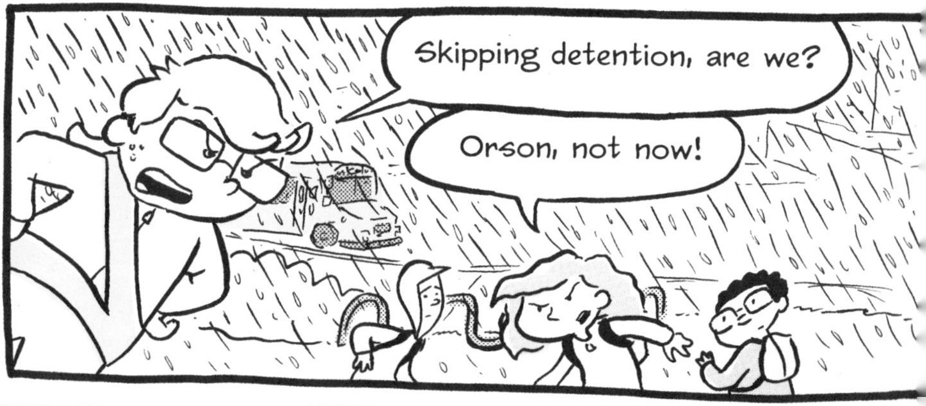
Skipping detention, are we?
Orson, not now!

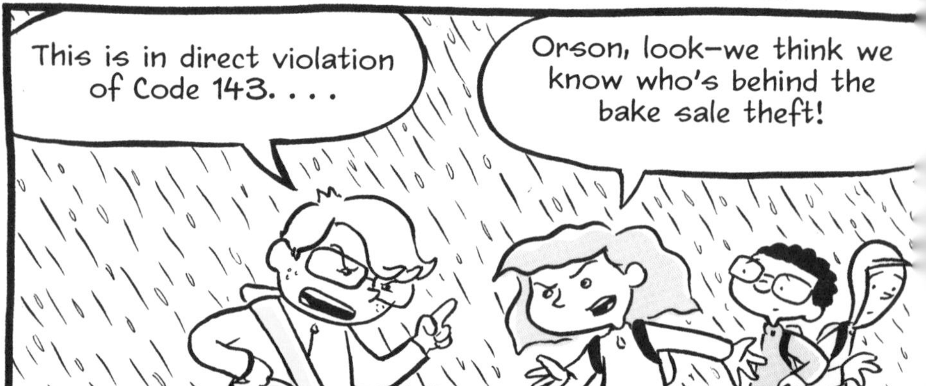
This is in direct violation of Code 143. . . .
Orson, look—we think we know who's behind the bake sale theft!

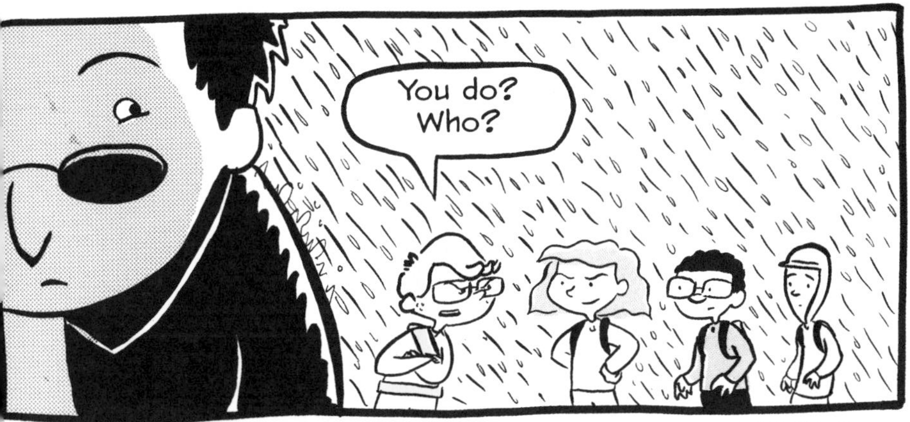
You do? Who?
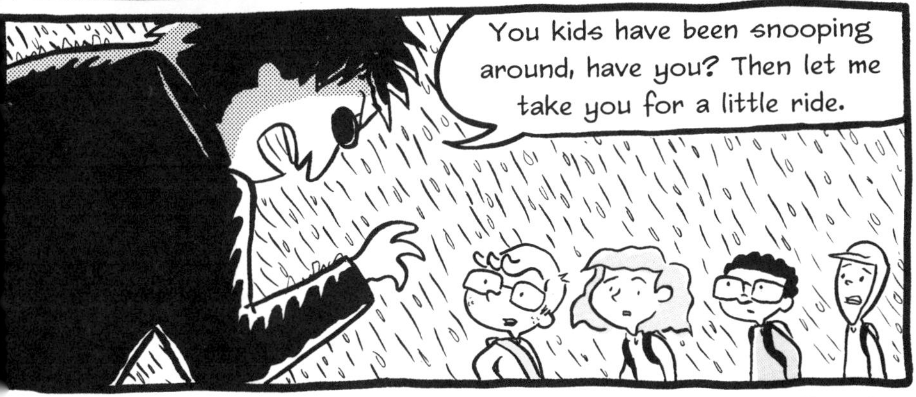
You kids have been snooping around, have you? Then let me take you for a little ride.
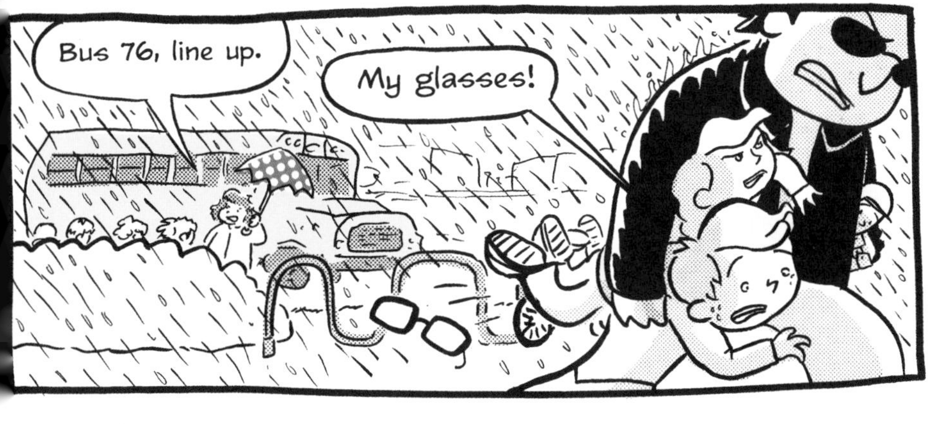
Bus 76, line up.
My glasses!

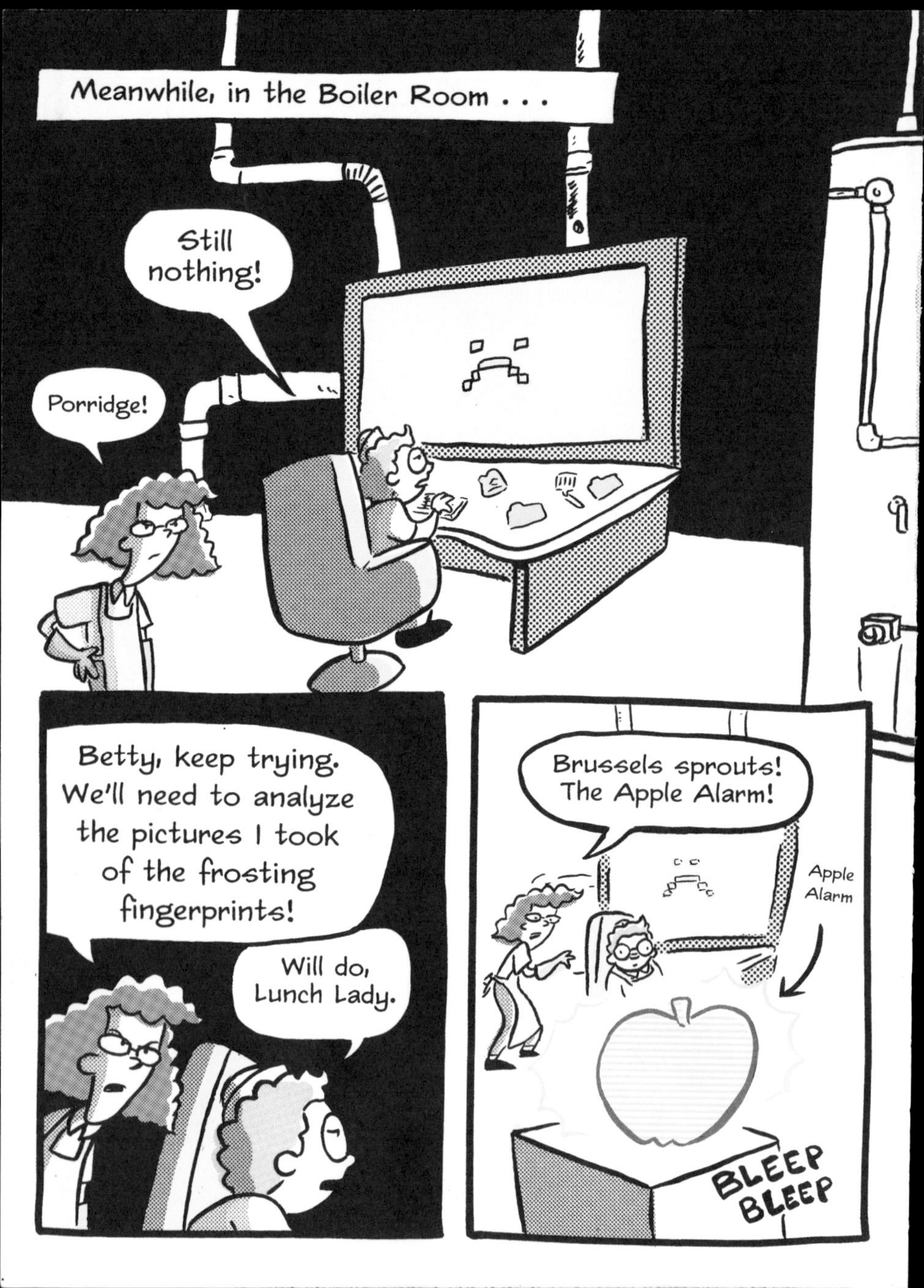
Meanwhile, in the Boiler Room . . .
Still nothing!
Porridge!
Betty, keep trying. We'll need to analyze the pictures I took of the frosting fingerprints!
Will do, Lunch Lady.
Brussels sprouts! The Apple Alarm!
Apple Alarm
BLEEP BLEEP

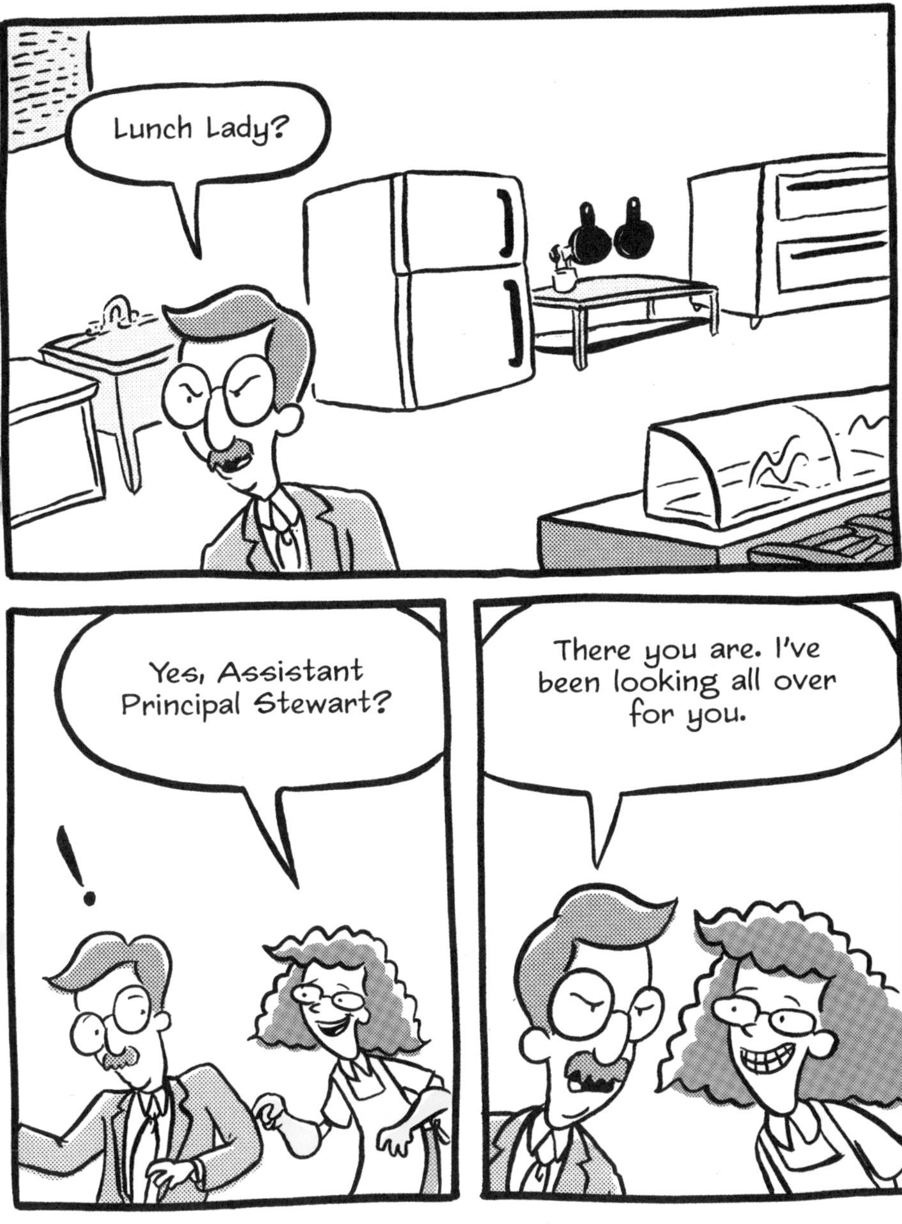
Lunch Lady?
!
Yes, Assistant Principal Stewart?
There you are. I've been looking all over for you.

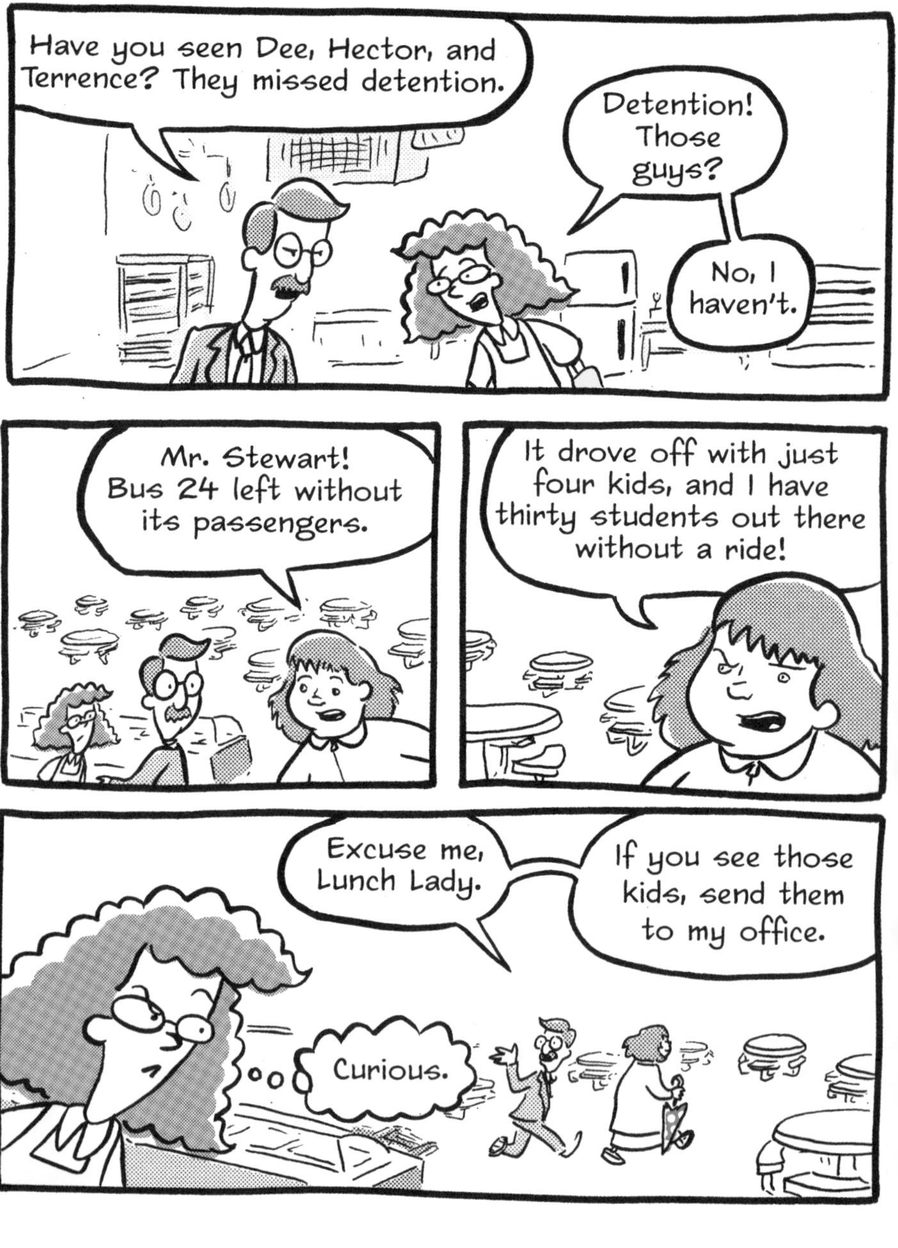
Have you seen Dee, Hector, and Terrence? They missed detention.
Detention! Those guys?
No, I haven't.
Mr. Stewart! Bus 24 left without its passengers.
It drove off with just four kids, and I have thirty students out there without a ride!
Excuse me, Lunch Lady.
If you see those kids, send them to my office.
Curious.

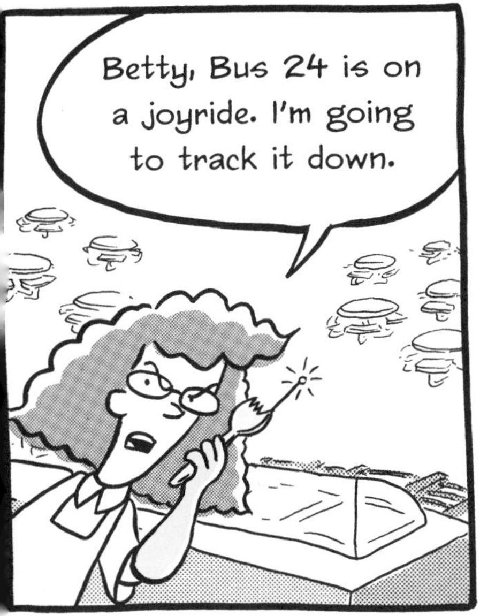
Betty, Bus 24 is on a joyride. I'm going to track it down.
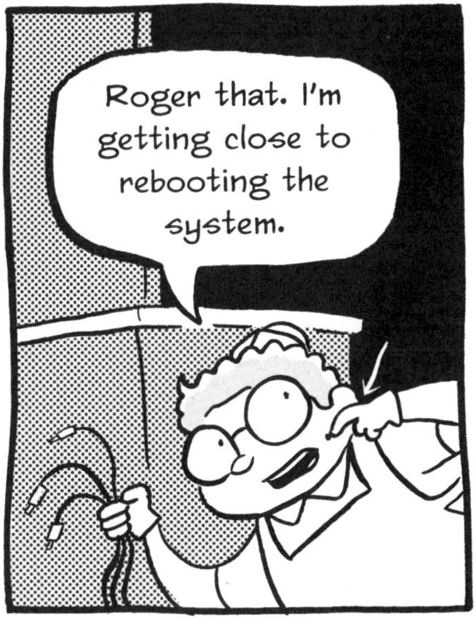
Roger that. I'm getting close to rebooting the system.
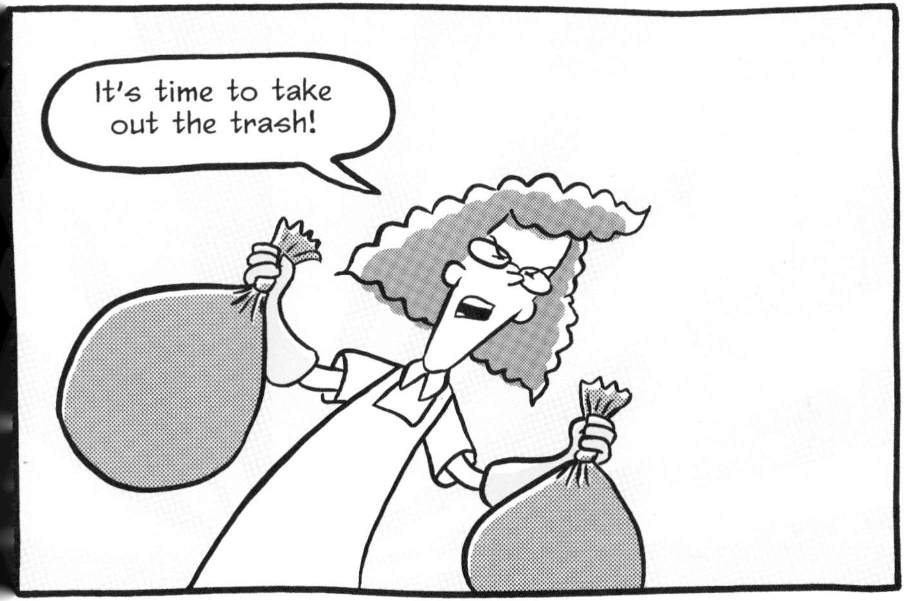
It's time to take out the trash!

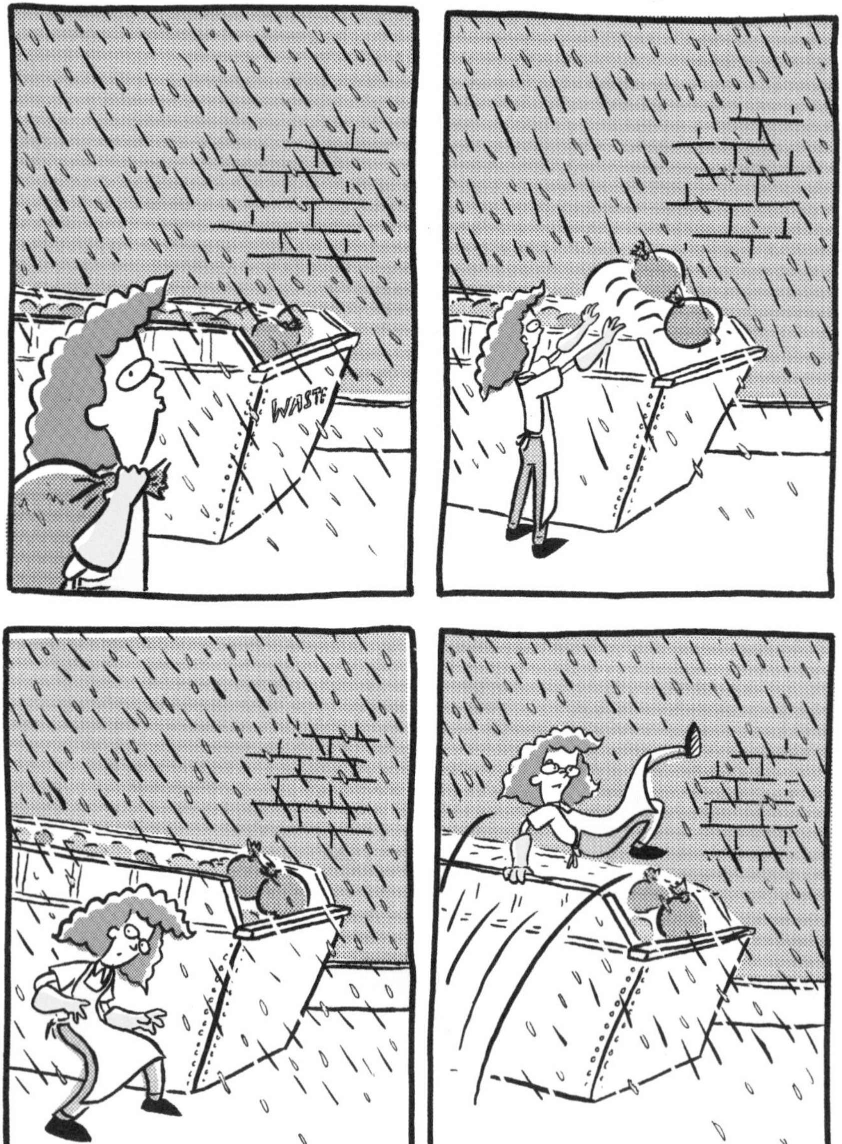
WASTE

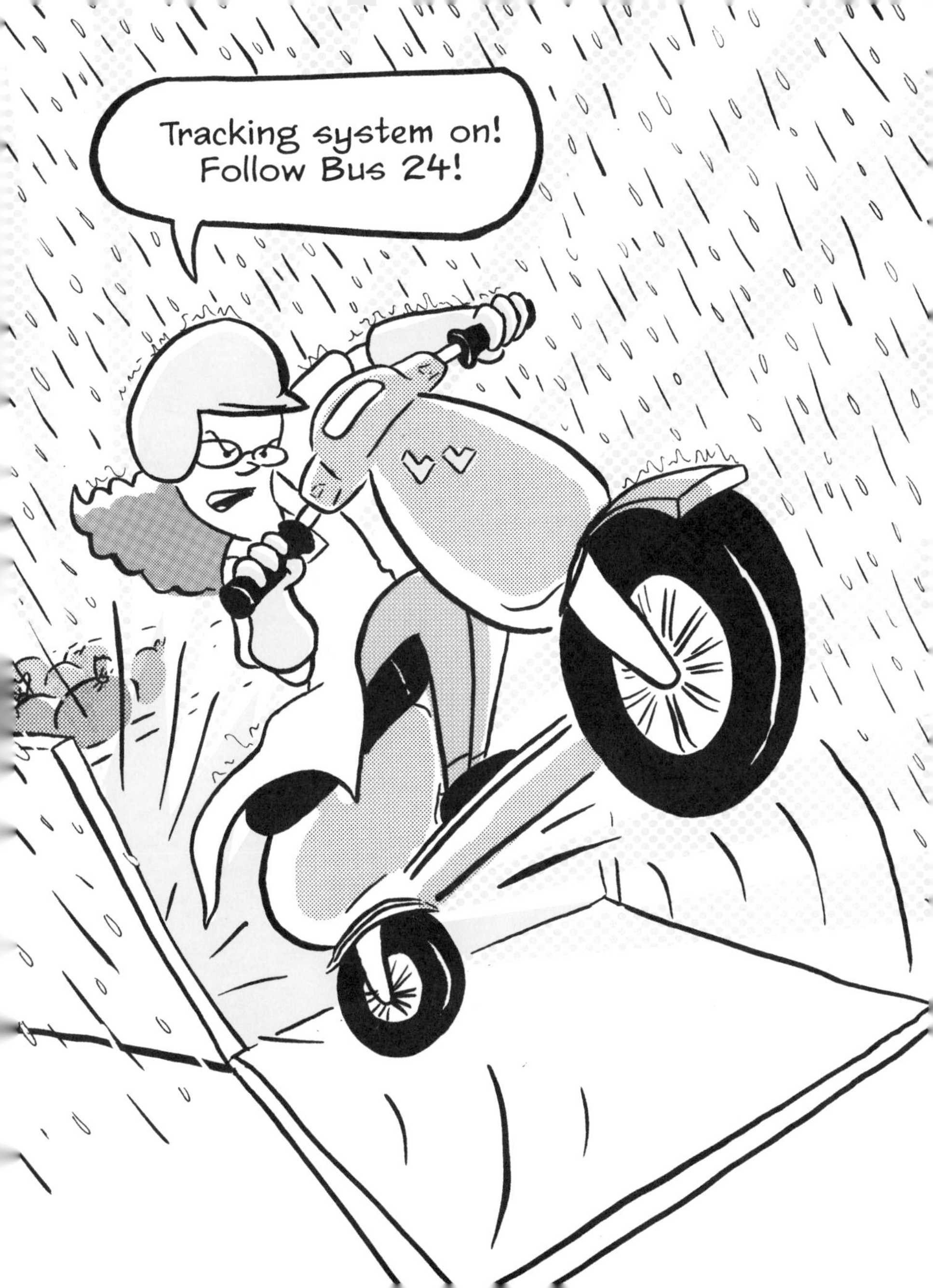
Tracking system on! Follow Bus 24!

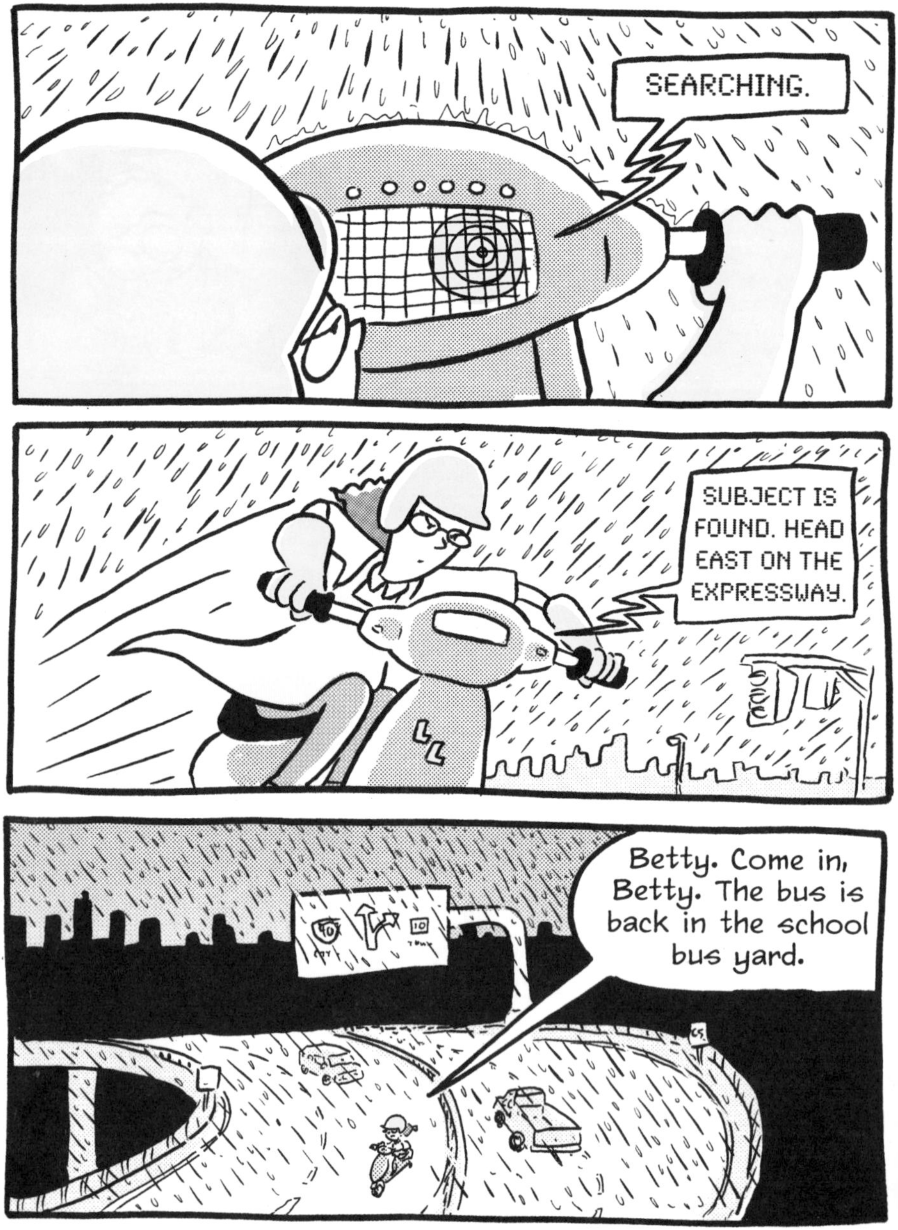
SEARCHING.
SUBJECT IS FOUND. HEAD EAST ON THE EXPRESSWAY.
Betty. Come in, Betty. The bus is back in the school bus yard.

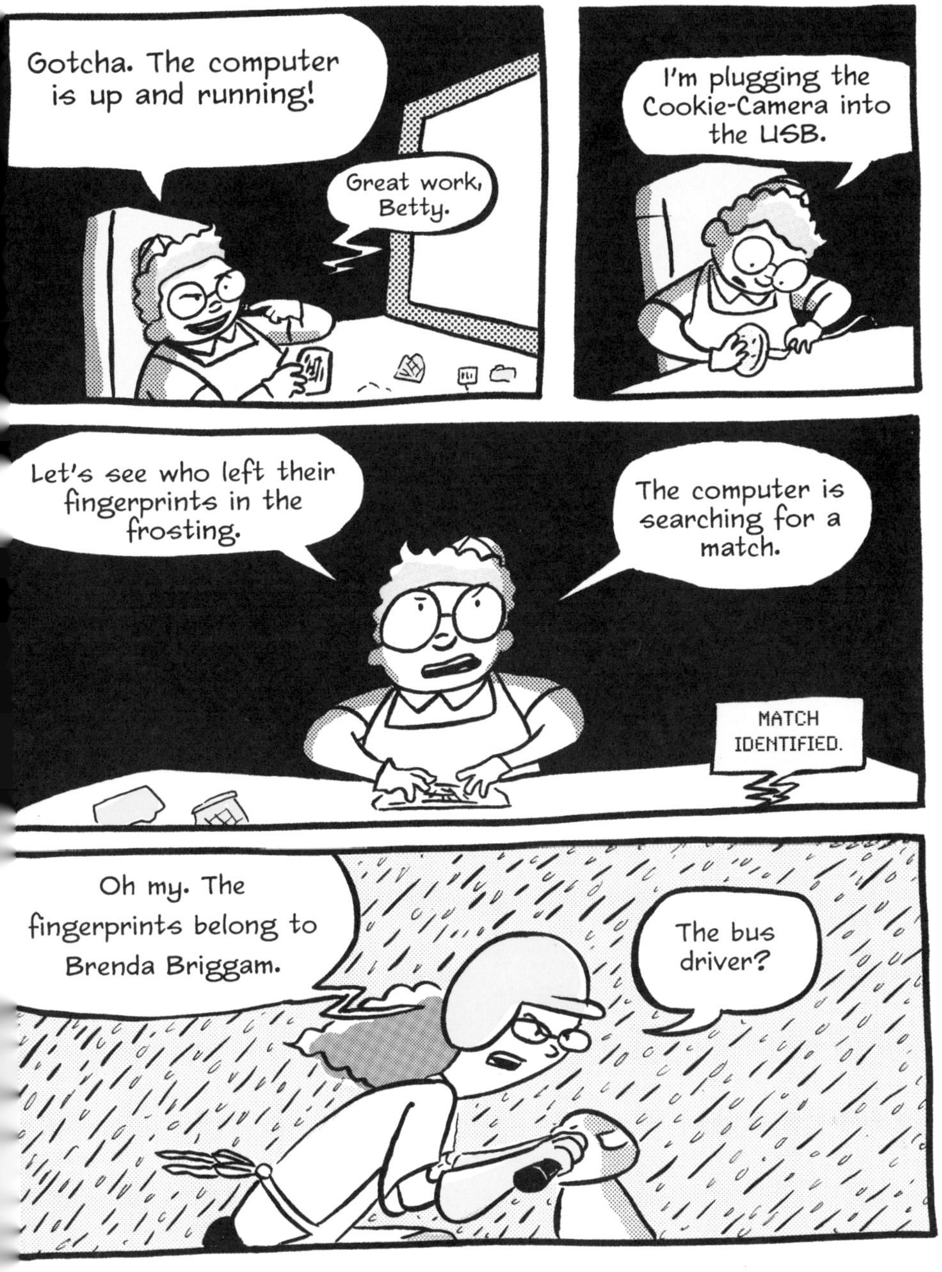
Gotcha. The computer is up and running!
Great work, Betty.
I'm plugging the Cookie-Camera into the USB.
Let's see who left their fingerprints in the frosting.
The computer is searching for a match.
MATCH IDENTIFIED.
Oh my. The fingerprints belong to Brenda Briggam.
The bus driver?

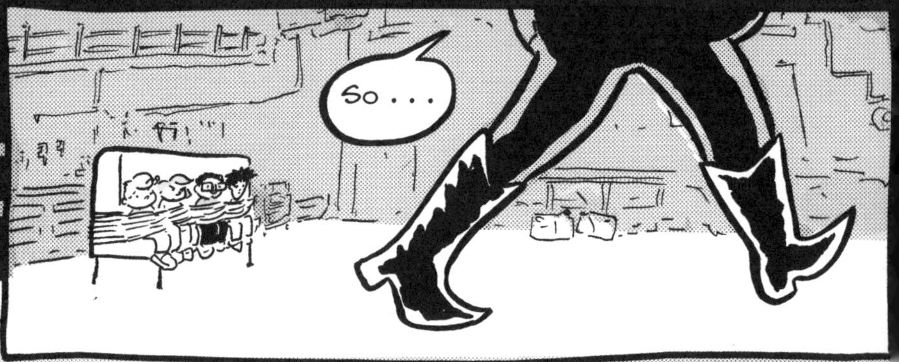
So . . .

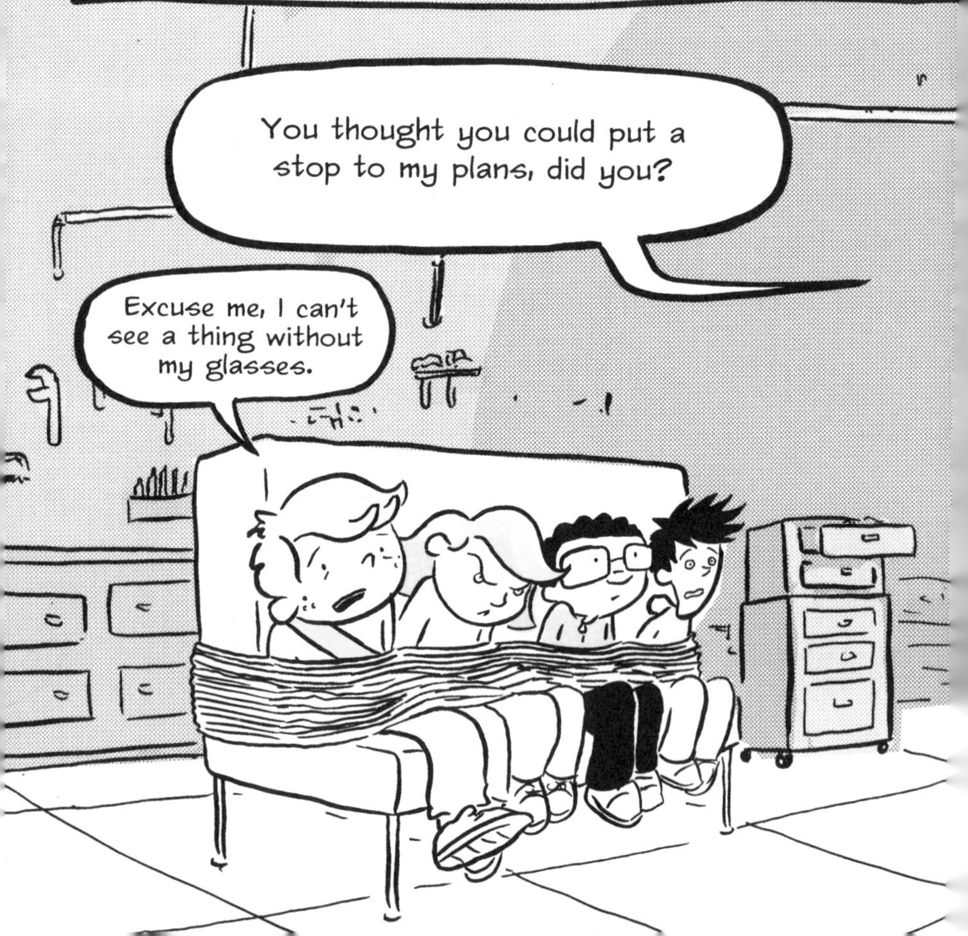
You thought you could put a stop to my plans, did you?
Excuse me, I can't see a thing without my glasses.

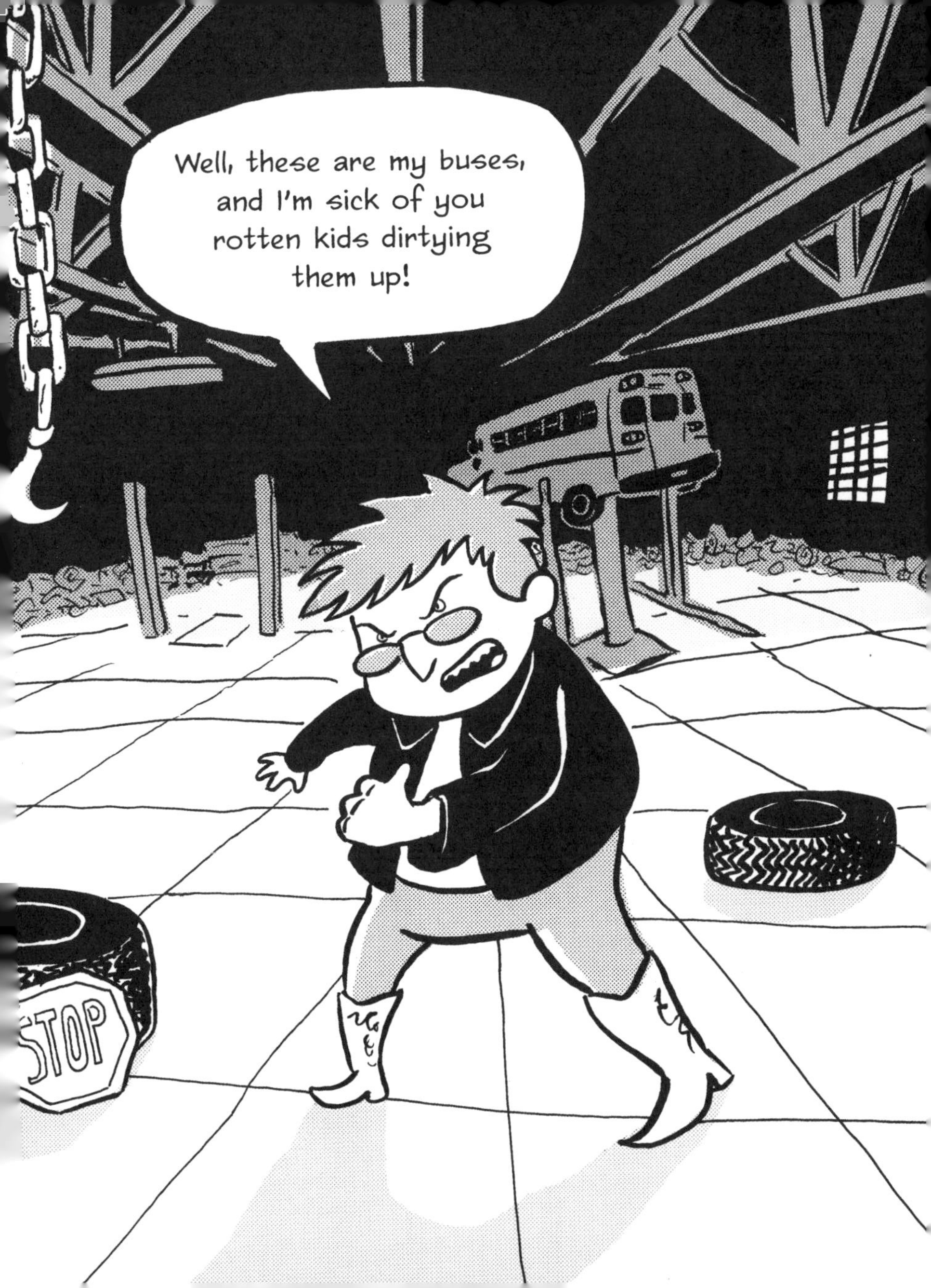
Well, these are my buses, and I'm sick of you rotten kids dirtying them up!
STOP

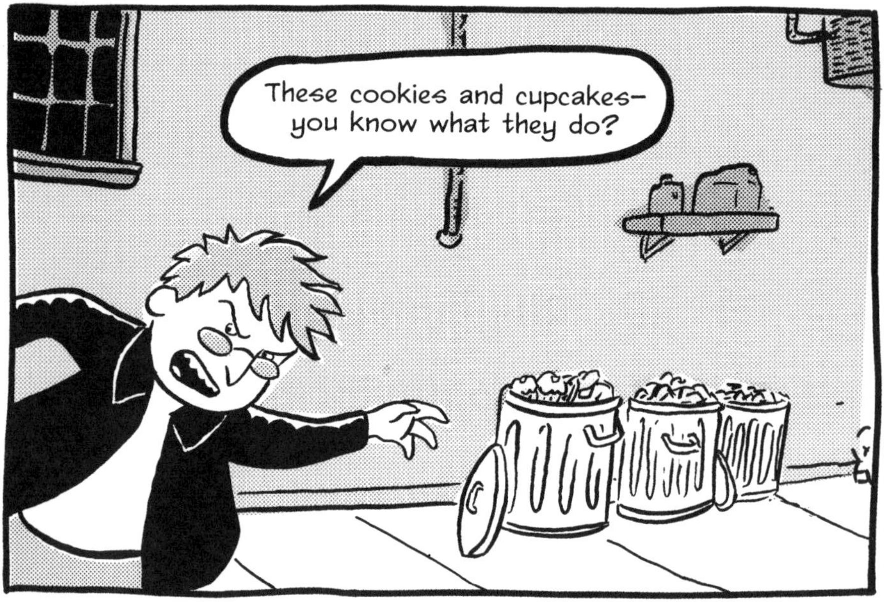
These cookies and cupcakes– you know what they do?

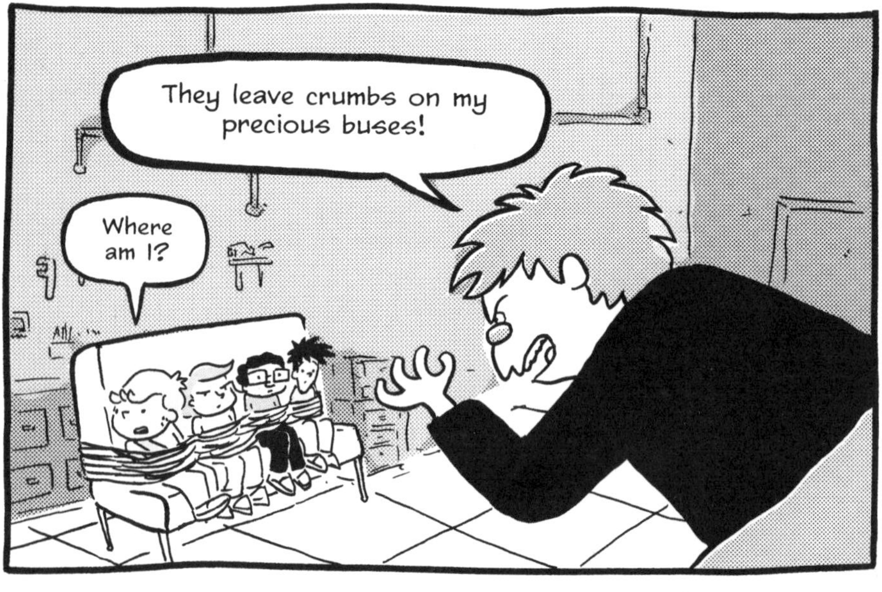
They leave crumbs on my precious buses!
Where am I?

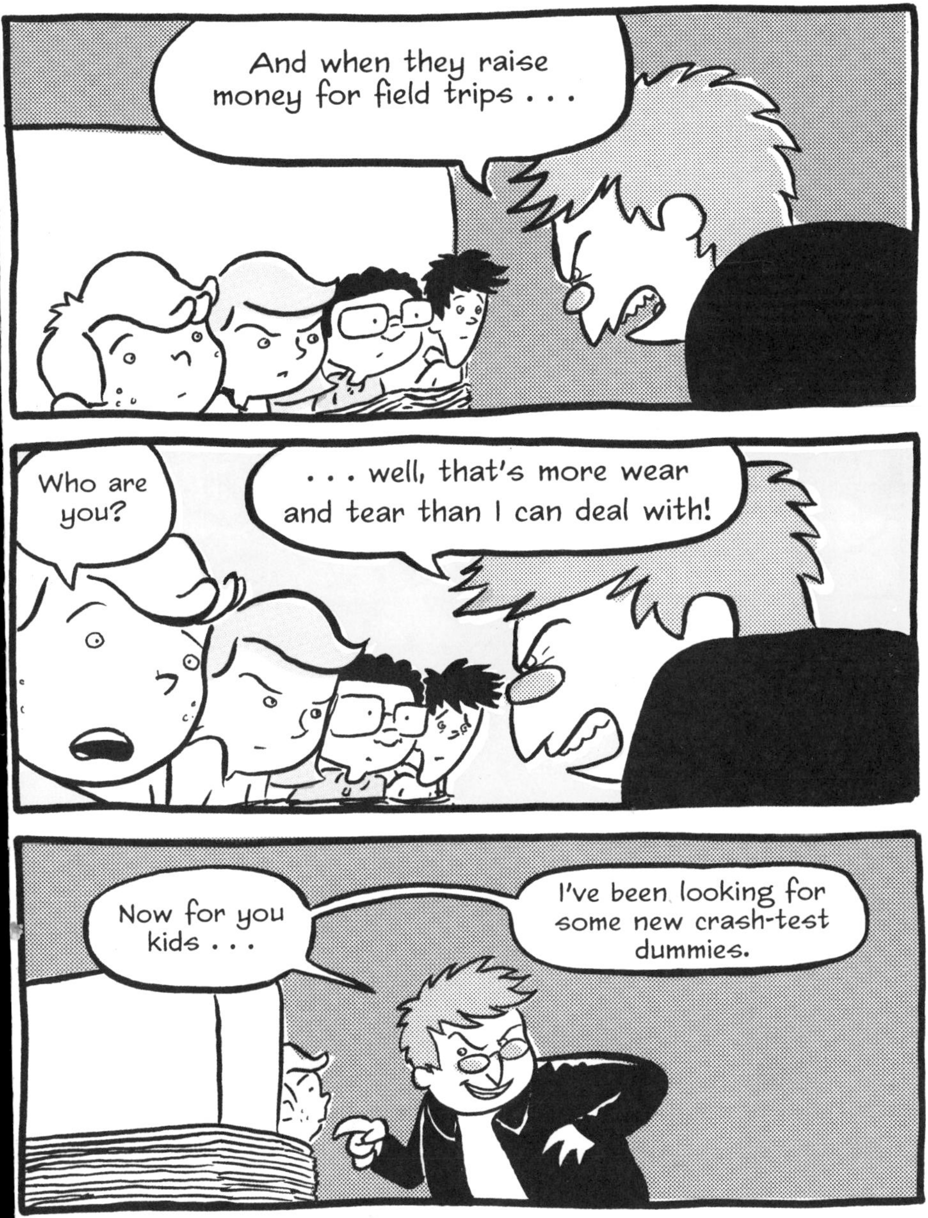
And when they raise money for field trips . . .
Who are you?
. . . well, that's more wear and tear than I can deal with!
Now for you kids . . .
I've been looking for some new crash-test dummies.

Betty, I'm atop the garage in the school bus yard!
Now to find bus driver Brenda.
I'm on my way!

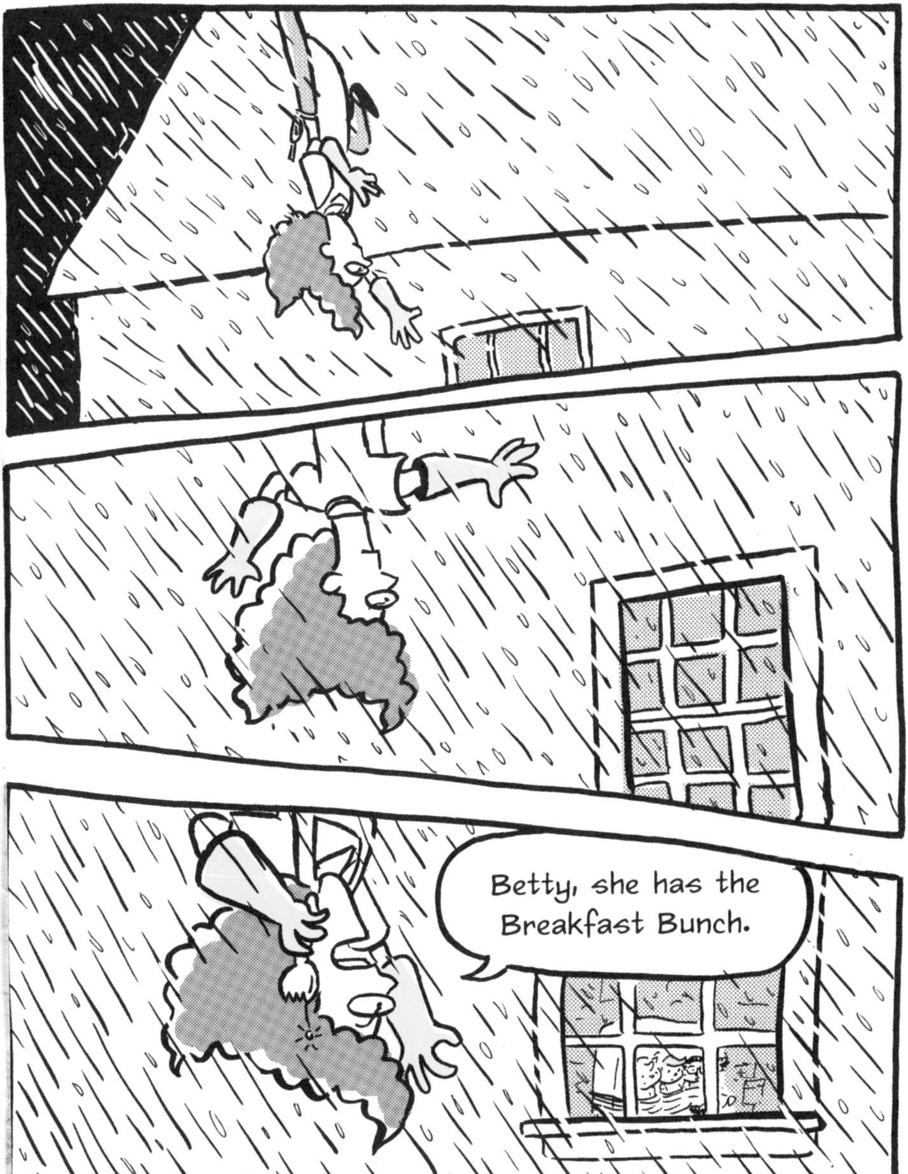
Betty, she has the Breakfast Bunch.

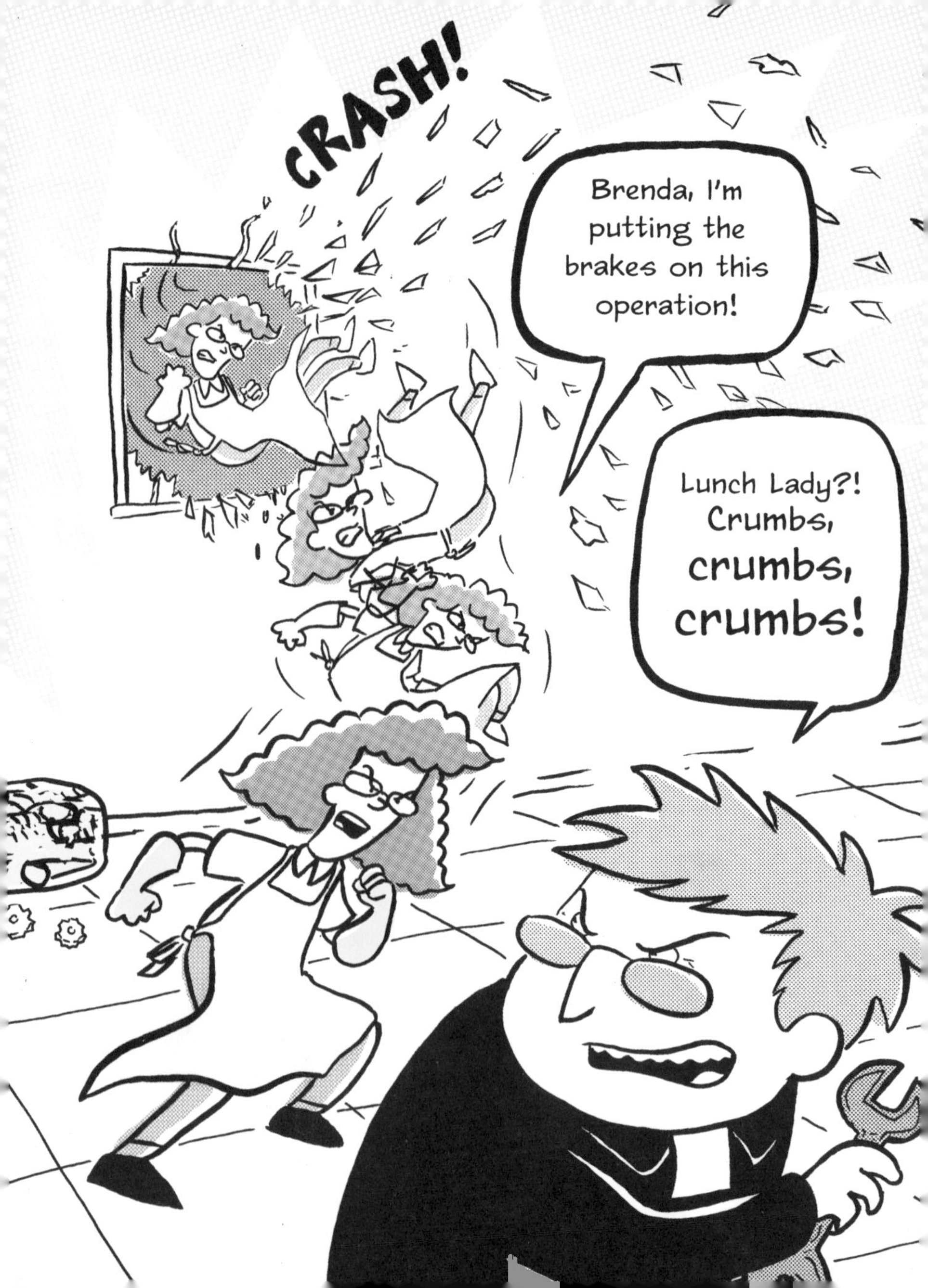
CRASH!
Brenda, I'm putting the brakes on this operation!
Lunch Lady?! Crumbs, crumbs, crumbs!

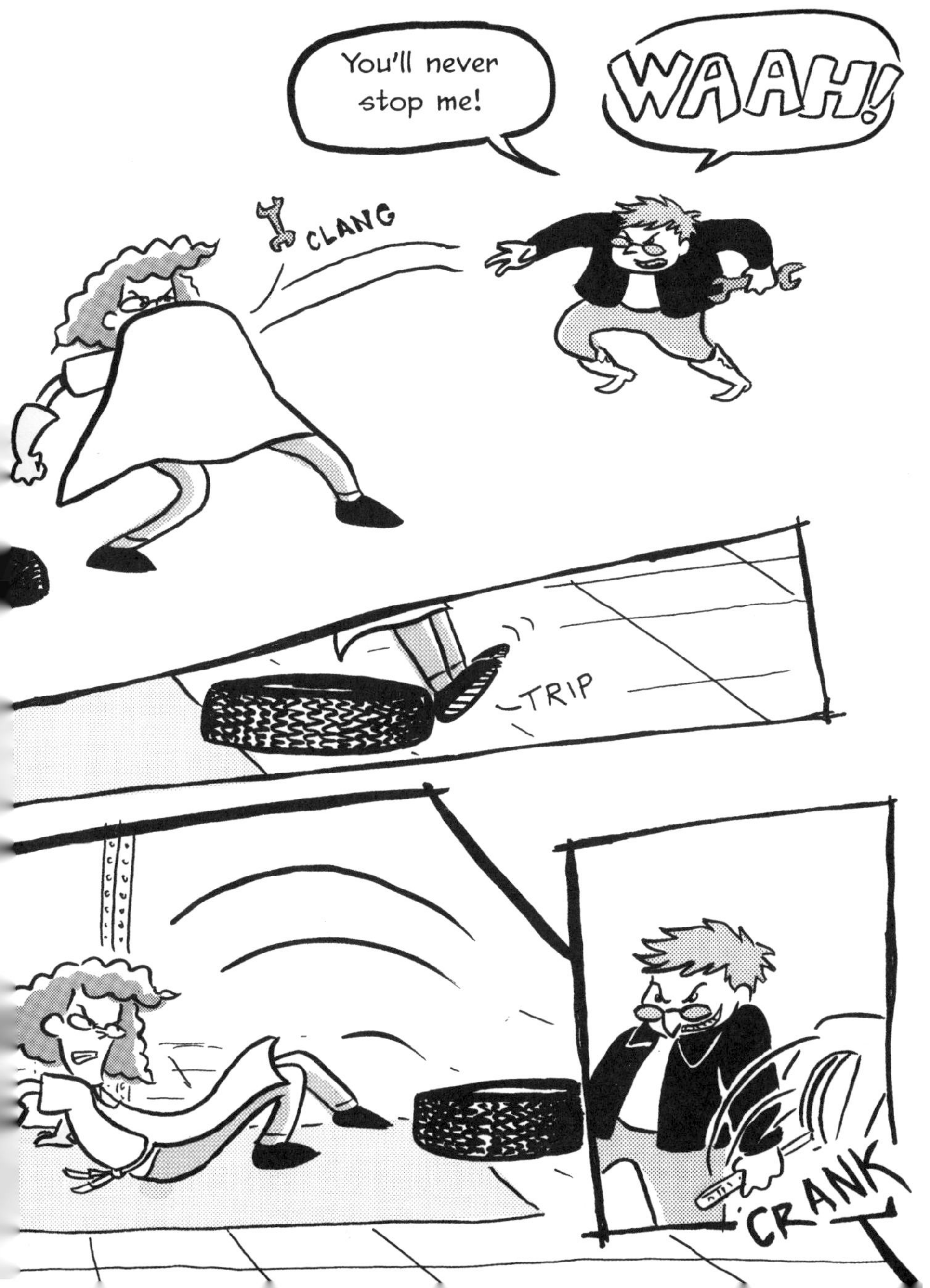
You'll never stop me!
WAAH!
CLANG
TRIP
CRANK

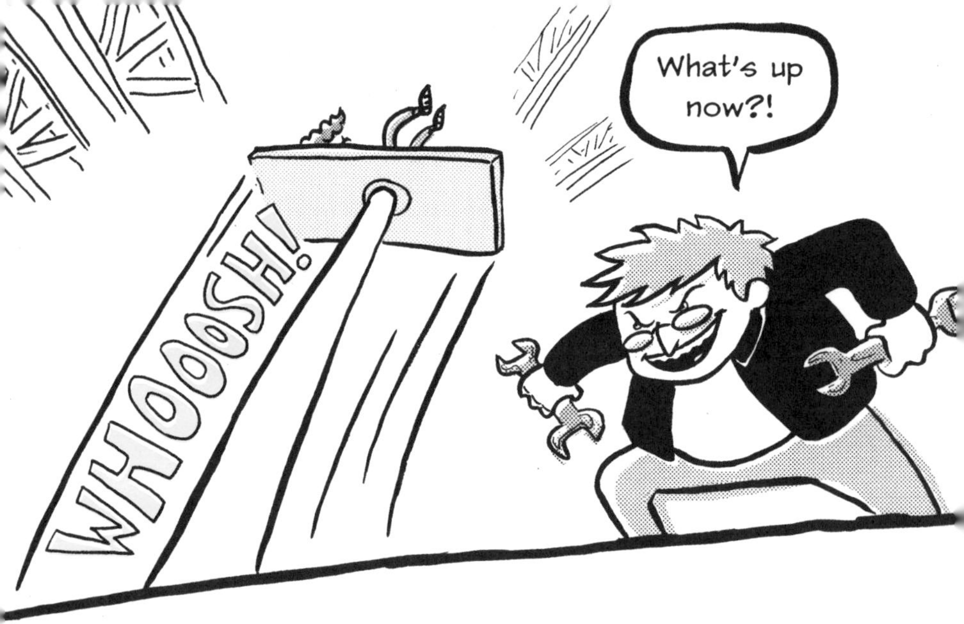
WHOOOSH!
What's up now?!

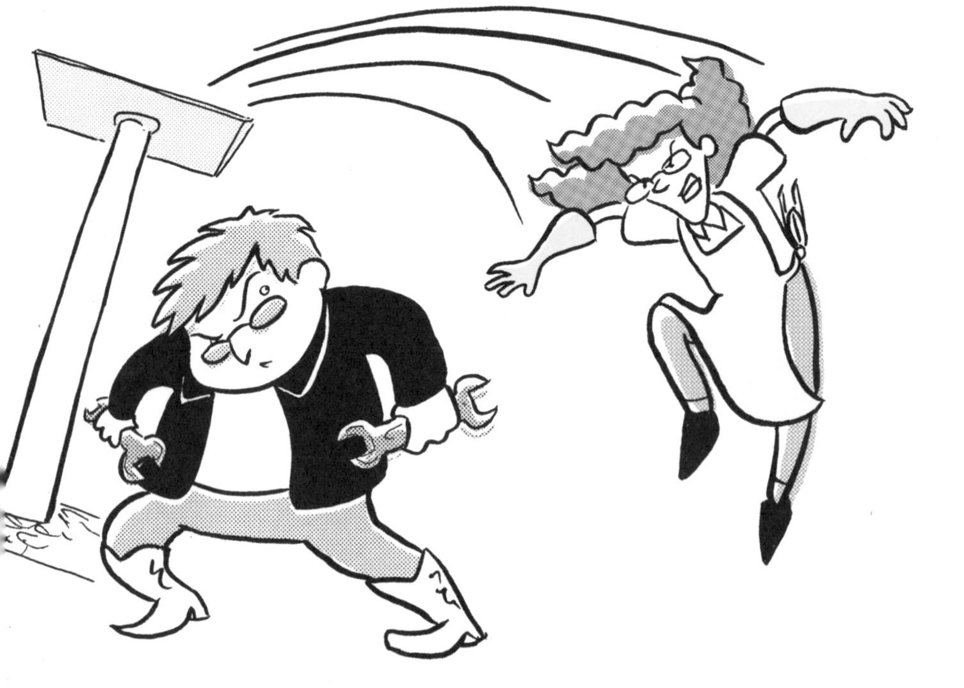

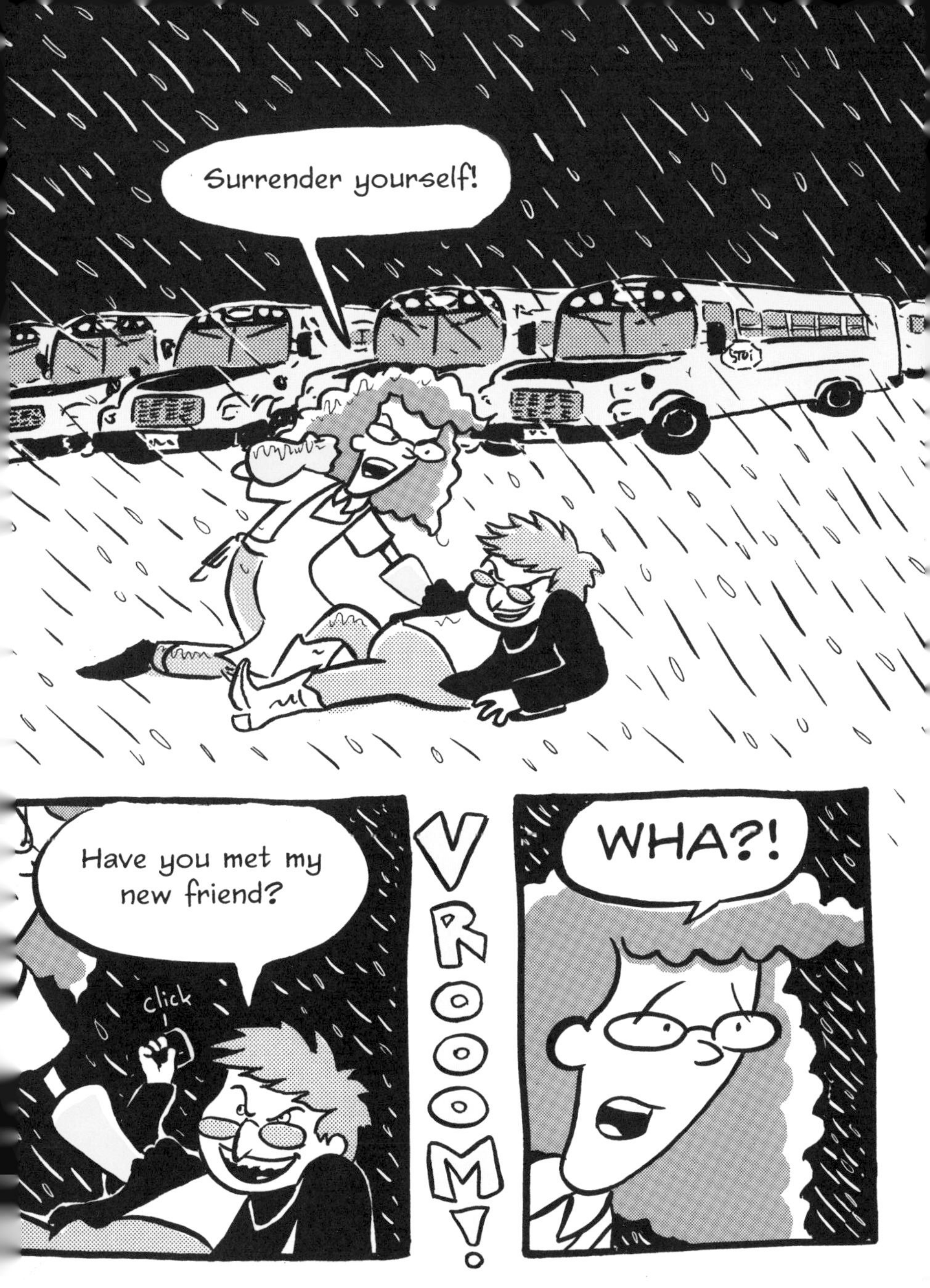
Surrender yourself!
Have you met my new friend?
click
VROOOOM!
WHA?!

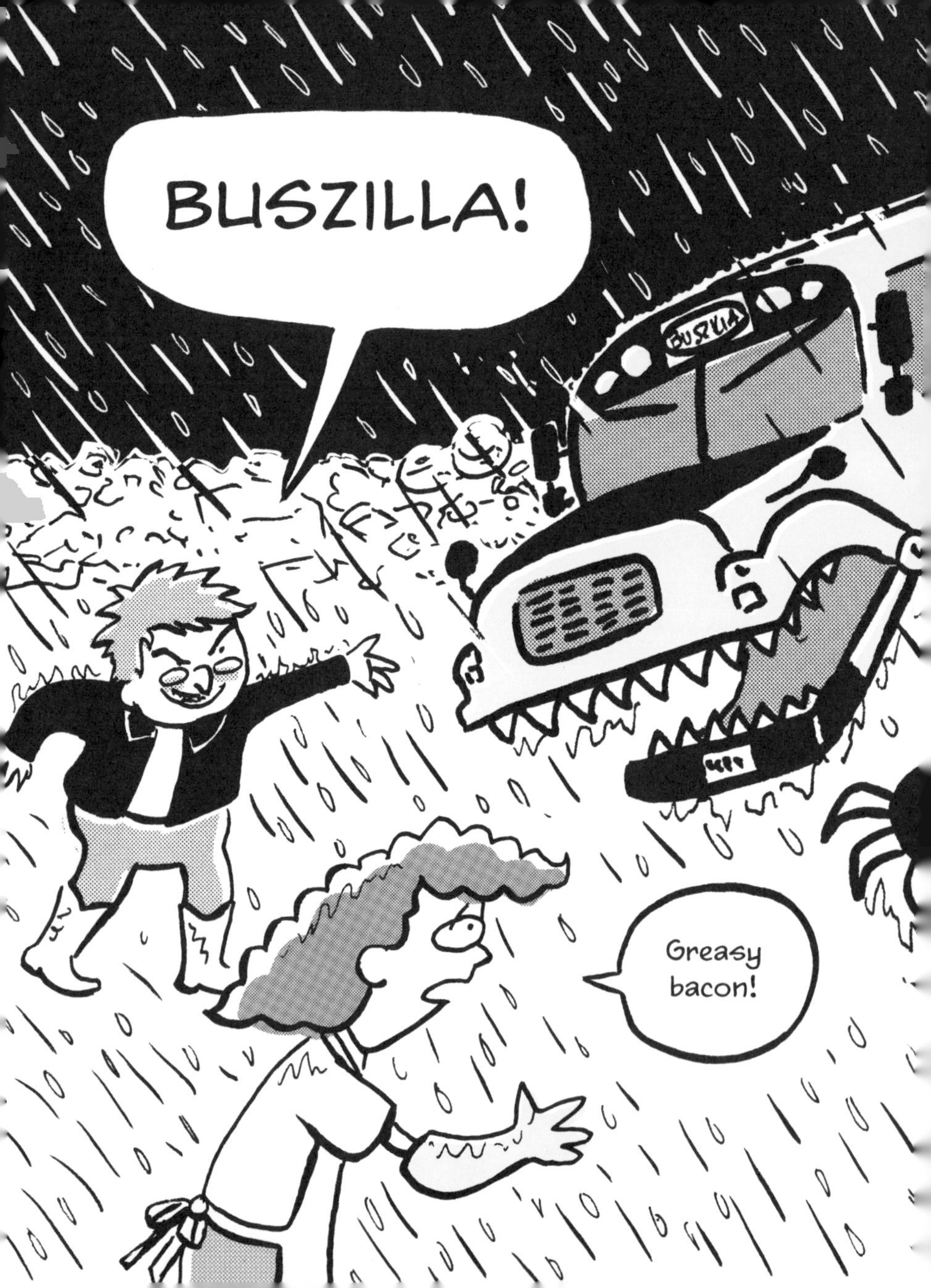
BUSZILLA!
Greasy bacon!

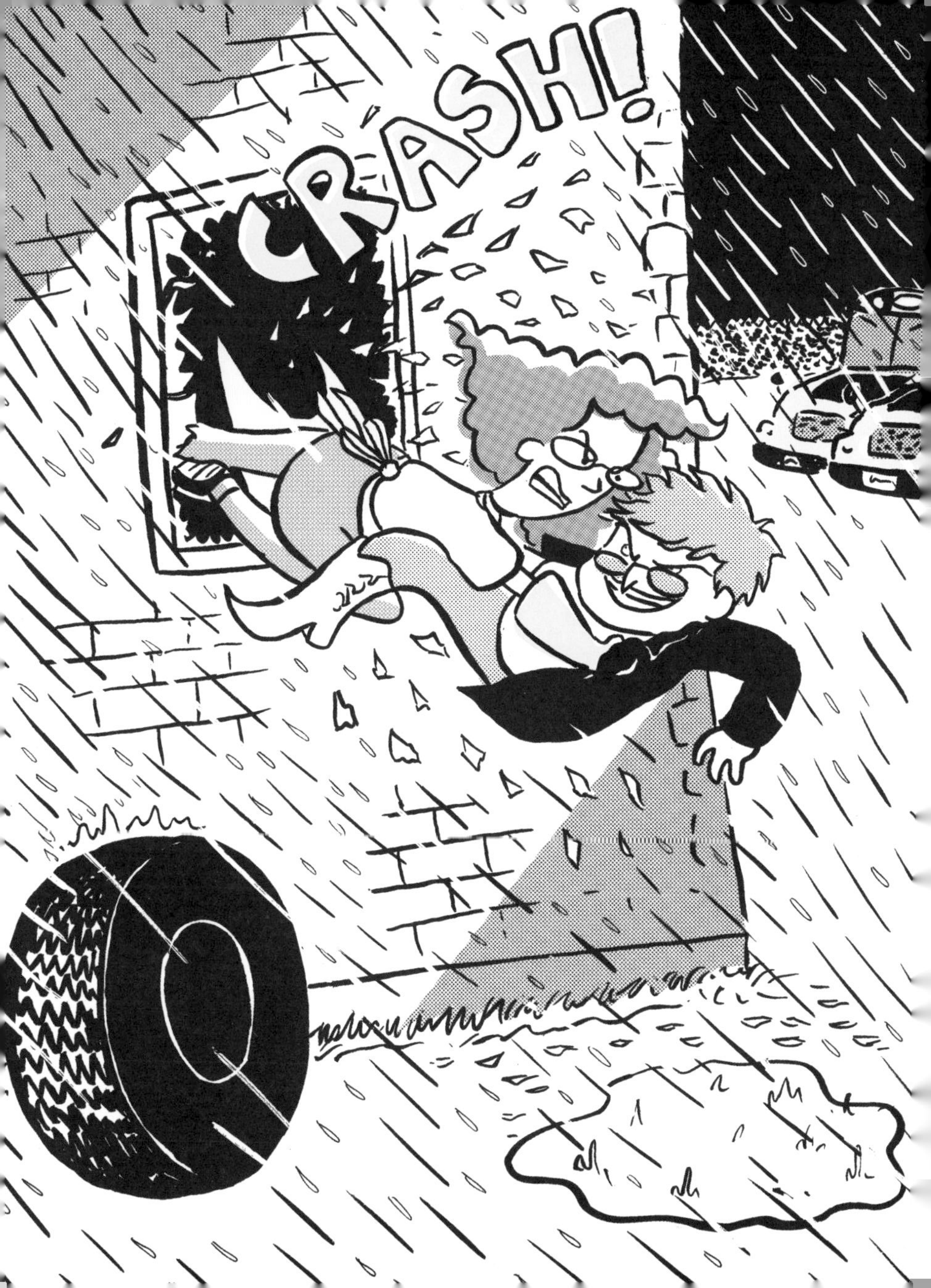
CRASH!

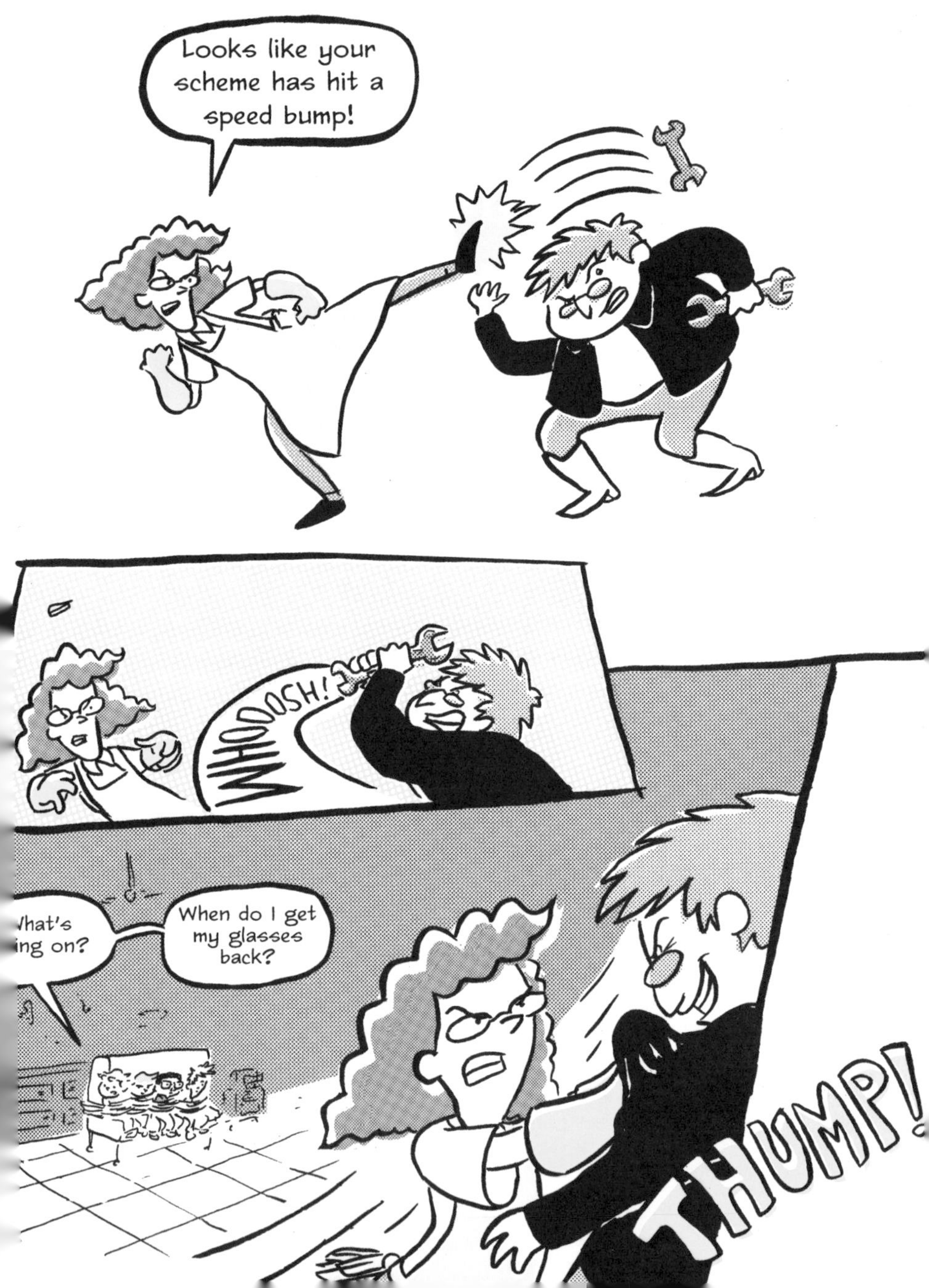
Looks like your scheme has hit a speed bump!
WHOOOOSH!
hat's
ing on?
When do I get my glasses back?
THUMP!

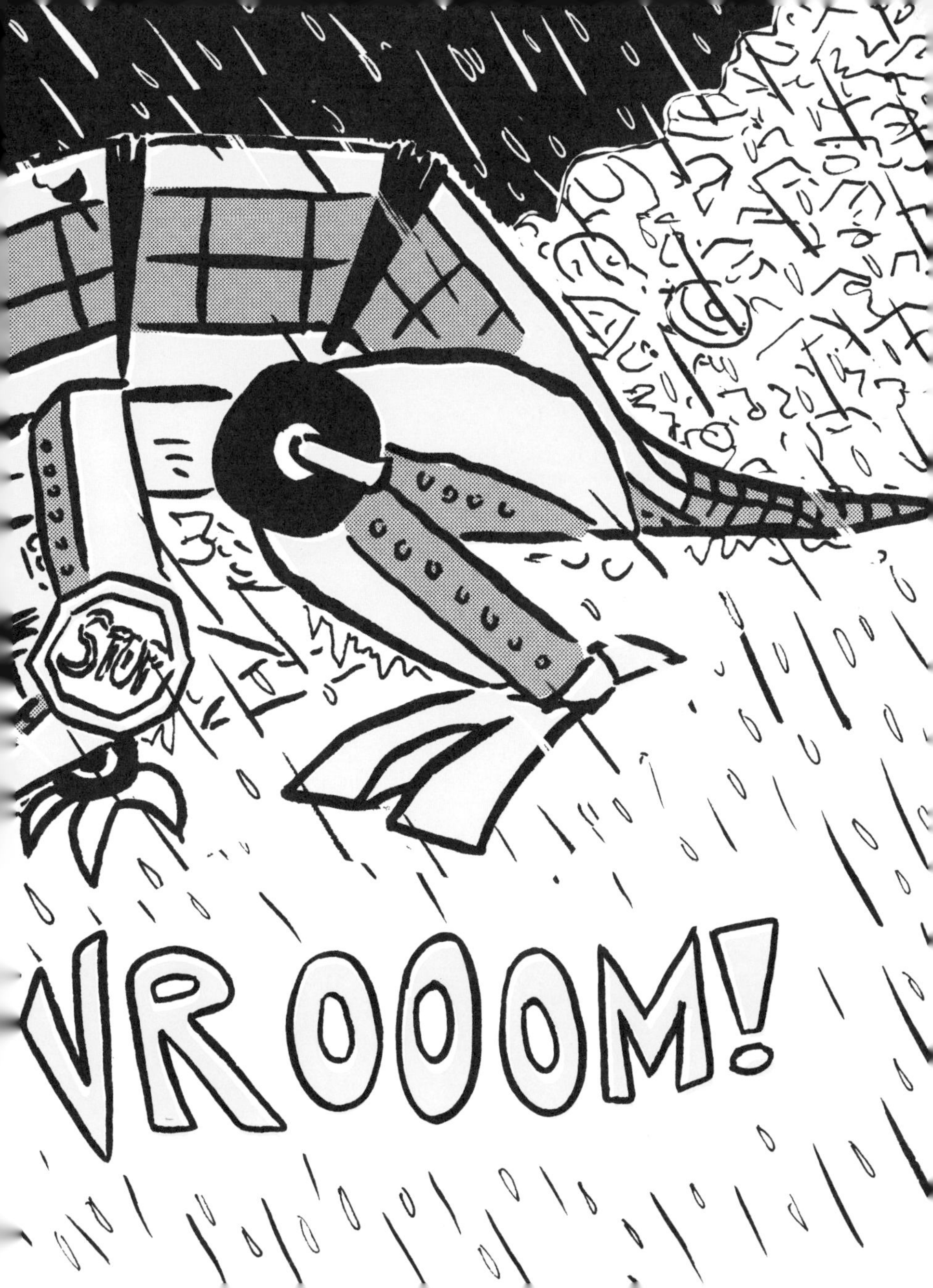
VROOOM!

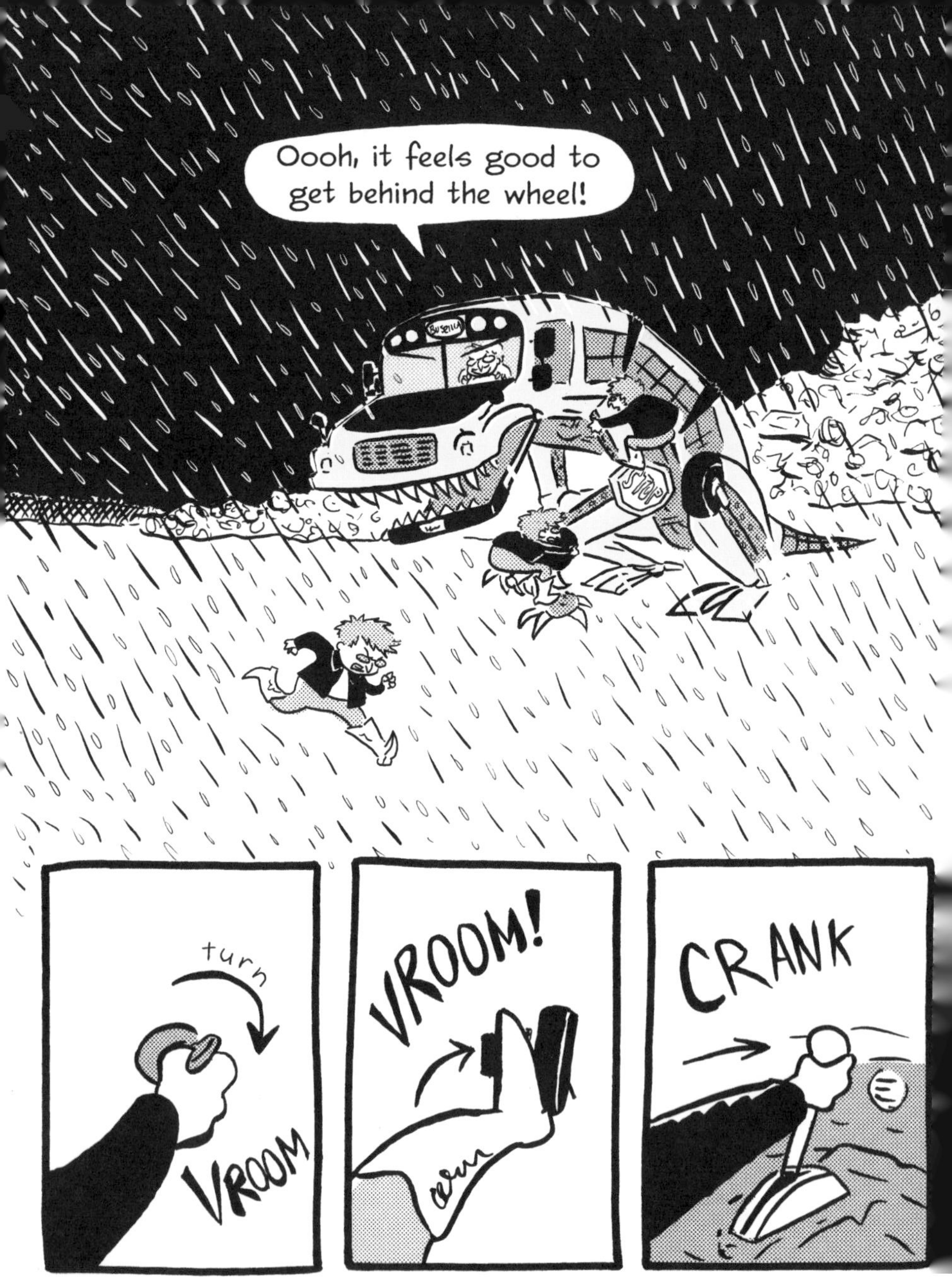
Oooh, it feels good to get behind the wheel!
STOP
turn
VROOM
VROOM!
CRANK

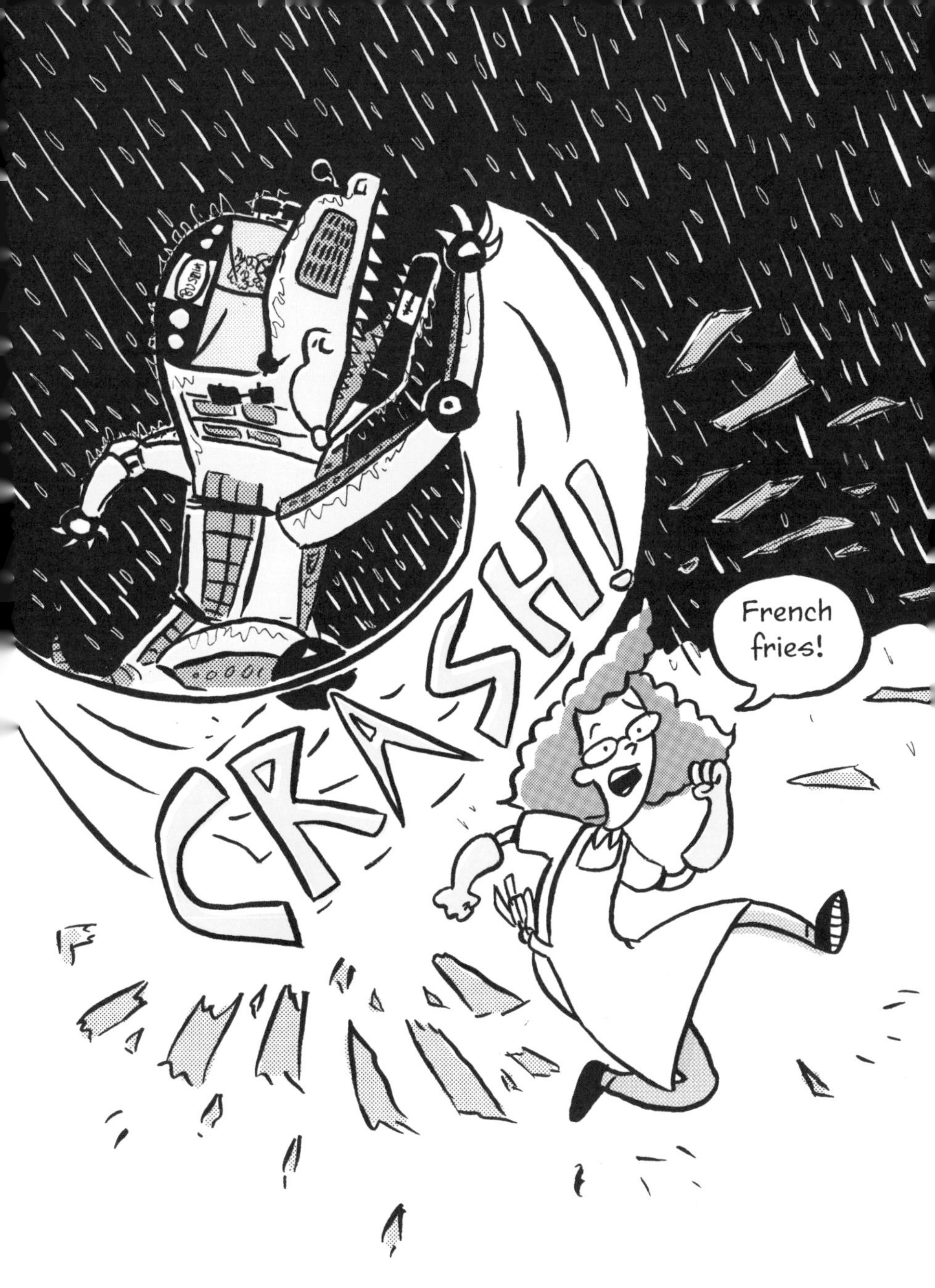
CRASH!!
French fries!

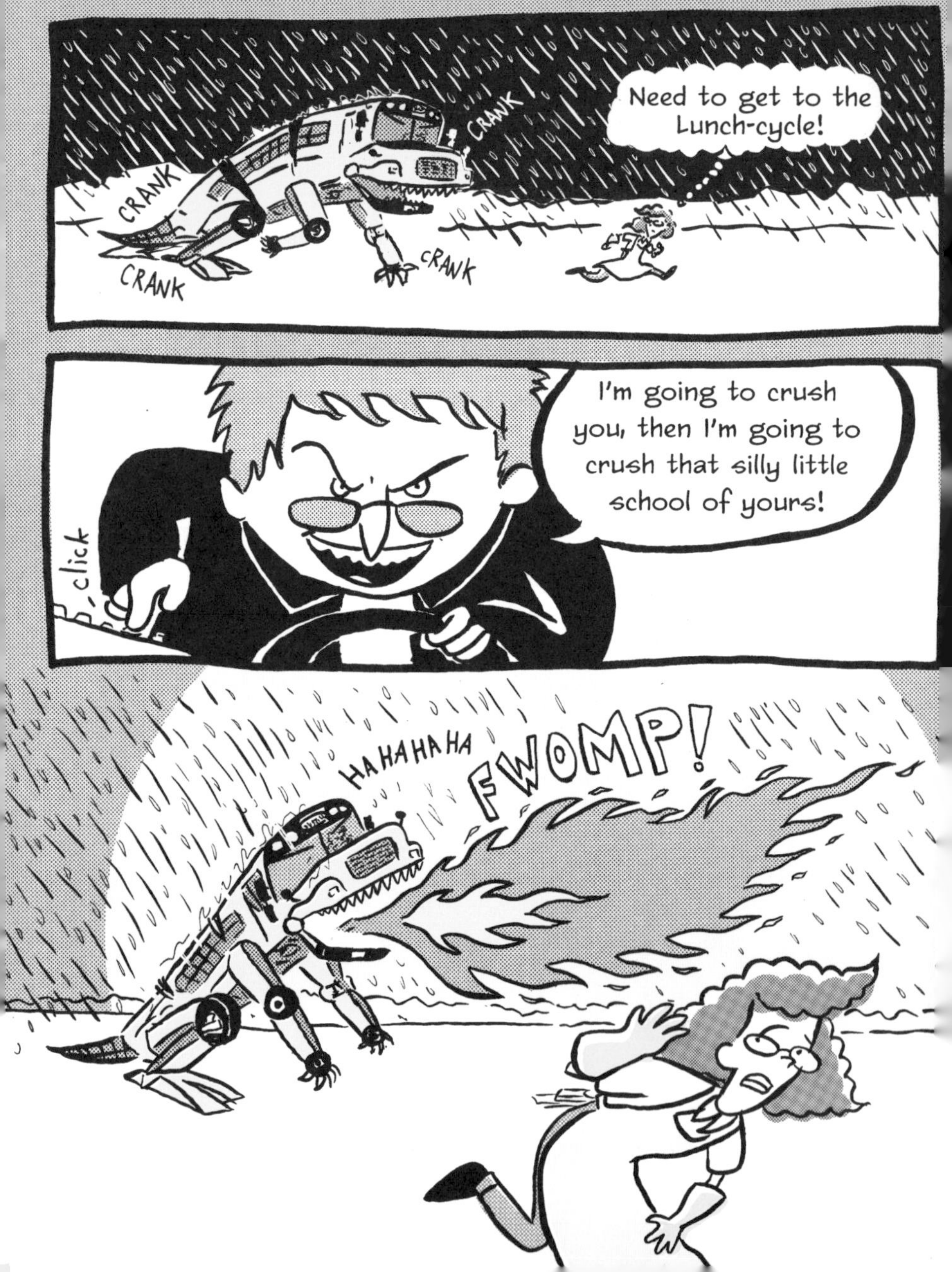
CRANK
CRANK
CRANK
CRANK
Need to get to the Lunch-cycle!
click
I'm going to crush you, then I'm going to crush that silly little school of yours!
HAHAHAHA
FWOMP!

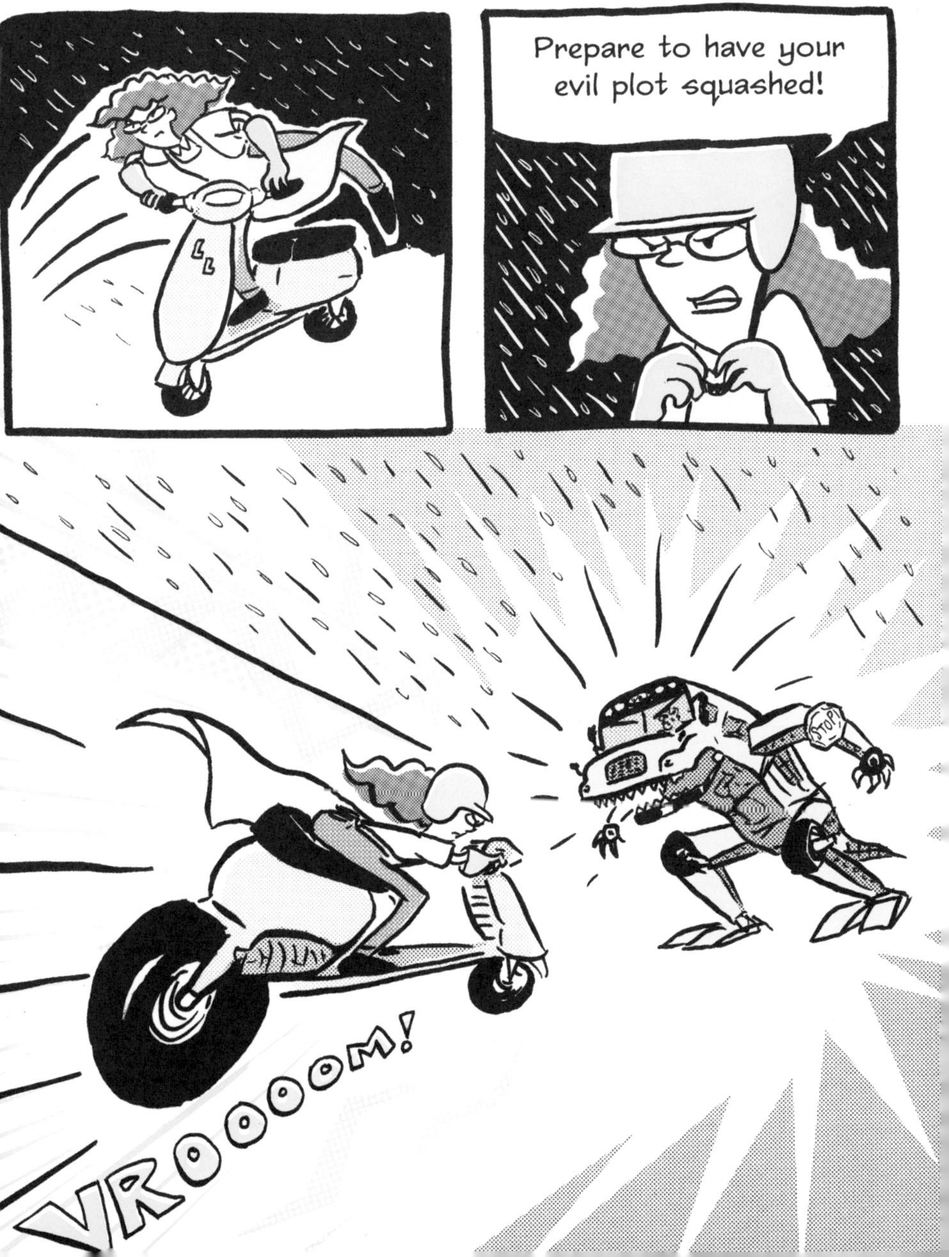
Prepare to have your evil plot squashed!
STOP!
VROOOOOM!

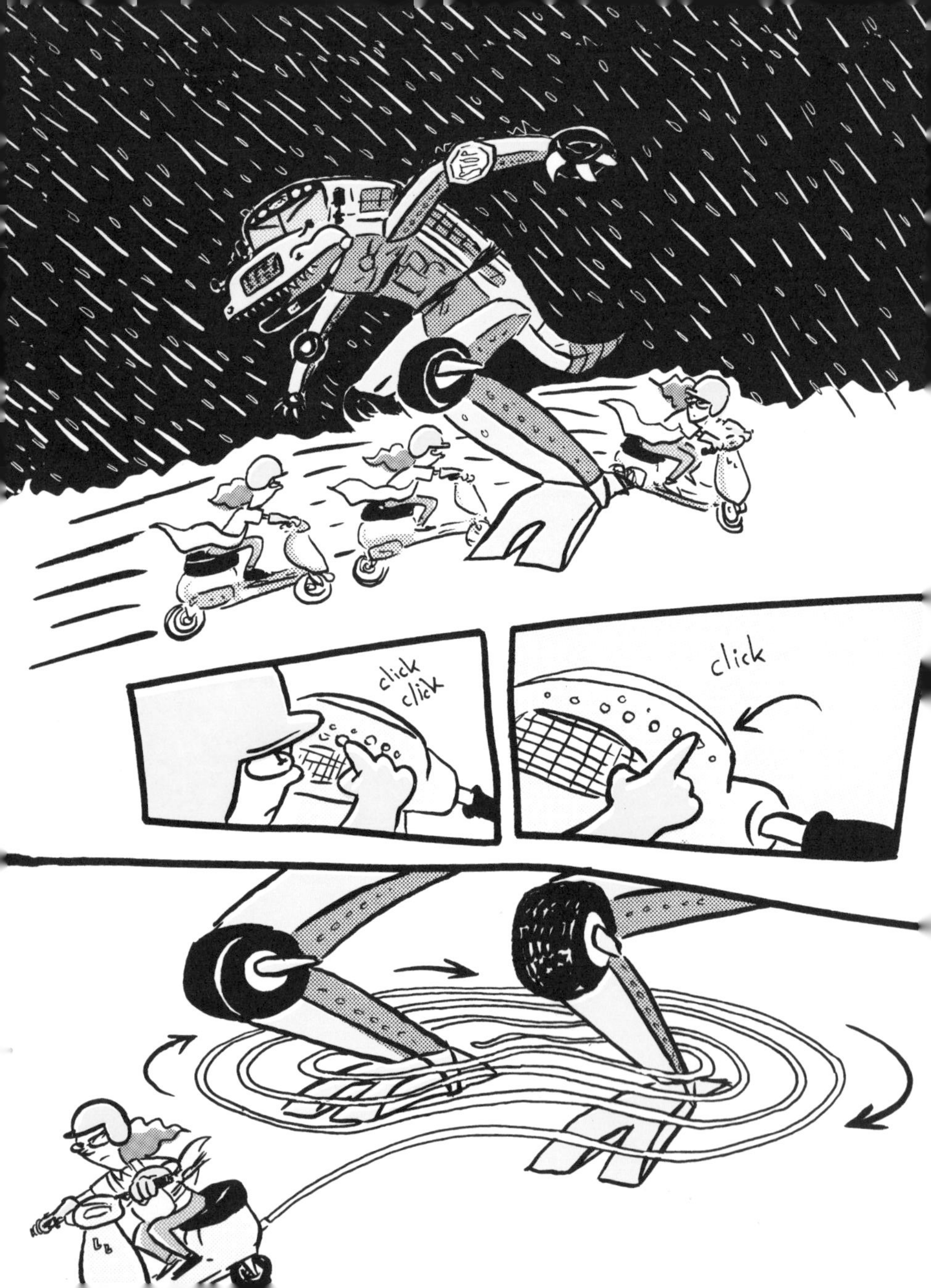
click
click
click

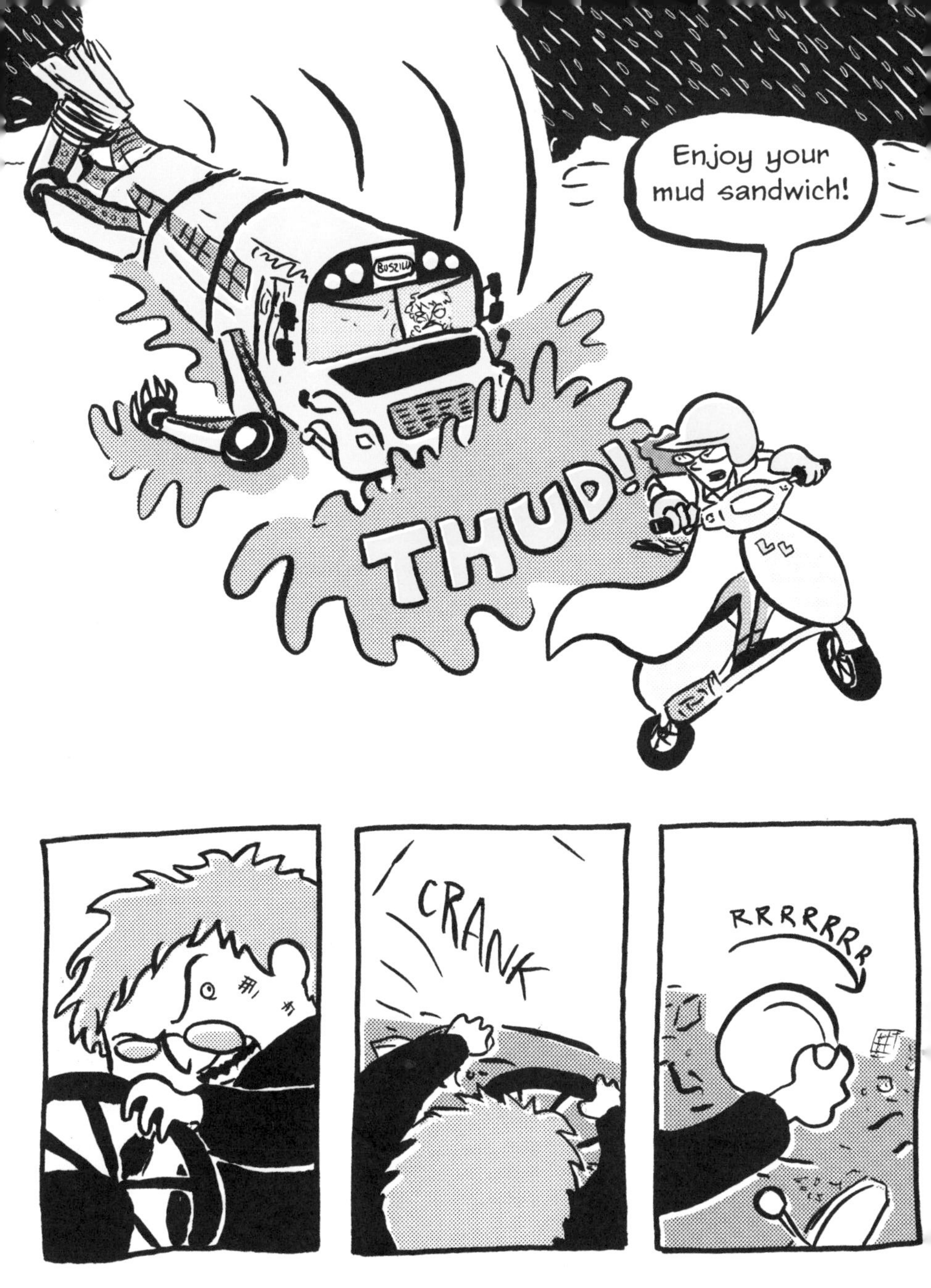
Enjoy your mud sandwich!
THUD!
CRANK
RRRRRRR

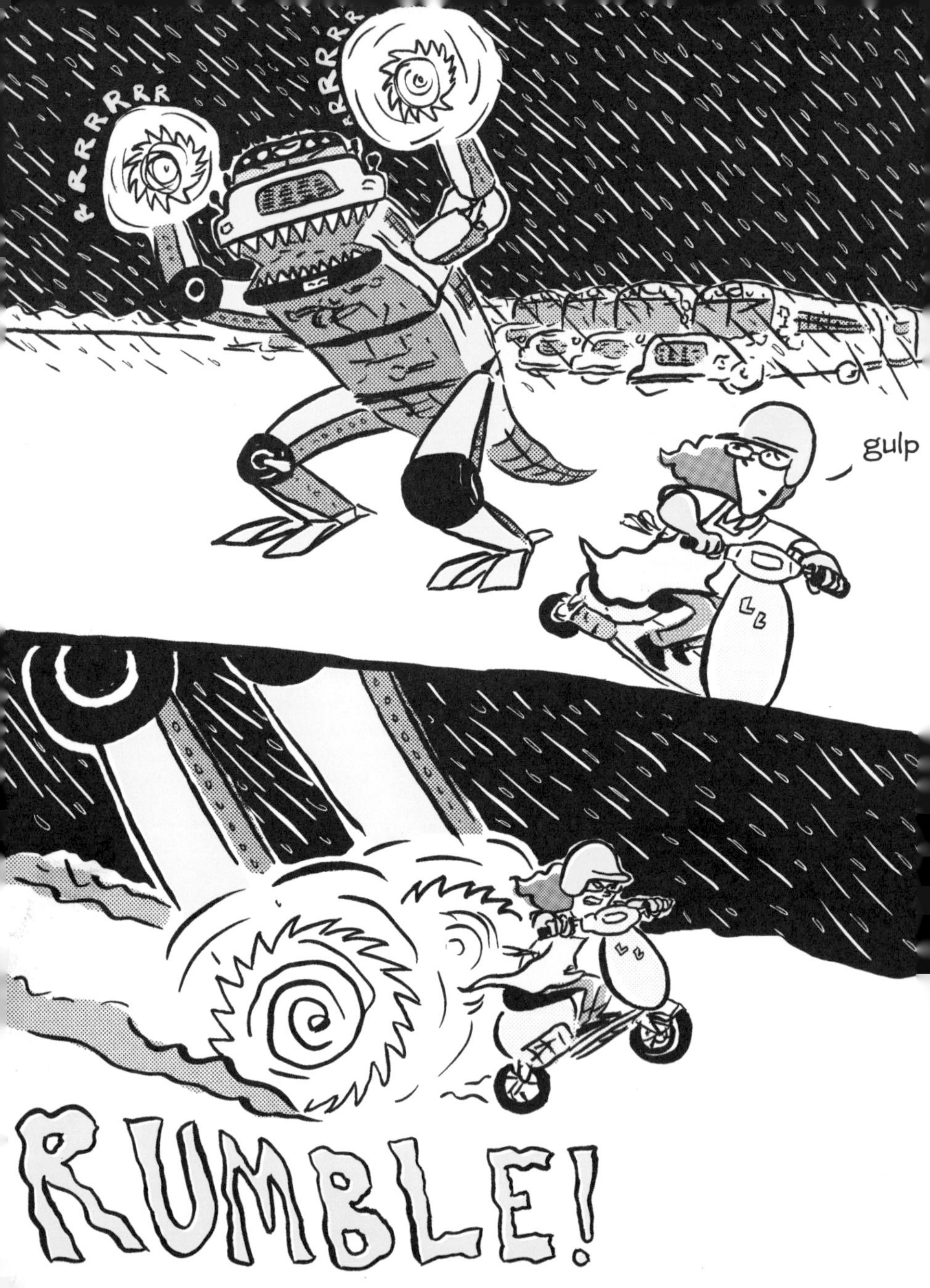
RRRRRRR
RRRRRRR
gulp
RUMBLE!

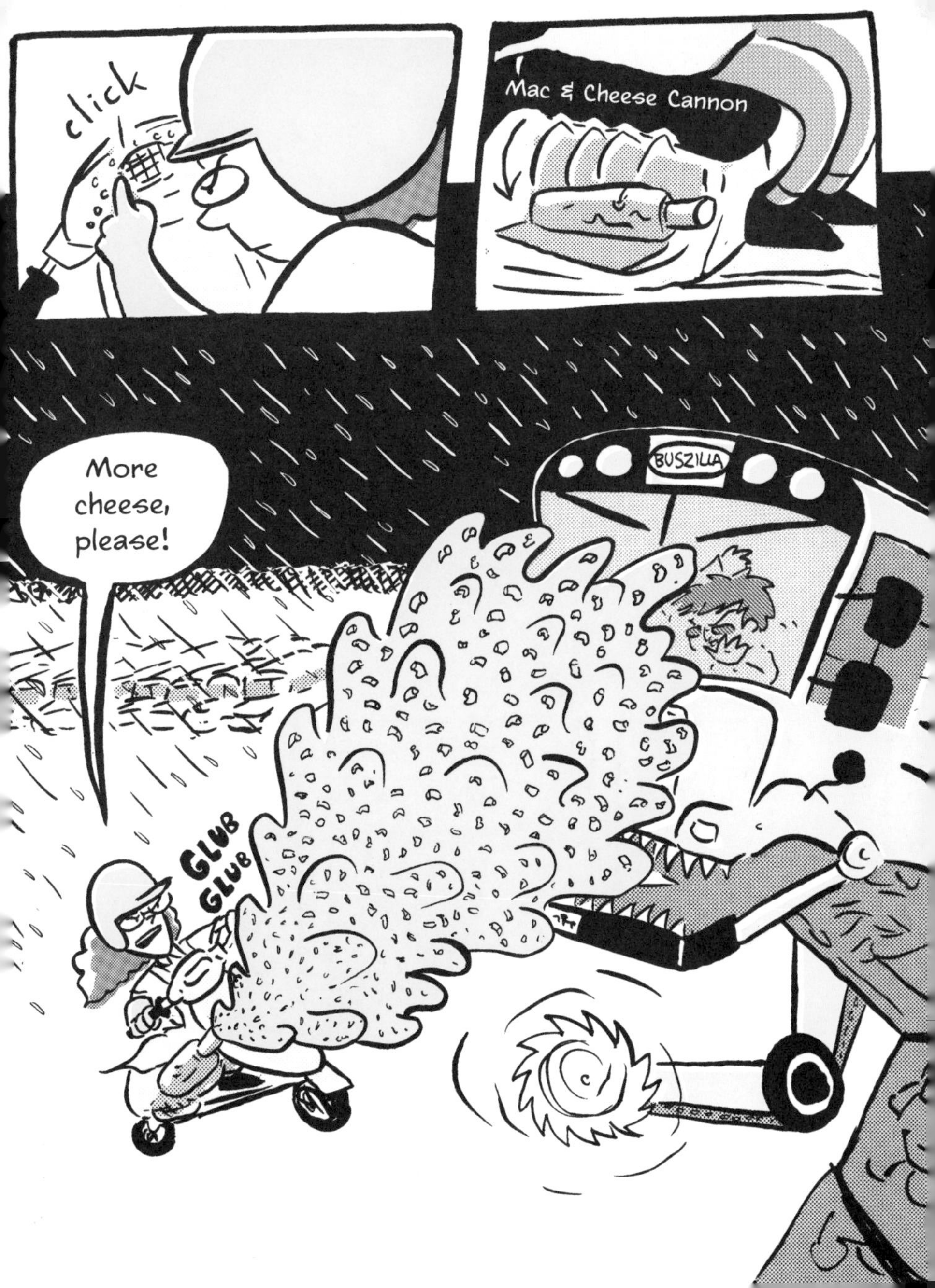
click
Mac & Cheese Cannon
BUSZILLA
More cheese, please!
GLUB GLUB

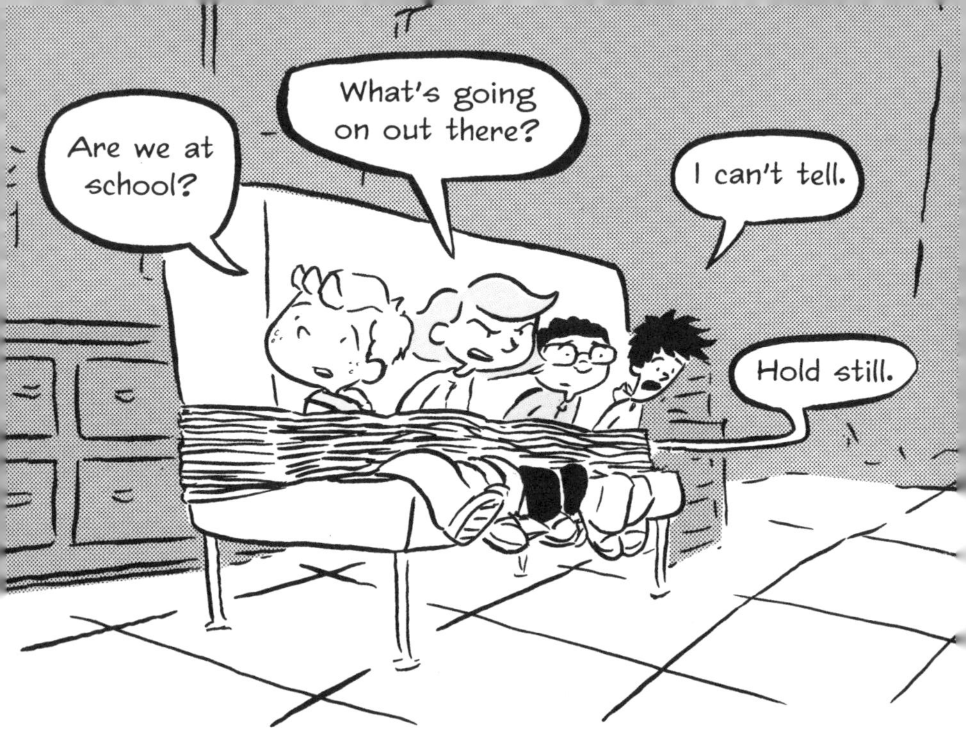
Are we at school?
What's going on out there?
I can't tell.
Hold still.

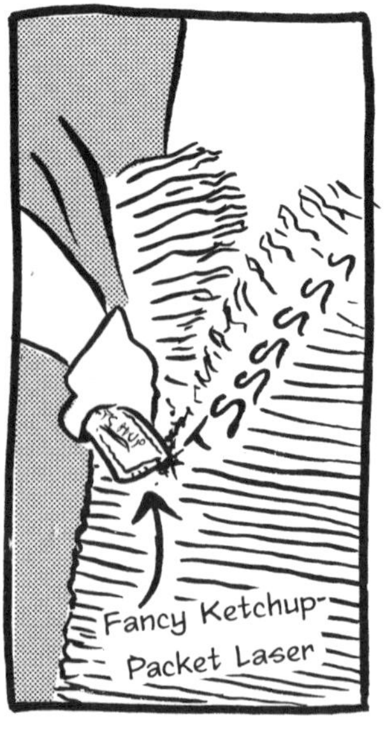
TSSSSSSS
Fancy Ketchup-Packet Laser

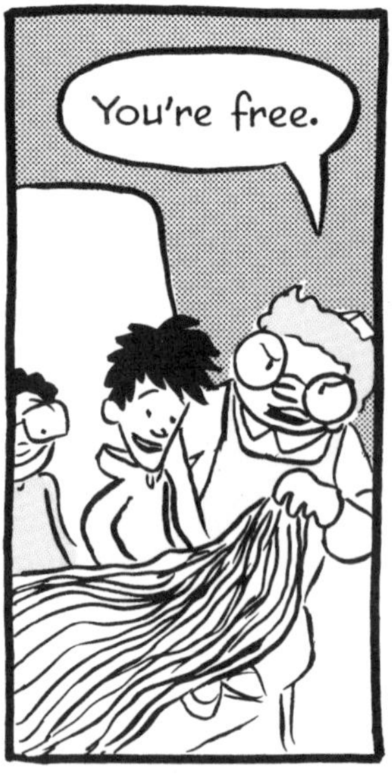
You're free.

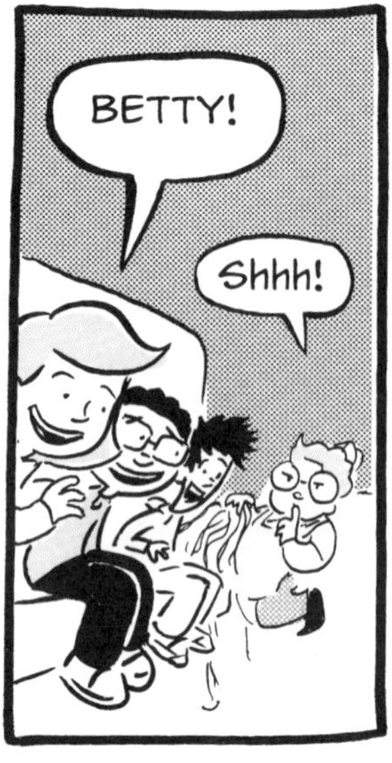
BETTY!
Shhh!

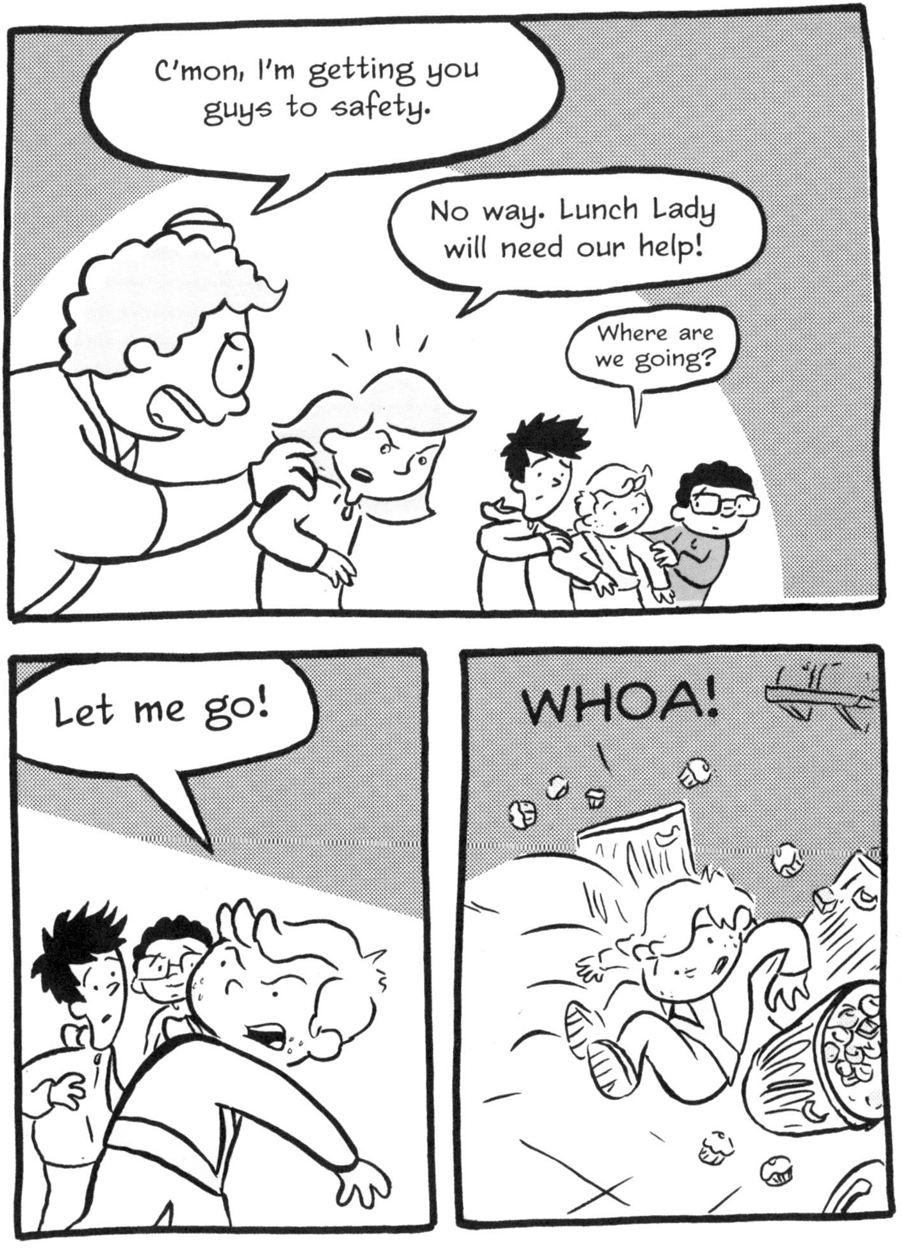
C'mon, I'm getting you guys to safety.
No way. Lunch Lady will need our help!
Where are we going?
Let me go!
WHOA!

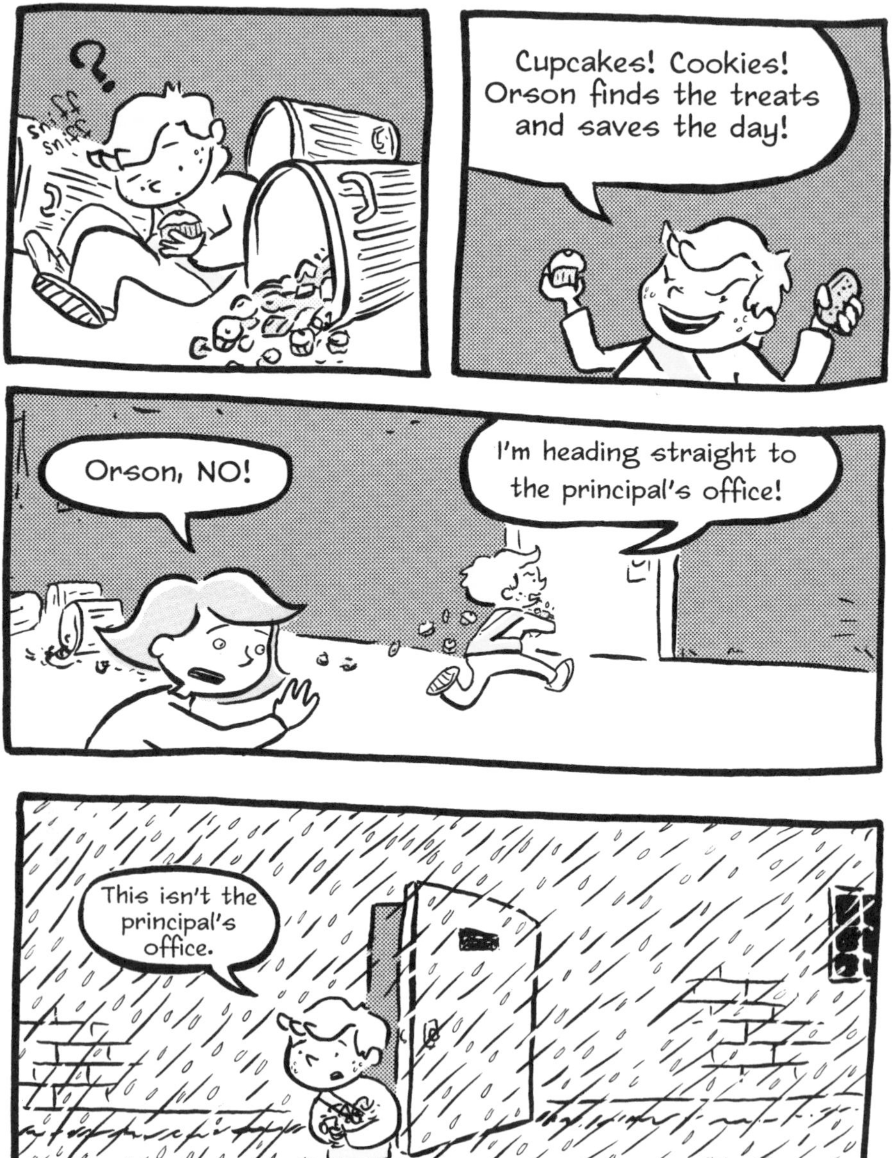
sniff sniff
Cupcakes! Cookies! Orson finds the treats and saves the day!
Orson, NO!
I'm heading straight to the principal's office!
This isn't the principal's office.

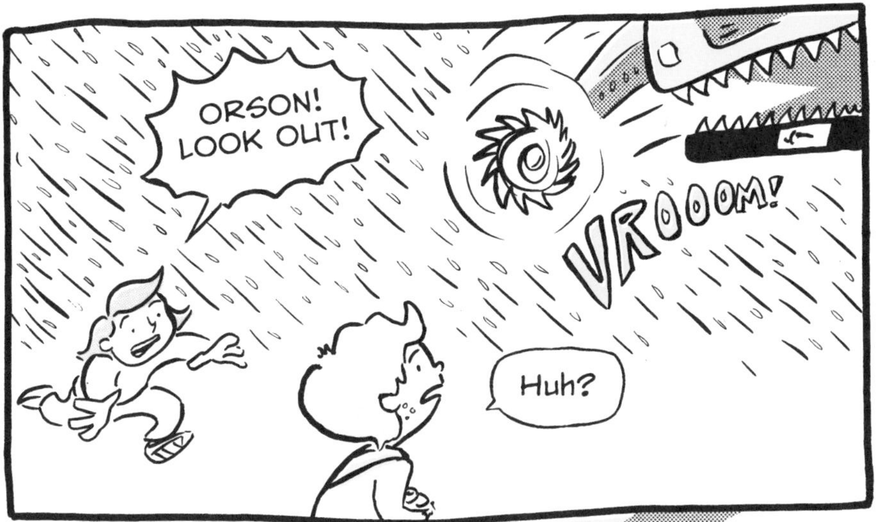
ORSON! LOOK OUT!
VROOOM!
Huh?
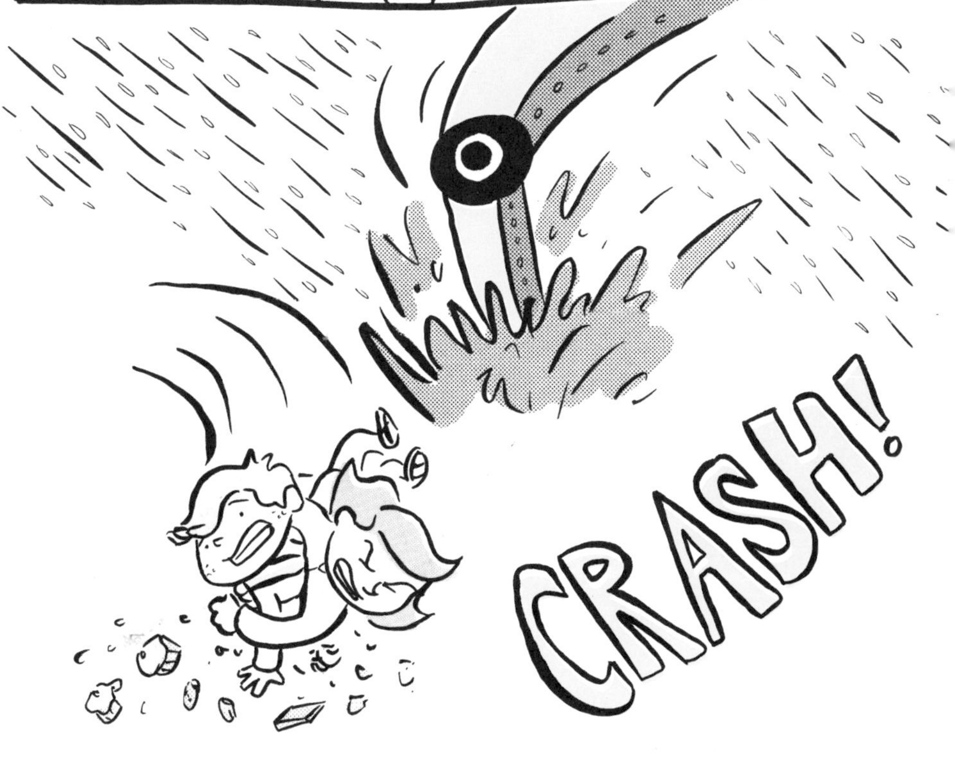
CRASH!

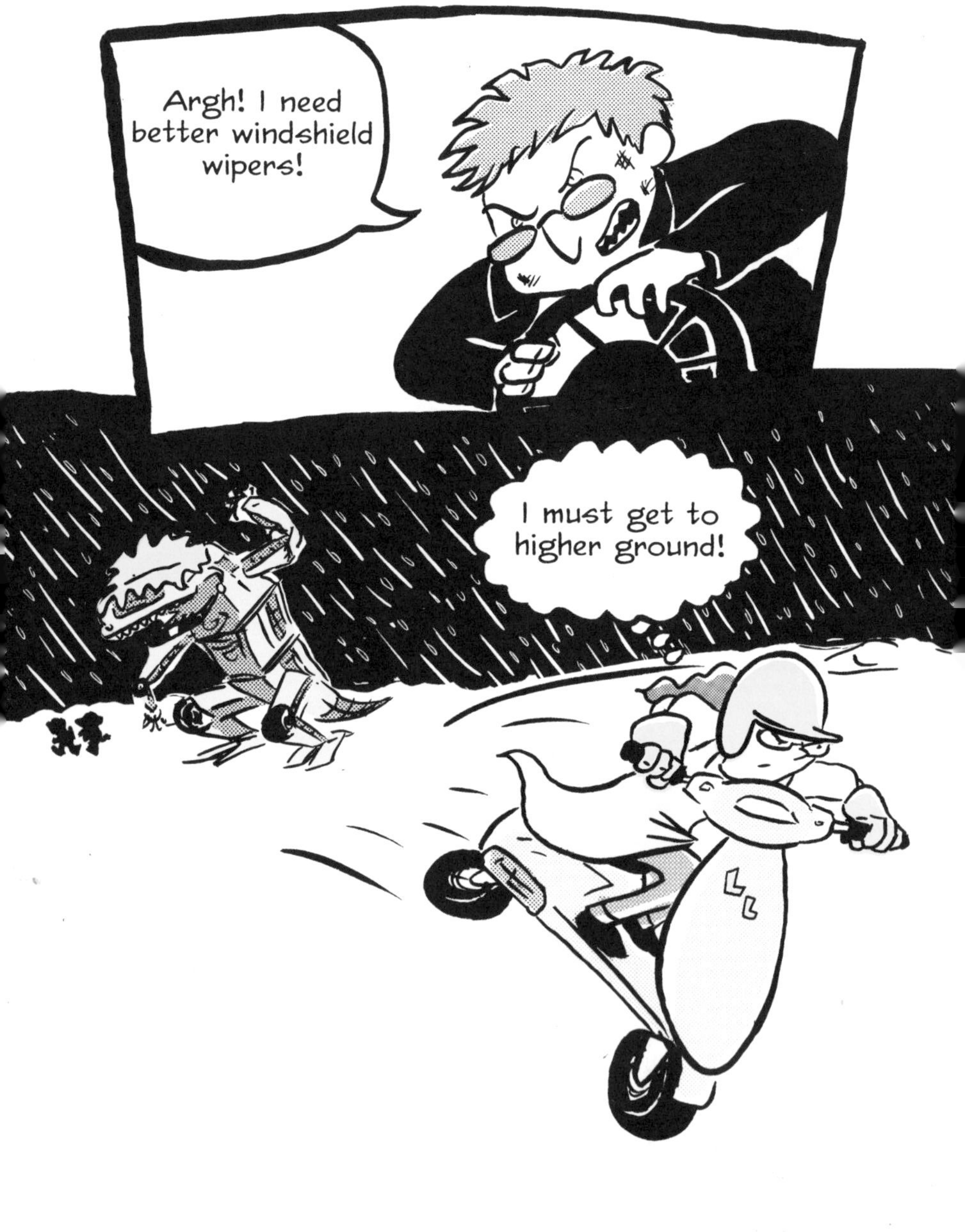
Argh! I need better windshield wipers!
I must get to higher ground!

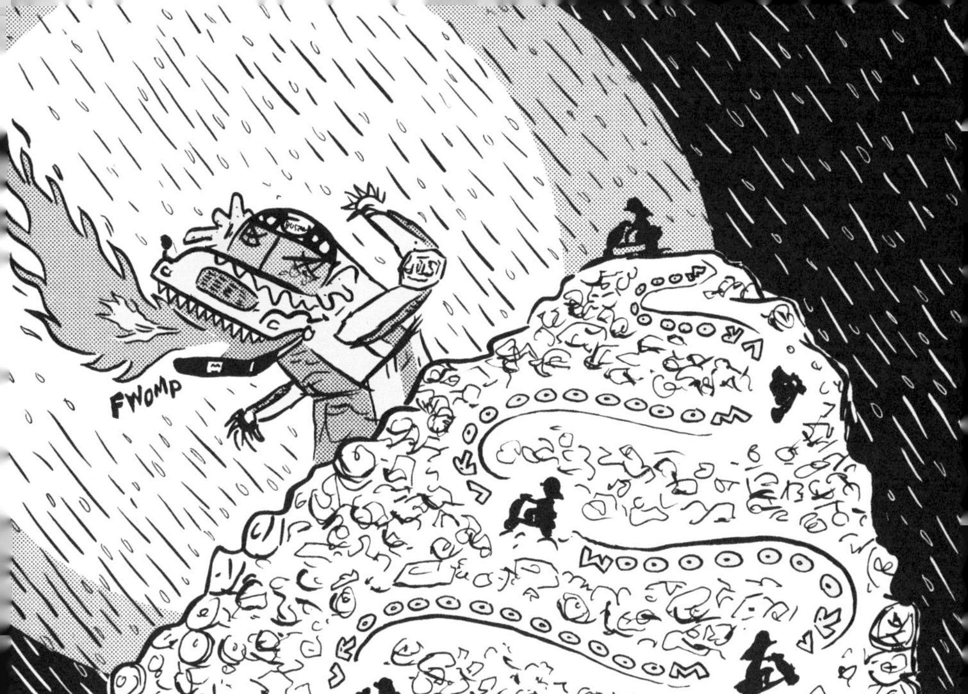
FWOMP

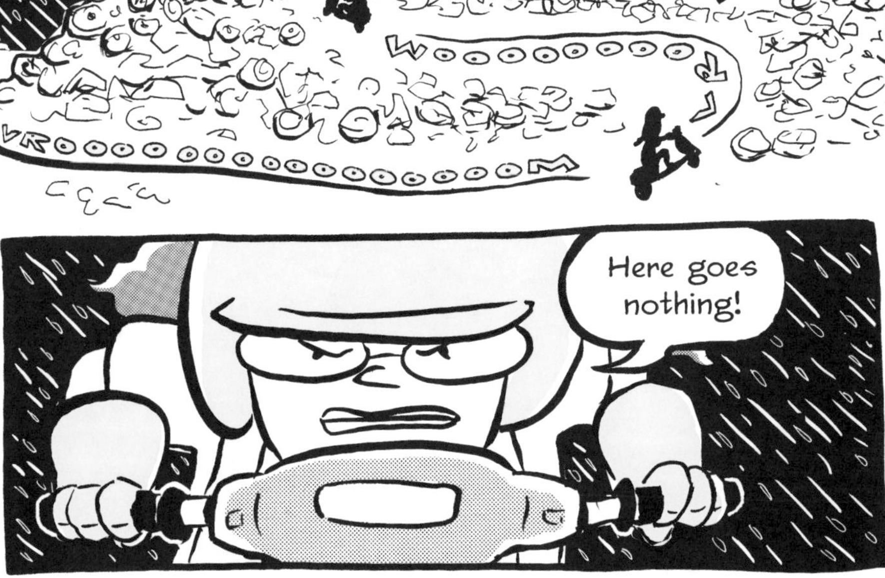
Here goes nothing!

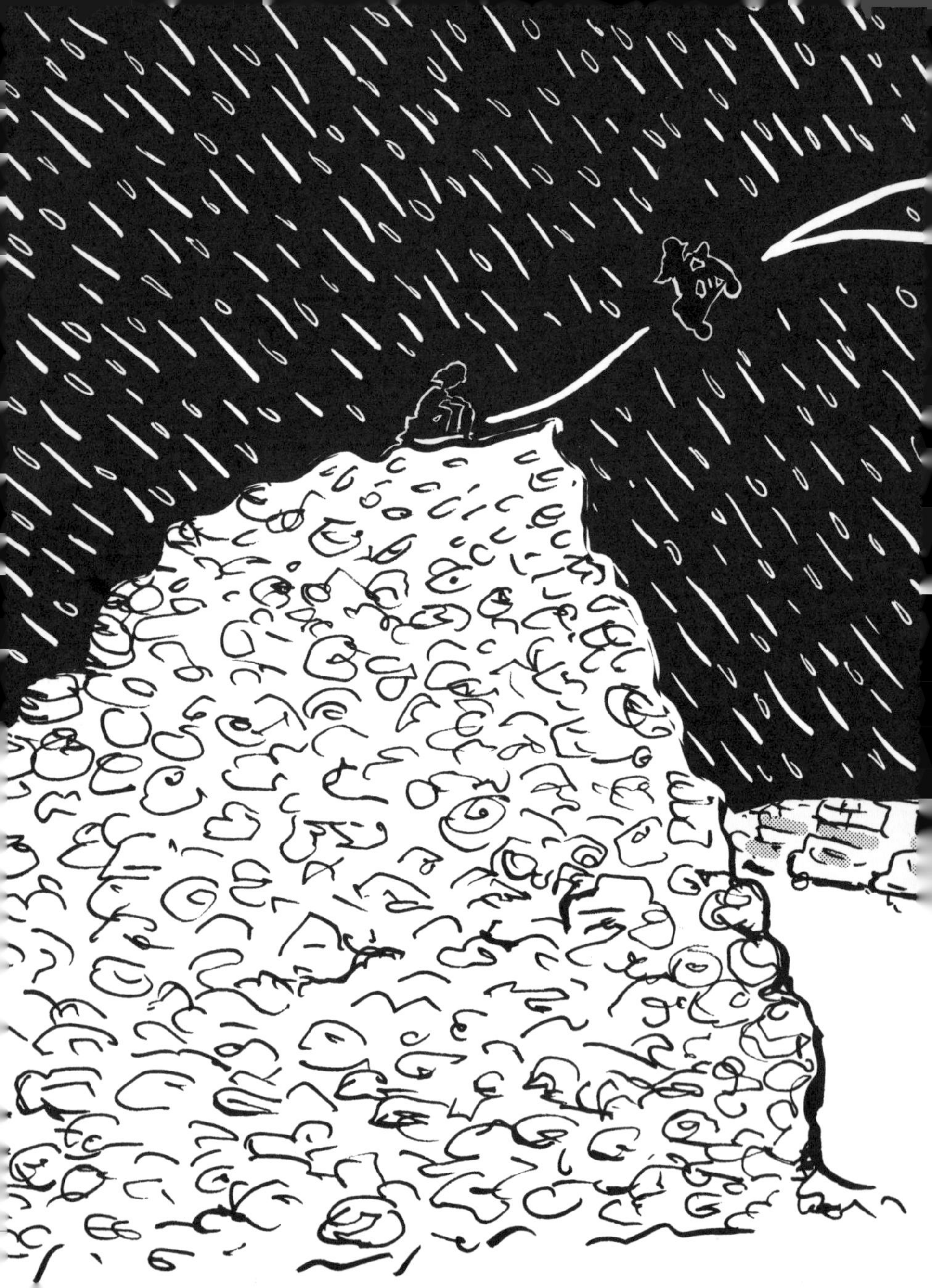

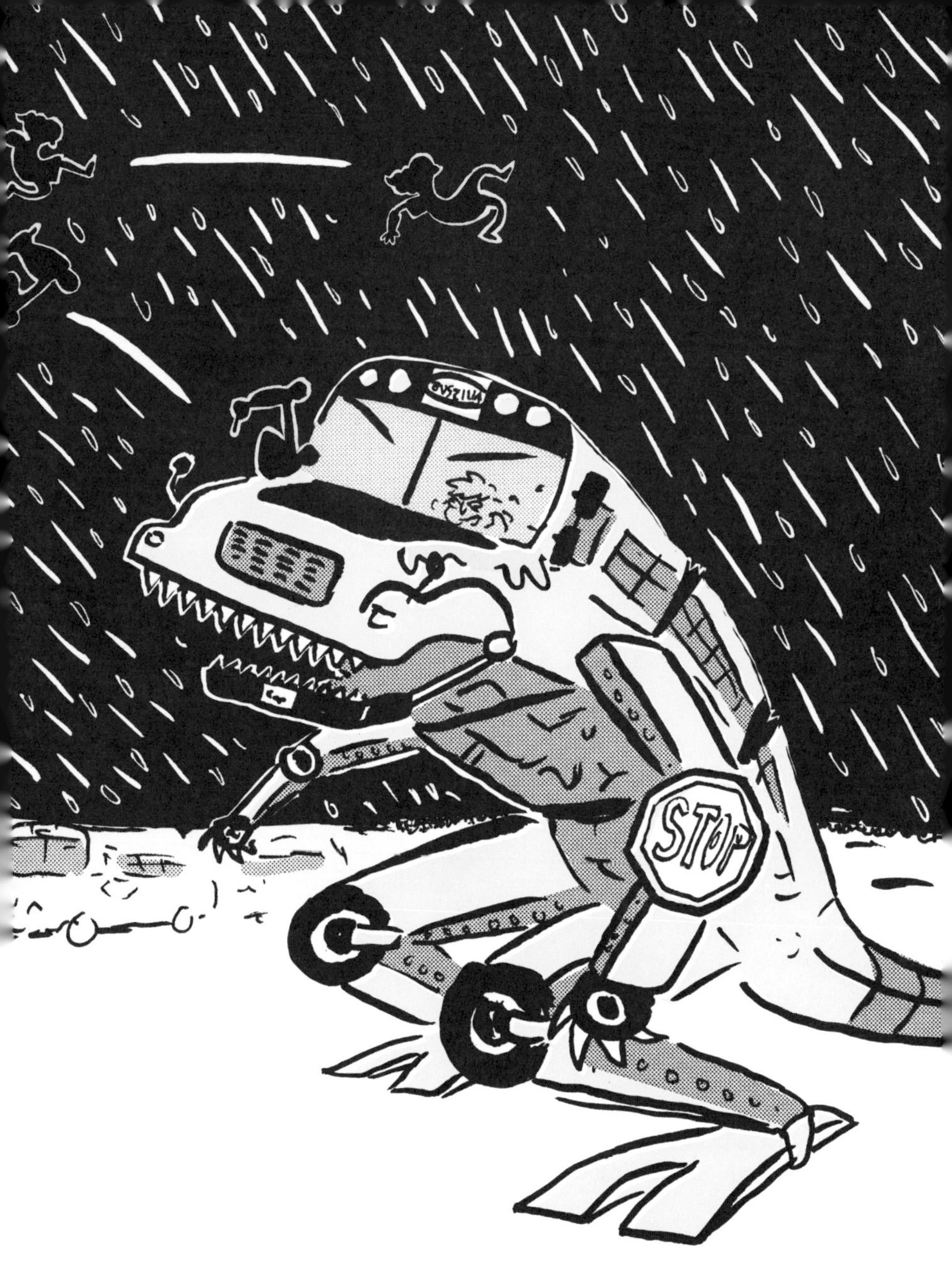
STOP

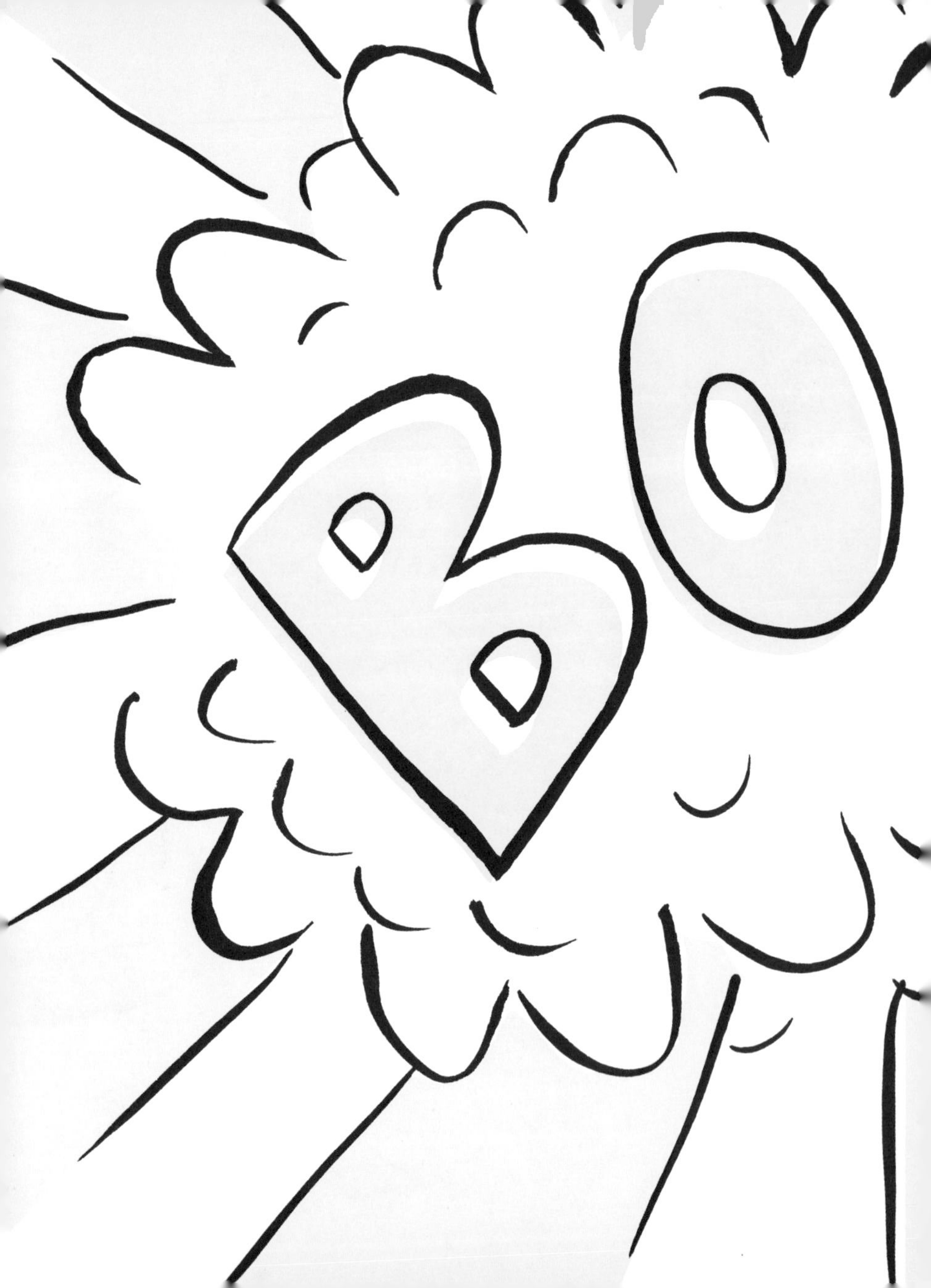
BO

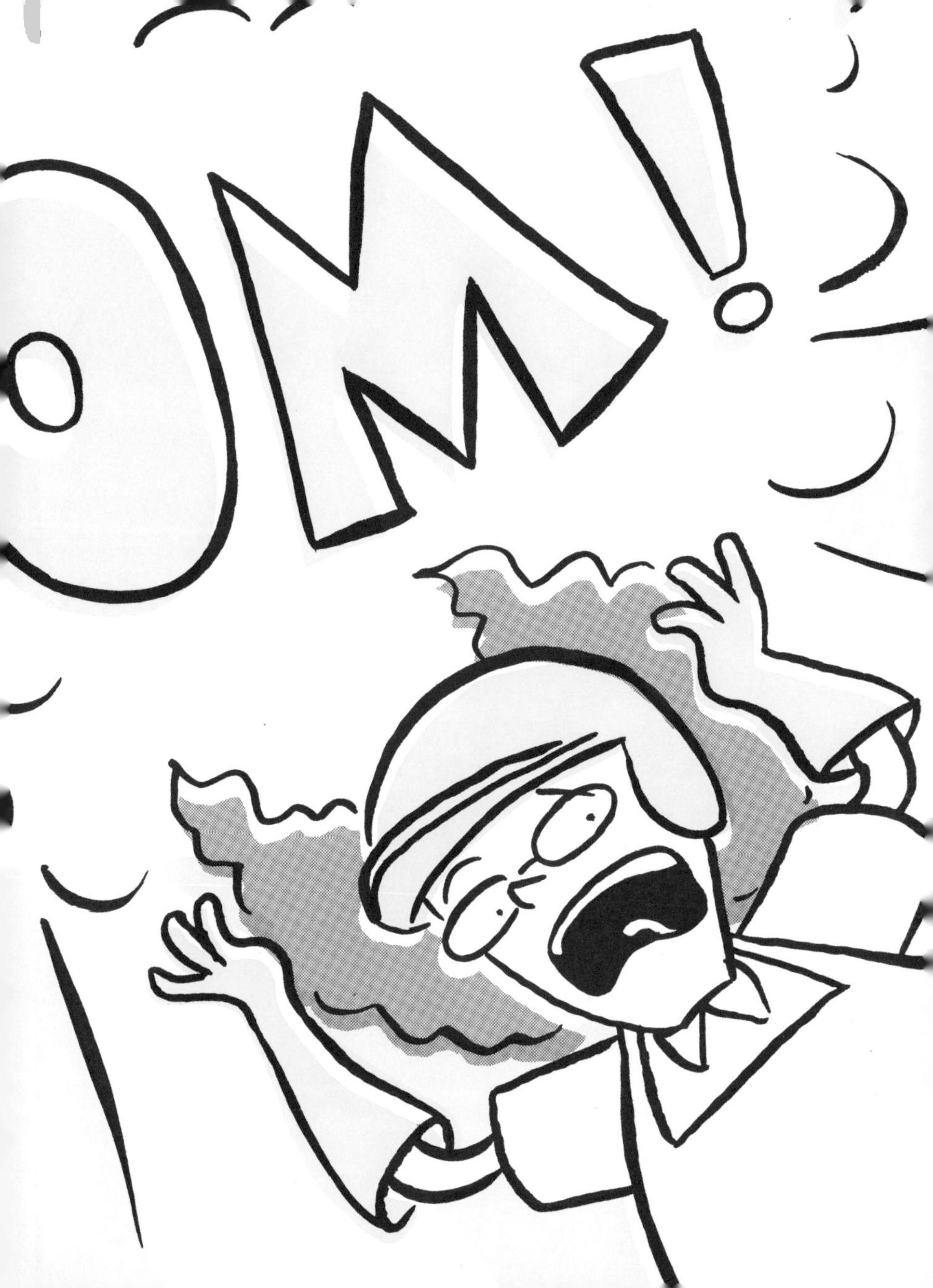
OM!

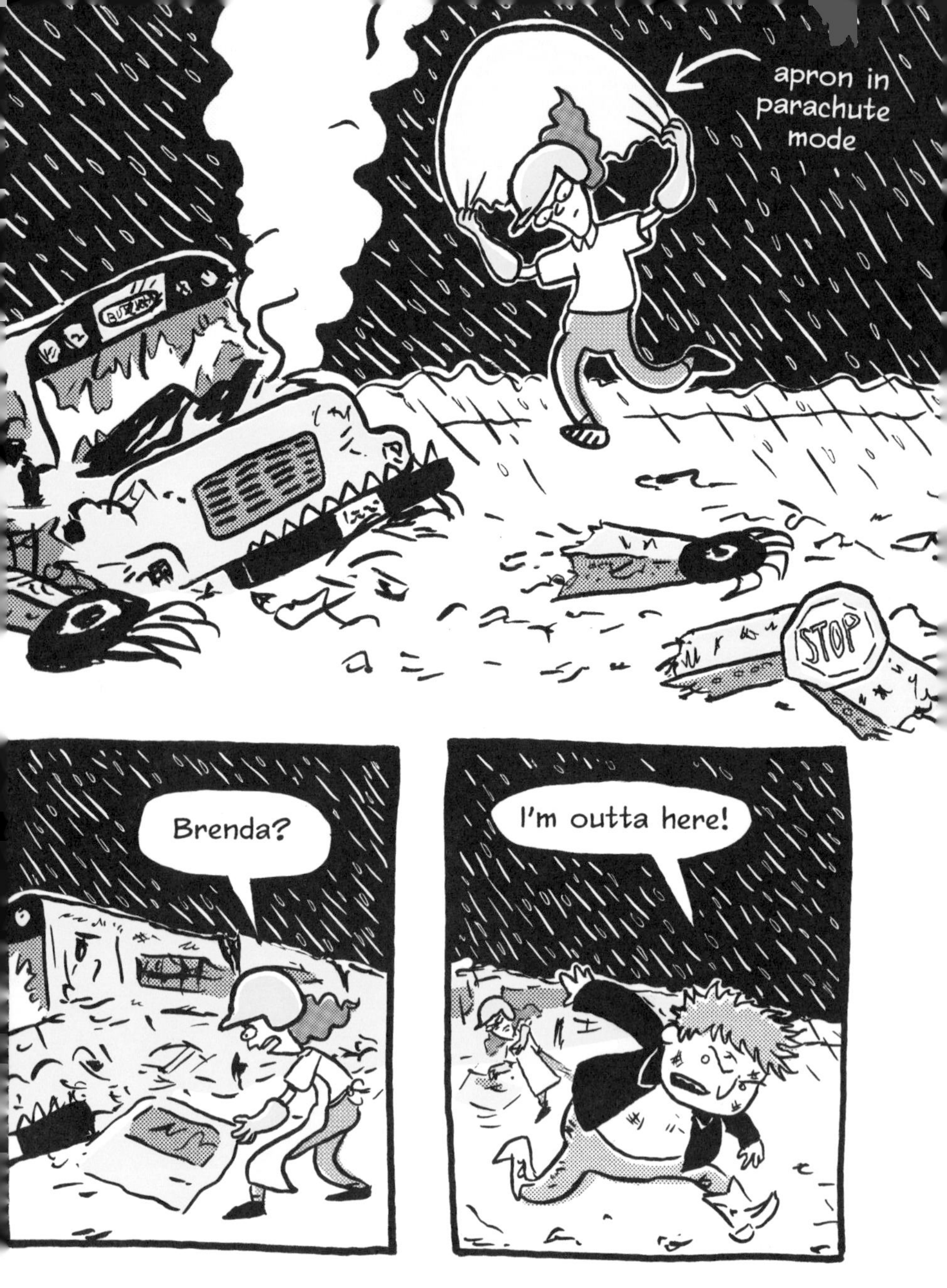
apron in parachute mode
STOP
Brenda?
I'm outta here!

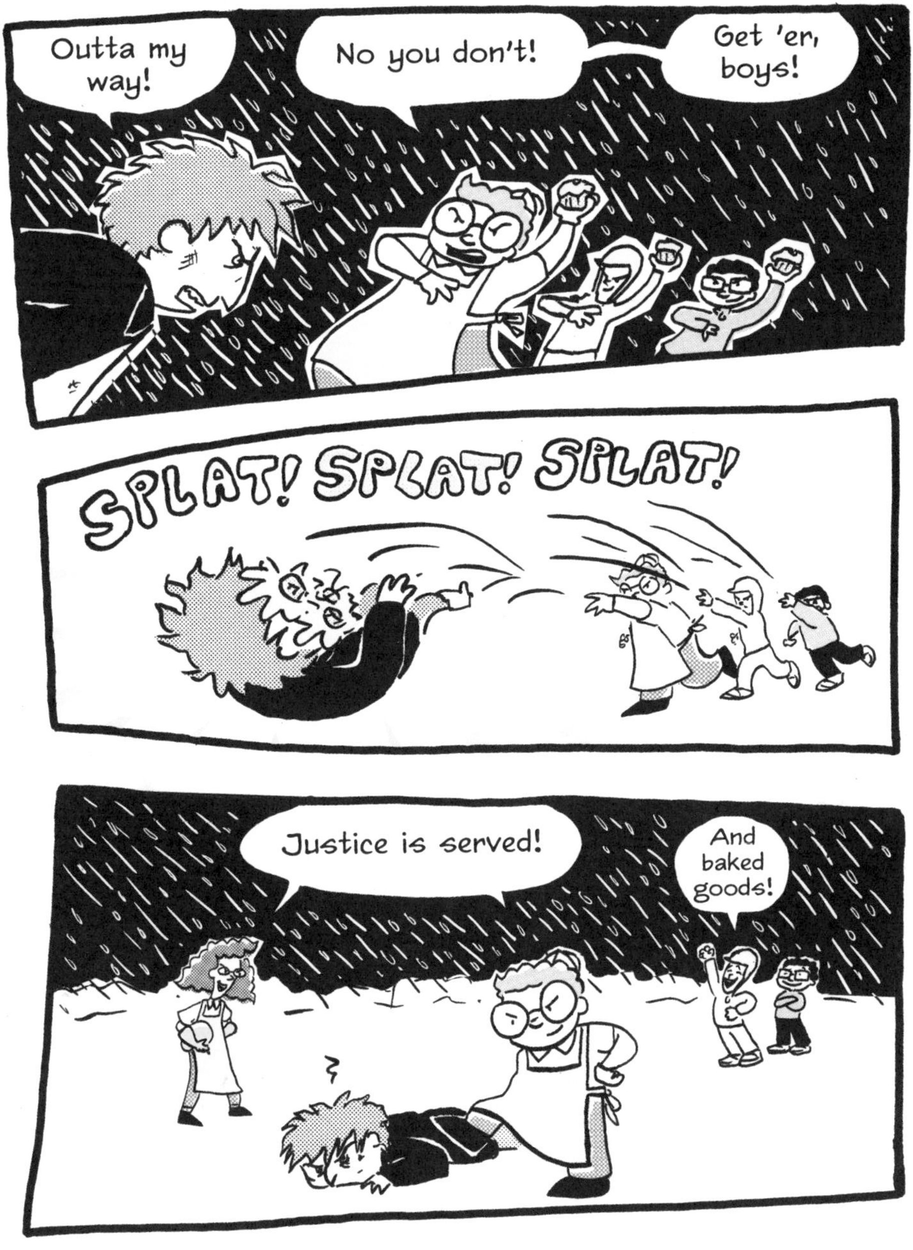
Outta my way!
No you don't!
Get 'er, boys!
SPLAT! SPLAT! SPLAT!
Justice is served!
And baked goods!

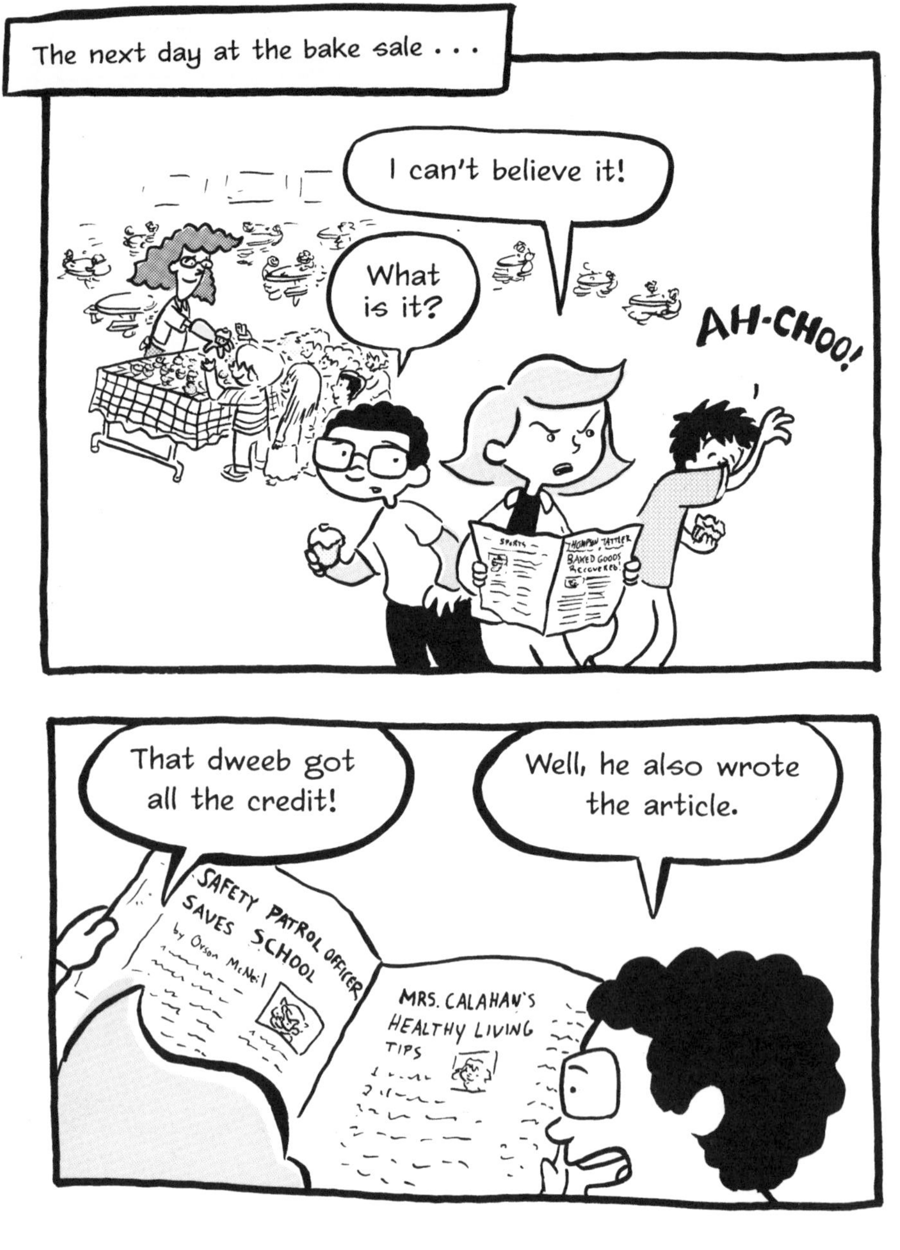
The next day at the bake sale . . .
I can't believe it!
What is it?
AH-CHOO!
SPORTS
BAKED GOODS RECOVERED!
That dweeb got all the credit!
Well, he also wrote the article.
SAFETY PATROL OFFICER SAVES SCHOOL
by Orson McNeil
MRS. CALAHAN'S HEALTHY LIVING TIPS

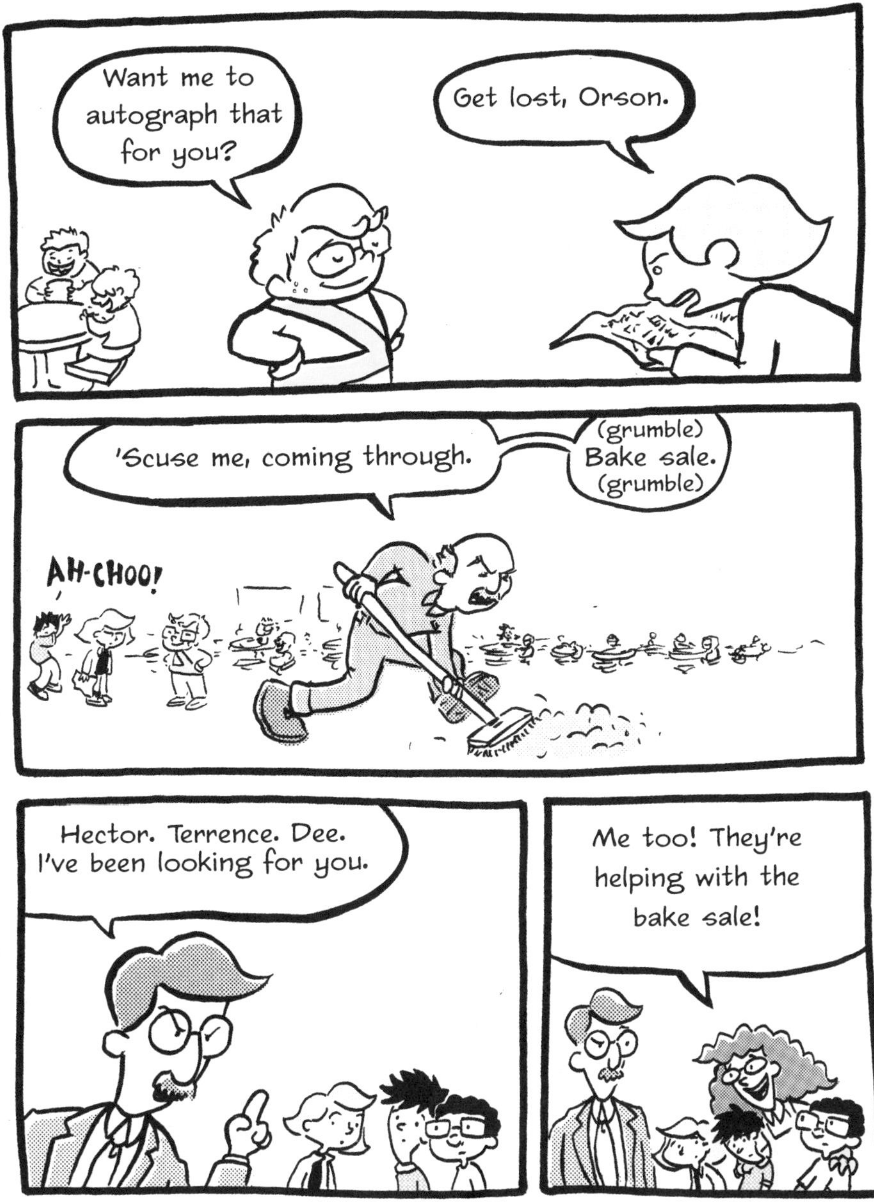
Want me to autograph that for you?
Get lost, Orson.
'Scuse me, coming through.
(grumble) Bake sale. (grumble)
AH-CHOO!
Hector. Terrence. Dee. I've been looking for you.
Me too! They're helping with the bake sale!

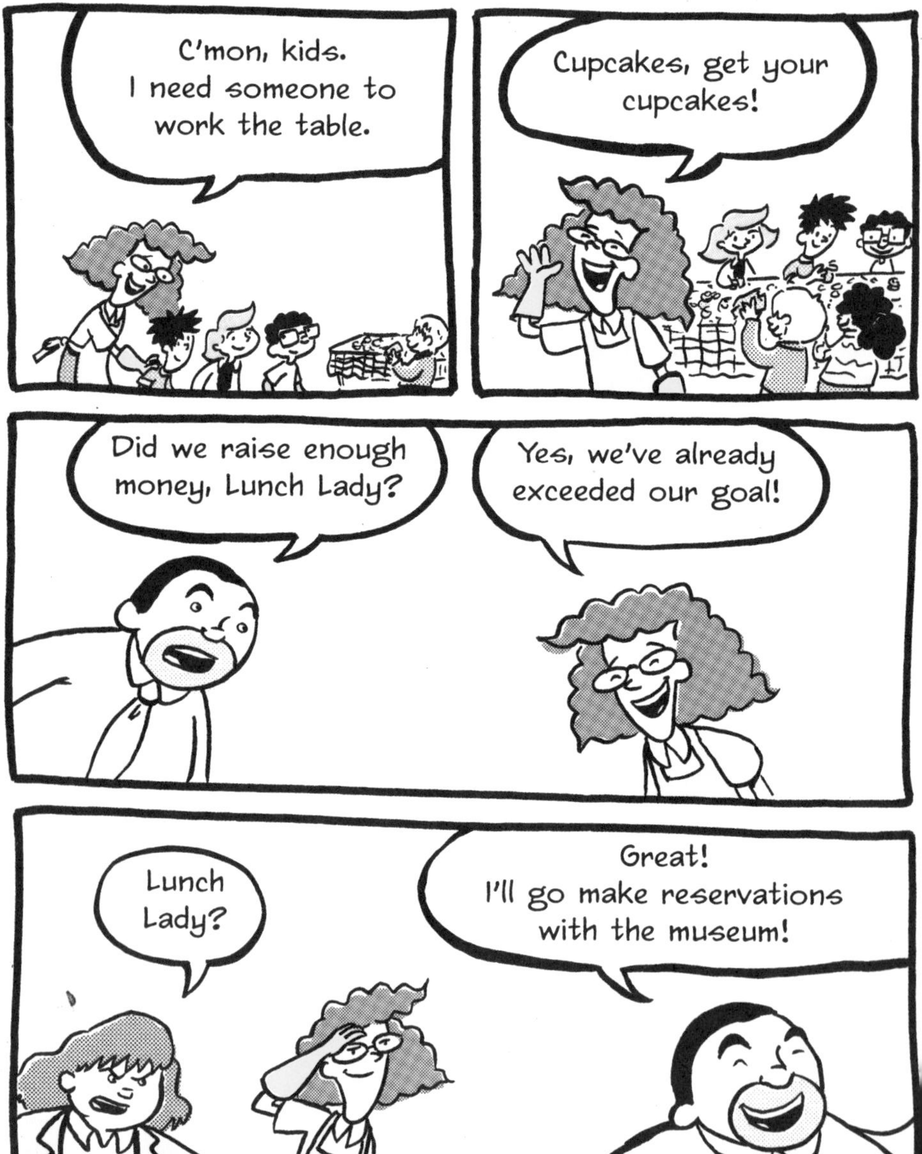
C'mon, kids.
I need someone to work the table.
Cupcakes, get your cupcakes!
Did we raise enough money, Lunch Lady?
Yes, we've already exceeded our goal!
Lunch Lady?
Great!
I'll go make reservations with the museum!

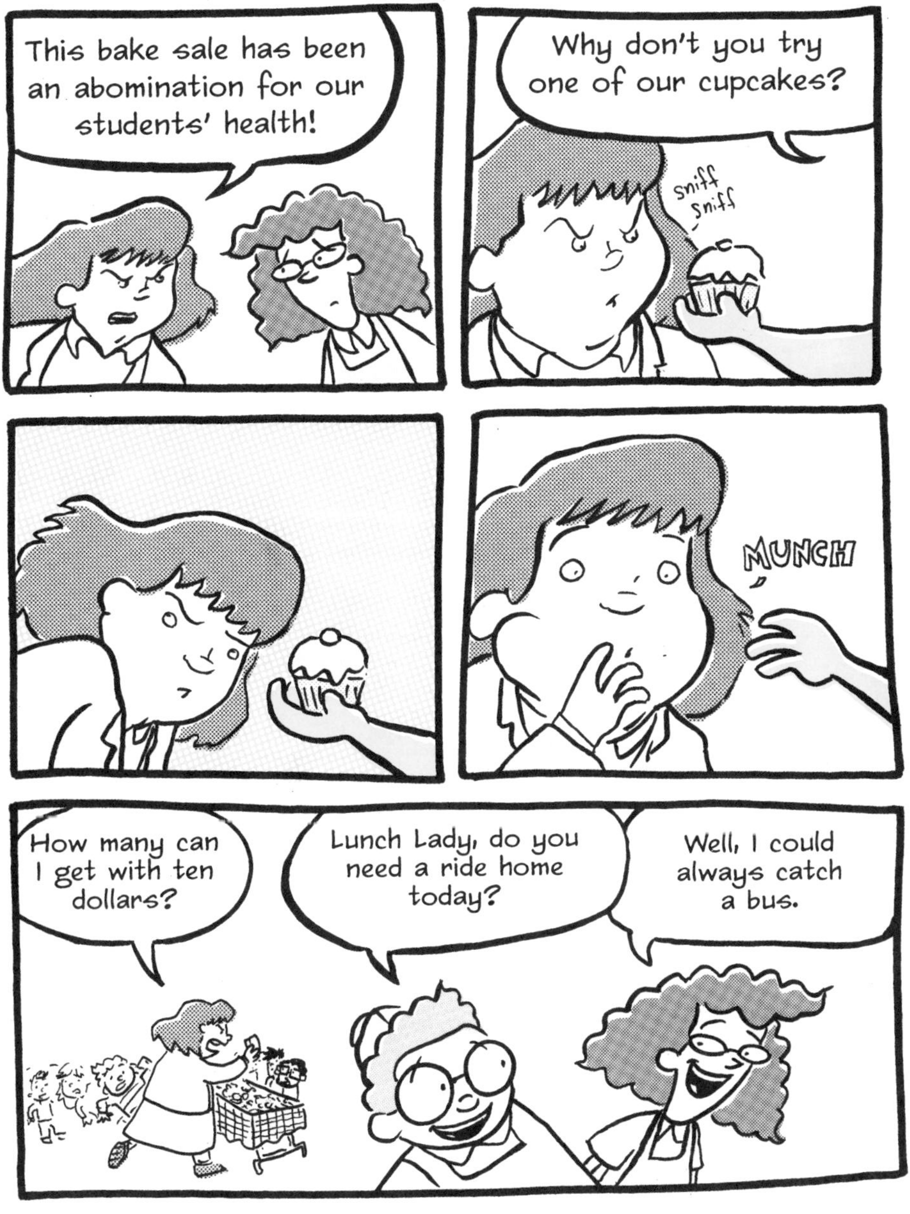
This bake sale has been an abomination for our students' health!
Why don't you try one of our cupcakes?
sniff sniff
MUNCH
How many can I get with ten dollars?
Lunch Lady, do you need a ride home today?
Well, I could always catch a bus.

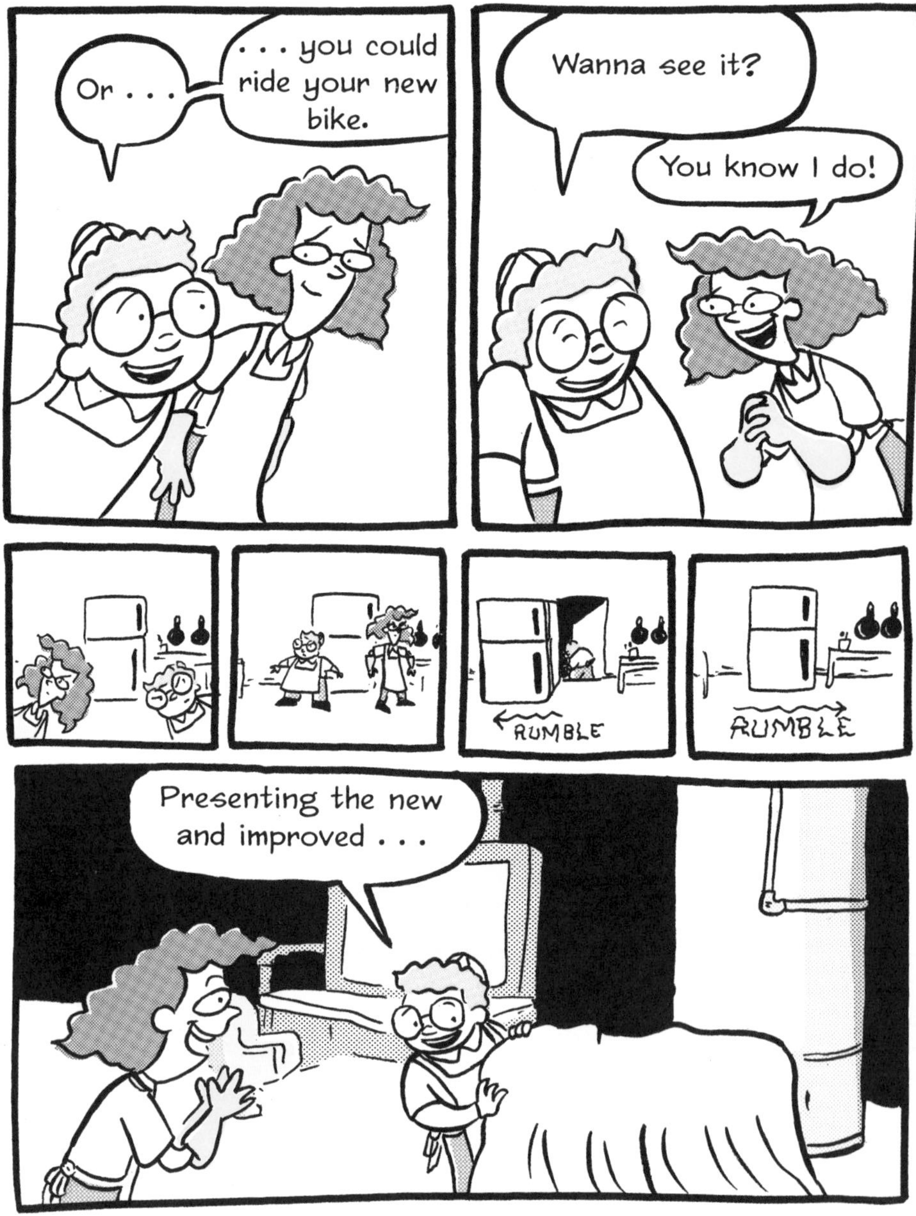
Or . . .
. . . you could ride your new bike.
Wanna see it?
You know I do!
RUMBLE
RUMBLE
Presenting the new and improved . . .

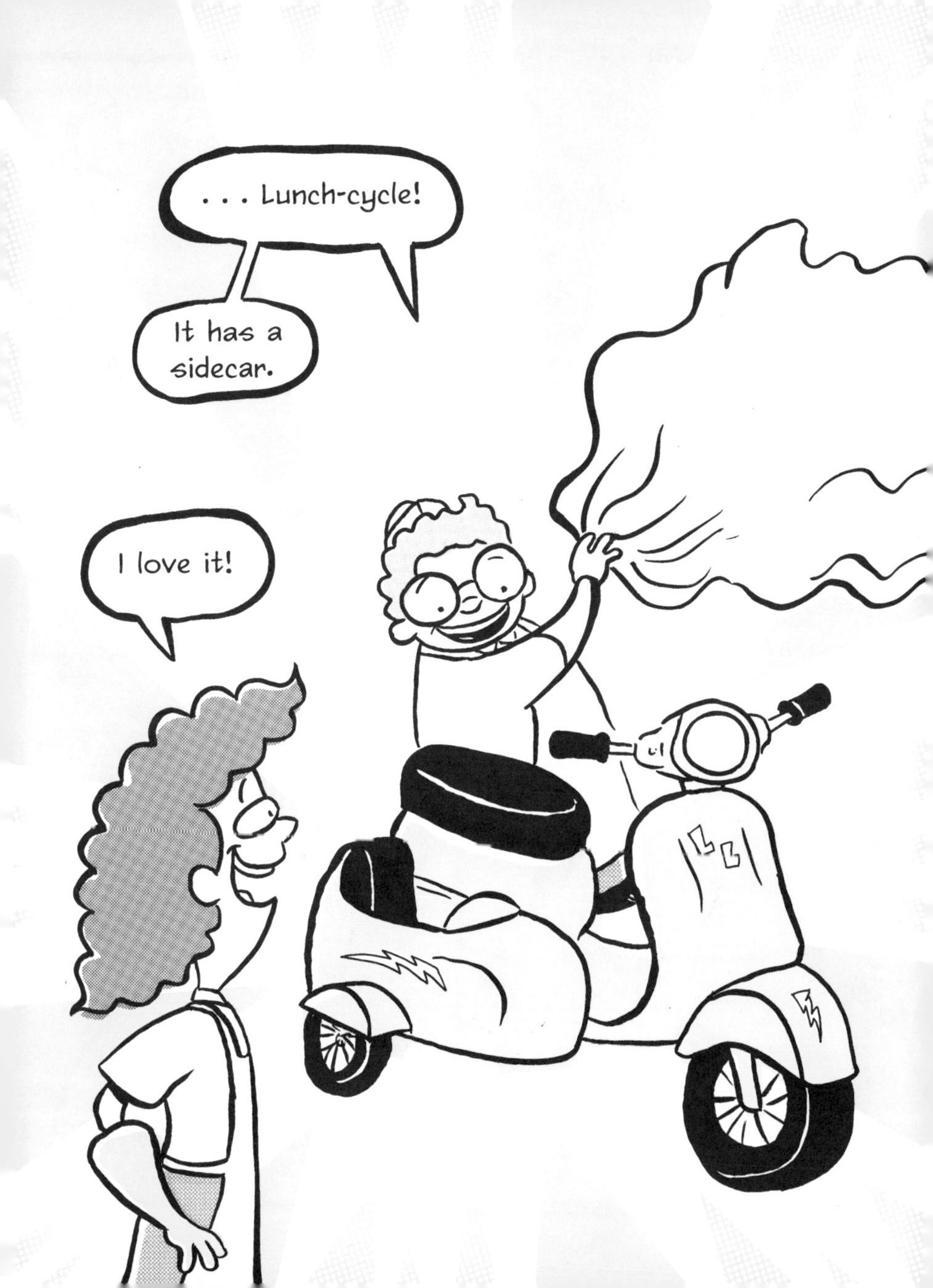
. . . Lunch-cycle!
It has a sidecar.
I love it!

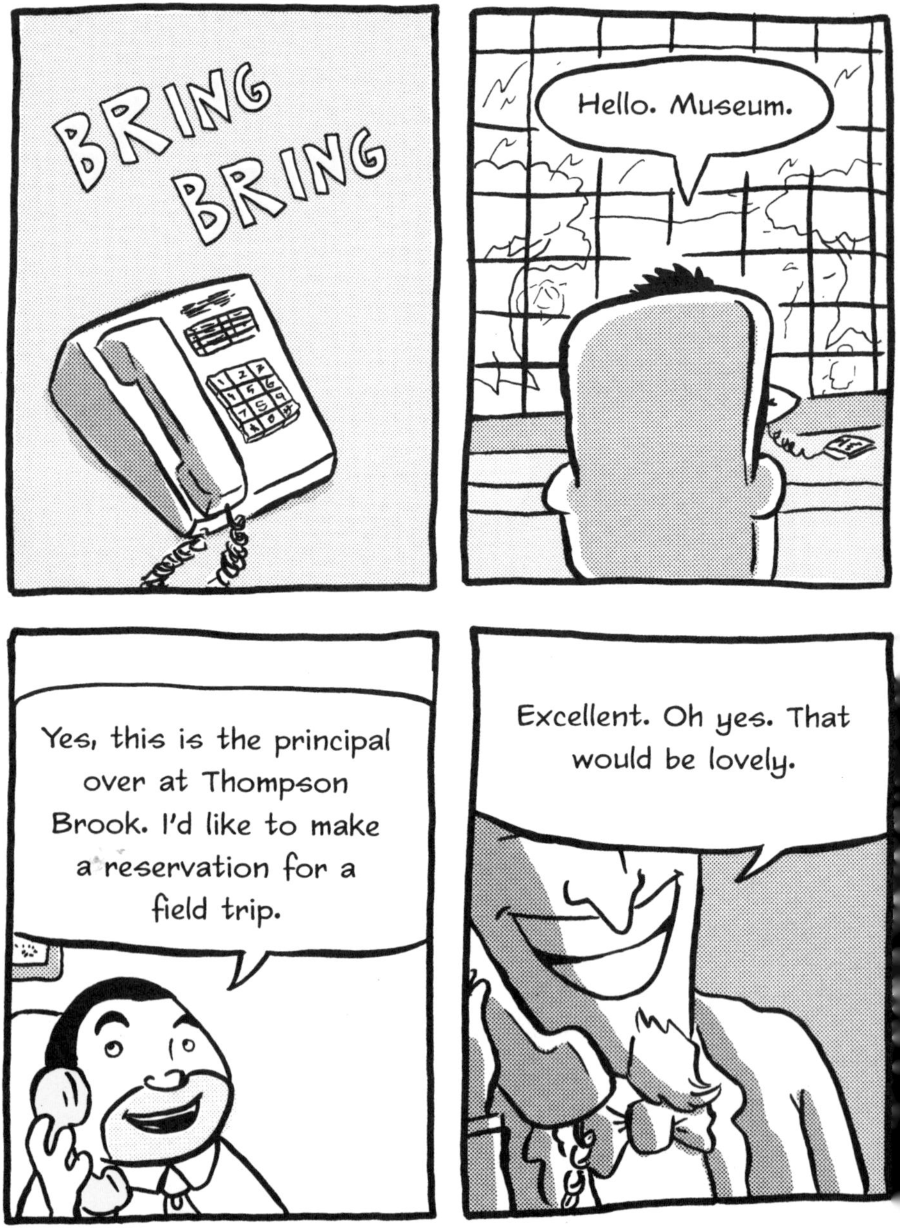
BRING
BRING
Hello. Museum.
Yes, this is the principal over at Thompson Brook. I'd like to make a reservation for a field trip.
Excellent. Oh yes. That would be lovely.

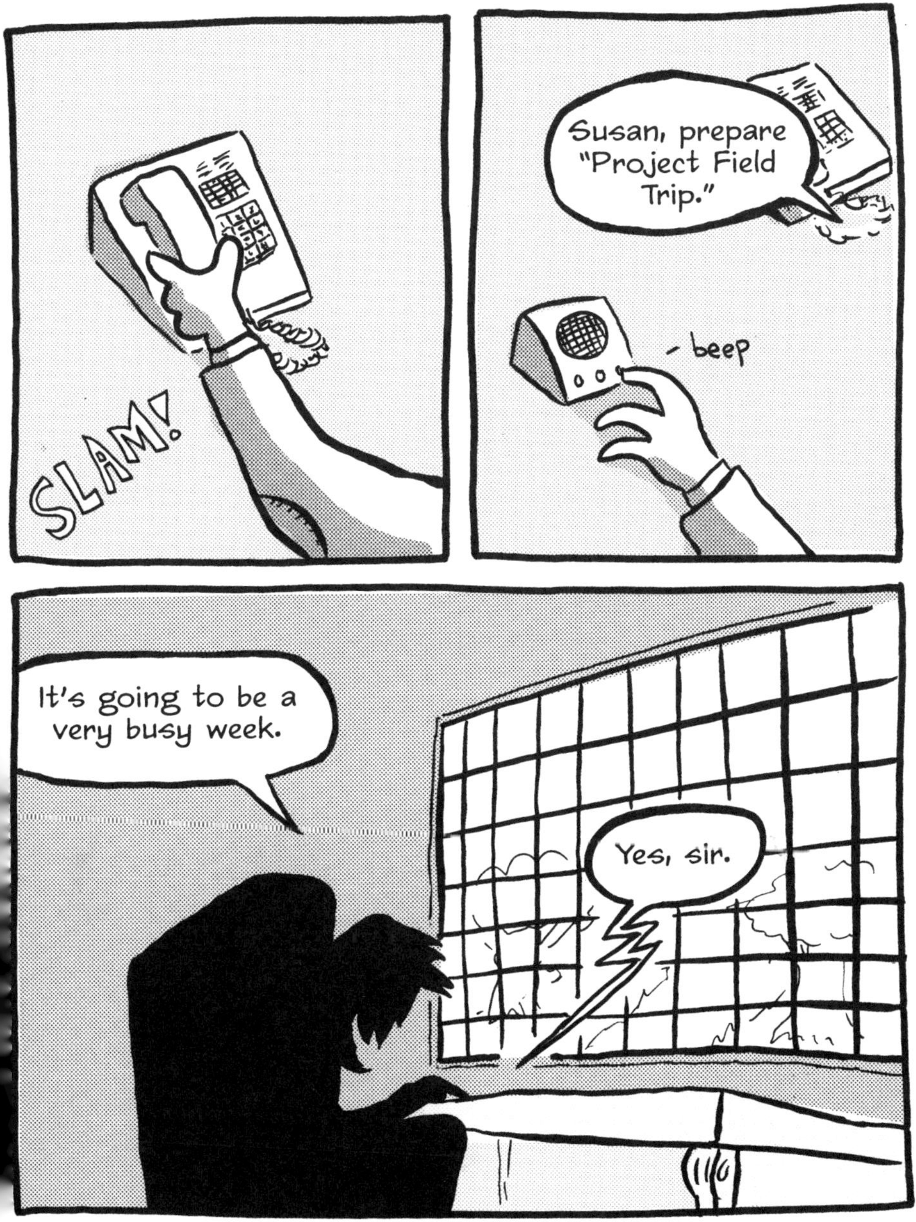
SLAM!
Susan, prepare "Project Field Trip."
- beep
It's going to be a very busy week.
Yes, sir.

FOR RICH AND DAWN
–J.J.K.

The author would like to acknowledge the color assist in this book by Joey Weiser.

THIS IS A BORZOI BOOK PUBLISHED BY ALFRED A. KNOPF

Visit us on the Web! www.randomhouse.com/kids

Educators and librarians, for a variety of teaching tools,
visit us at www.randomhouse.com/teachers

Library of Congress Cataloging-in-Publication Data
Krosoczka, Jarrett J.
Lunch Lady and the bake sale bandit / Jarrett J. Krosoczka. — 1st ed.
p. cm.
Summary: Lunch Lady, Betty, and the Breakfast Bunch must figure out who is stealing the goods from the bake sale.
ISBN 978-0-375-86729-3 (trade pbk.) — ISBN 978-0-375-96729-0 (lib. bdg.)
1. Graphic novels. [1. Graphic novels. 2. School lunchrooms, cafeterias, etc.—Fiction.
3. Stealing—Fiction. 4. Schools—Fiction. 5. Mystery and detective stories.] I. Title.
PZ7.7.K76Ltm 2010
[Fic]—dc22
2010012781

The text of this book is set in Hedgè Backwards.
The illustrations in this book were created using ink on paper and digital coloring.

MANUFACTURED IN MALAYSIA
December 2010
10 9 8 7 6 5 4 3 2 1

First Edition